When the Bough Breaks

M. C. WILKINSON

Paperback ISBN: 978-1-5356-0936-4
Hardcover ISBN: 978-1-5356-1028-5

Prologue

"Rock-a-bye baby in the tree top. When the wind blows, the cradle will rock. When the bough breaks, the cradle will fall, and down will come baby, cradle and all."

The dark-haired woman sang to the newborn infant while running her fingers through the baby girl's fine brown hair.

"I never liked that nursery rhyme, but I think it's fitting for you."

There came a clicking noise, as if a door somewhere was being unlatched. The woman's attention was momentarily drawn away from the baby girl. The woman pulled out a note pad and went to half a dozen babies in the large room full of hundreds. The woman gently turned the left forearm of each baby with her delicate hands. After looking at each arm, the woman quickly jotted a note about each. She heard another click, this time closer. She whipped her head around, looking over her shoulder with fear in her hazel eyes. There were dark figures entering at the far end of the nursery room. The sound of boots stomping upon the gray tile floor echoed through the low hum of slumbering babies. The woman hurried back over to the first baby, to whom she had sung the lullaby. She reached into the cradle and gently turned the baby girl's forearm, revealing a tattoo of lines and numbers upon the fragile skin. The black barcode tattoo stood out vividly against the porcelain-white skin of the baby. There was not enough time to transcribe the number tattooed in her notepad because the soldiers had spotted the woman and they grew nearer like wolves stalking their prey. The woman ripped a single sheet of paper out of her notepad before she folded the paper and inserted it into an envelope. She tucked the envelope into one of the pockets on her white smock.

"You are the hope for the future. Be strong, my little angels," the woman whispered to the room of babies before running out the door farthest from the huntsmen. The dark figures pursued her quietly, but swiftly. A few hours later, people in similar white smocks entered the large nursery and removed all of the babies the woman had touched and documented, all except the baby girl with gray eyes and fine brown hair. The woman had not had enough time to write that baby's number down in her notebook. The baby girl now lay sleeping peacefully, dreaming of a bright future yet to come.

Chapter 1

"Alabaster, dear, it is time to wake up," lulls a soothing voice.

I feel a soft, warm hand brush across my ivory cheek, pushing a few loose strands of brown hair out of my face. I open my eyes to see the familiar face of my mother smiling down on me. Her eyes are as gray as a storm cloud seconds before it breaks. I smile back and stretch my arms out wide. When my arms leave the warm safety of the blanket, I see a vivid black tattoo upon the delicate skin of my left wrist. I yawn before pulling my arms back into the warmth of my crisp white blanket. I have seen this barcode tattoo my entire life, so I do not give it a second thought, but the stark contrast of black and white always catches my eye.

"It is a big day for you, so I made you a special gift."

My mother reveals a light-blue bundle wrapped with a single piece of white twine tied off in a simple bow. I smile with delight as I quickly pop out of bed and eagerly take the gift. I do not receive gifts often.

They are banned. I gently pull one end of the twine, which causes the bow to easily give way. I savor every second as I unfold the crisp light-blue cotton material. I hold in my hand the standard uniform for my new job, which I have been training for since I turned three. I feel a little let down after the built-up excitement. Before my smile can falter, my mother excitedly grabs the bottom hem of the T-shirt and turns it inside out. There, craftily embroidered into the fabric about two inches above the hem, is a tiny emerald-green butterfly. It is no bigger than my pinky nail. My mother is very talented indeed, because there is no trace of the hidden gift visible on the outside of the fabric. She and I know anything that could visibly set me apart from others is forbidden and severely punished. My smile widens and I feel the gentle sting of tears, but I hold them back. I have never been a crier.

"Oh, Mother, it is beautiful. Thank you," I whisper as I wrap her in a grateful embrace.

"Happy sixteenth birthday, sweetheart. Hurry and get dressed. Breakfast is already on the table." My mother rises from my bed to leave, but turns back to me before she is out the door. "Oh, by the way, try to get an extra shirt so you can keep this one for always. You will never see it again if it gets into the laundry."

My mother smiles as she stays in the doorway gazing at me for a moment longer. Other than the eighteen-year gap, she and I are identical. We both share the same eyes, sterling-gray of a storm cloud, light-brown hair flows long and lusciously down our backs before coming to an end at our hips, and we both have skin as white as snow. The truth is, we are identical all the way down to a genetic level. We are Clones. Each of us was created for a specific purpose in our city. Each Clone is given certain genetic attributes to help them thrive in their Essential Function, which is their job, their purpose. There are only five different base genetic models amongst the Clones, three are male, two female.

I smile and admire the butterfly. I rub the special gift pinched between my index finger and thumb. It is so soft. I wonder where she got the thread. There seem to be golden flecks when the light catches the gift just right. My mother inhales like she is going to speak, so I look up to her perch in the doorway. She does not say anything; however, there is a slight flash of something in her eyes, but it is gone before I can determine what it is. Regret maybe? Or perhaps fear? She smiles one more time before she leaves me alone to get ready.

My mother is not my real mother; I do not have a real mother, as I was created in a laboratory somewhere within the city. Each Clone spends nine months in an incubator after they are genetically designed for whichever Essential Function needs to be filled. It is impossible for a Clone to reproduce anyway; we are all created sterile. My real name is not Alabaster either. All I have is a number, my Clone number, which is number A14B45T3R, and it is found under the barcode tattooed upon my left wrist. Clones are not given names or any title that would make us more like the People. We are each given our Clone number tattoo on the soft side of our left wrist shortly after being removed from our incubators. Each Clone number is a combination of letters and numbers to help the People keep track of who is who. There are only two people who know me as Alabaster, my mother and my best friend, Boston.

Boston is another contraband I must keep secret, even from my mother. Clones are not allowed to have friends; it is banned. There are many things that are banned. It is hard to forget, as there are signs posted everywhere to remind us.

No Clone shall be named

No Clone shall wear adornment

No Clone shall own any possessions

No Clone shall harm any of the People

No Clone shall fraternize with another

No Clone shall ever say no to one of the People

The last rule makes all the others a gray area. I see the signs so often, I do not even notice them anymore. I do not know for certain, but I believe every Clone has a secret illegal indulgence or rebellion. I have a hard time accepting the fact that my mother and I are the only ones who enjoy breaking the rules by hugging and giving each other the rare gift. I would never ask another Clone, but none would admit to it anyway. I would never admit my illegal tendencies to anyone, Clone or Person. If the People ever find out, there are severe consequences.

I quickly head to the bathroom to get ready for my first official day of my Essential Function. The door is closed and it sounds like water is running through the pipes. Apparently, someone else has already claimed the shower. I will have to forego one this morning. Instead, I head back to my room to dress.

I met Boston at school. He is designed for the same Essential Function as me, so we have been in the same classes our entire lives. We were created to be nurses in the city's only hospital. That is not our only thing in common. We also share the same birthday. That really is not a big deal because every Clone shares the same birthday. It is one of the ways the People reassure the lack of individuality of the Clones. Whether or not we were actually born on the same day remains a mystery to me, but it is what I have been told.

To everyone else, Boston is known only as Clone number 6O5T0N. I began calling him Boston when we were in our second year of studies. We were five at the time. It came to pass one day when we were paired off to practice taking vitals. I do not know what had come over me, as my mother had continuously instilled a sense of fear of the People. A fear of them discovering my secret name, or any other illegal thoughts, feelings, ideas, or individualistic traits. However, for one reason or another, I gave Boston his name, and shared my own with him. We rarely use our forbidden names, because we do not want others to overhear, nor do we wish to receive the subsequent punishment for the offense.

Once in my room, I remove my modest off-white nightgown and begin to pull on my new uniform. After I am done getting dressed, I leave my small bedroom again, and head down the narrow halfway. The soft soles of my tennis shoes create a hollow pitter-patter as they hit the bland linoleum floor. There is no carpet in my house, linoleum is easier to clean. I pass three other bedrooms on my way to the kitchen. Each exactly like my own, minimal. As a Clone, I am not allowed to own anything. In other words, I do not need anything to hold my belongings, a change of clothes, a watch, jewelry, photos, or trinkets. A clean nightgown is provided every evening, and a clean uniform and undergarments are provided each morning. The used clothing is sent down a laundry chute, where I can only assume it is laundered and sent back. There are also places in most buildings where a Clone can receive a new set of clothing, in case of accidental soils. During my yearlong internship, I generally found myself replacing my scrubs several times a day. The laundry situation is the reason why my mother wants me to find an abandoned shirt to wear instead of my new shirt with the special embroidered gift.

Our dwelling has a laundry chute at the end of the hallway before it opens to the kitchen. As I pass the small square panel, I hold my tattooed wrist up to a small light. A red line crosses my barcode and the panel opens with a soft beep. I insert my nightgown and proceed down the remaining short distance of the hall once again. I can hear the panel softly slide shut and the whirlwind sound of a vacuum as it takes my laundry away.

Each Clone bedroom has only a cot and a small bedside table to hold an alarm clock. The alarm clock is not considered a possession, because punctuality is of great importance to a Clone. The People do not want Clones who are unreliable.

The bathroom is now unoccupied, so I enter and close the door for some privacy. There is a small mirror and also a camera in the left corner of the closet-sized room. Every room in our dwelling is equipped with security cameras, as well as every street corner, and inside every building. There are a few blind spots my mother showed me, but they are sparse. The People want to make sure we Clones stay in line.

I nimbly run my fingers through my long hair. We have a single hairbrush for my family unit to share, but my hair is usually tangle free. I would rather use my fingers because I like how soft my hair feels against my skin as it spills through. In a matter of seconds, my long hair is in a perfect French braid and tied off with a hair band that is the same shade as my hair so that it blends in. Hair bands are not considered a possession, as they are essential in the de-individualization of each Clone, and they keep a Clone's hair neat and out of the way. Both female types are required to pull their hair back into a braid of some sort so we all look the same. However, we are not required to wear the exact same braid. The People get tired of us all looking exactly alike, which is why there is more than one base genetic type of Clone. This is also why we can braid our hair in several different ways, as long as it is a single braid down the center of our back.

When I feel my appearance is up to the required standards, I leave the bathroom to continue on to the kitchen for breakfast. It is the only other room in the dwelling. There is no living room, no television, and no couch to relax on. After all, the time I am in my dwelling is spent either sleeping or eating. I do not get free time to spend at my leisure. A typical day in the life of a Clone is wake, eat, work, eat, work, eat, sleep, and repeat. There is no vacation time, no sick time, no holidays off, and no pay. No one in the city is paid, not even the People. As a Clone of age, I will now be expected to complete my Essential Function daily, and for that I will be fed and clothed. No one is left wanting. Many of the People also work, but it is not a requirement like it is for a Clone. They are given whatever they want, regardless of their role within the city.

As I enter the small kitchen, my nose is filed with the rich aroma of coffee. Along with my alarm clock, the coffee pot is another item which could be considered a possession, but in my opinion it is an essential part of my daily life. Before joining the three other Clones already seated at the small square metal table, I fill a cup with the steaming black liquid. Even though the coffee is boiling hot, I take a big gulp. The burning sensation down my throat brings my body to full attention.

"Clone A14B45T3R, you had better eat quickly. It would not be proper to be late on your first day." Mother never uses the secret name she gave me in front of others, especially not my father.

The only talking usually heard in this house is when my father tells someone to stop doing something he considers illegal before he reports them to the authorities. I do not doubt he would turn any one of us in without hesitation. I think he would likely turn himself in if he broke a rule, even if it were an accident.

I take the vacant cold metal chair between my mother and younger brother. My brother's warm caramel eyes look down into his half-eaten bowl of oatmeal. I rarely see them, as he usually has his face buried in his blue bound textbook, which currently rests under his cocoa-skinned hand. When he is not reading the book, it is usually sitting next to him with a hand holding it close. Sure enough the book is sitting next to his bowl with a heavy hand guarding it right now. He will be starting his yearlong internship today. I do not know the exact function of his job, as we are not allowed to talk about such things, but his book is titled *Solar Energy Sciences and Engineering Applications.*

I give my mother a polite smile and she winks at me. Across the table from me sits my father. He does not acknowledge my presence as usual. I am relieved because when he does acknowledge me it is only to bestow a judgmental look, which makes me sick to my stomach. He spoons his oatmeal whilst his coffee-brown eyes laboriously pour over a pile of paperwork. His inch-long blond hair is slicked to one side as his Clone type is mandated. There is no talking allowed at the table, especially when Father is here. He is rigidly committed to the laws handed down by the People.

Even though the People allow titles such as "mother," "father," "brother," and "sister" within a family unit, Father does not allow it. Our family unit was formed by the People. A family unit is formed so the young Clones are brought up and taught the rules a Clone is required to follow, as well as any taboos. Another important reason for the formation of the family units is that, until a Clone comes of an age to begin their Essential Function, they would be of no use to society and would not be deserving of the food which is provided.

Mother was assigned to Father when they were eighteen. They have never shared a bedroom and I am certain neither has any feelings toward the other. My brother and I are the first set of Clone children they have raised. My parents will likely be assigned one more set of children before they are removed from society. When Clones reach an age where the effects of age begin to take hold, they are removed from society. Gray hair sets one Clone apart from another, as do wrinkles, and arthritis prohibits the long hours of work required from a Clone. The average lifespan of a Clone is fifty years, but that varies drastically based on Essential Functions as well as Clone type. Both my mother and father have relatively easy jobs, so age will be slower to take a toll on them.

If Father knew what Mother and I say when no ears are present, he would be appalled, and would likely turn us in. From what Mother has told me, he is a clerk in one of the government buildings. He has never yelled at me or touched me, but the looks he can give are far more menacing.

Clones are genetically designed to be unaggressive. There is no violence amongst the Clones, with the exception of the third male type, which is specially designed for combat. Unlike the other four Clone types, each individual Police Clone looks slightly different than the next. They are all created from the same base genetic model, but due to the nature of their Essential Function, each bares visible scars as a result of brutal training methods. I have only seen a Police Clone once, and I am in no hurry to see one again. A few years ago, a Police Clone and a few People interrupted one of my classes and accosted my teacher. I still do not know what her crime was, but I never saw her again. That was yet another time a fear of the People, which my mother has been trying to ingrain into me, has been reinforced.

I quickly eat my oatmeal, which has become slightly cool, because it arrived right on time ten minutes ago. I rotate between the oatmeal and a halved orange with a sip of coffee in between. The other three members of my family unit are finished before me and have already left the table. Each cleared their own dishes, which they left neatly piled in a tub, awaiting mine to join before being sent away through the dish chute. I may not know much about the city and its inner workings, but I do know it moves fluidly like a well-oiled machine.

My father and brother both leave without a goodbye. After a few minutes, my mother also prepares to leave, and I follow in suit. My mother gives me an encouraging smile and conceals a gentle kiss on my forehead by bending over me to collect my dishes.

"Good luck, my dear Alabaster," she whispers before pulling away with my empty dishes in hand.

Even with the cameras, signs of affection like this are generally missed by the People. If someone picked up on the subtle action, we would both be promptly removed from society. There are a lot of subtle things missed by the People. I can tell Clones apart by subtle differences, as can most Clones. Each Clone carries themselves slightly different, some have subtly differing mannerisms, setting them apart. The easiest way I can tell each Clone apart is to look in their eyes. Every Clone's eyes look the same on the surface, but a deeper look seems to reveal something entirely different. The People are unable, or unwilling to look at us long enough to discover those differences. The People generally call us all by the simple title of Clone and do not even bother to call us by our assigned number.

I have always needed to be extra vigilant at blending in with other Clones, as I have a noticeable L-shaped scar on my chin. When I was three I was playing in the house with my mother. I have never been sure-footed and I tripped and fell. On my way down I hit my chin on the corner of one of the metal chairs in the kitchen. Luckily my mother was the only one present when the unfortunate accident occurred. She quickly cleaned my face and used super glue she had accidentally brought home from work to seal the gash. My mother did such a good job sealing the wound that it left only the slightest scar as a reminder. That was the day my mother began calling me Alabaster.

None of the People look close enough or long enough to notice such minute details, so I am relatively safe. But if a Person ever has a reason to look close, I will be in trouble. Clones with noticeable traits are removed from society.

I smile back at my mother and give her a slight nod. I can tell from the look in her eye that she cares deeply for me, but that is something a Clone would never dare speak of. We are genetically created not to love and not to desire love. I do not know if I love my mother or if she loves me, but I feel a fondness for her.

During my internship at the hospital last year I saw a family of People huddled around an elderly family member who had just passed away from this world. The family stood huddled together trying to ease the pain with warm embraces and sweet words.

Soft tears of loss could also be heard from my distant observation. I would likely have been punished if I were caught spying on the moment of mourning, but I was careful. I am uncertain if I would mourn the loss of my father or brother, but if I were never to see my mother or Boston again––I am unsure how I would feel. I suppose I may feel a loss, but I do not think I would be driven to tears. I cannot imagine either of them mourning me either.

My mother and I leave the house together and head down the street away from the endless expanse of tall green grass behind my dwelling. For as far as I can see, there is only the waist-high sea of greenish yellow. I know not of anyone who has stepped foot over the threshold and into the grass. There are no roads leading out into the green void, nor are there any foot trails. I also have no inkling of what may exist beyond, and would never dare ask. I can see the field from the small window in my bedroom. One night, I woke up to what sounded like someone calling my name from out in the field. It was not my mother's voice, but it was a woman's. The melodic sound of my name being sung drew me to the window. When I looked out of the small window, I thought I saw the fickle flickering of light deep in the field, but it was gone in a flash. I figure it was imagined or possibly the reflective eyes of a cat.

I stop walking when I reach the bus stop. I will need to wait for the city bus to take me deeper into the city where the hospital is. All of the Clone dwellings are located in the outer ring of our city. That way the People do not have to see us as often. Mother gives me one last look of encouragement before continuing down the cobblestone sidewalk. She is also a nurse, but was long ago claimed by one of the People.

The People can have whatever they want, Clones included. If a Person takes a fancy to one Clone, they claim it as their own, much like any other possession. Sometimes, like with my mother, the People are nice and gentle. However, more often than not, to be claimed by a Person is not as fortunate. Many Clones are claimed for the mere purpose of pleasure for the Person. The Clone could be tortured, raped, or killed without consequence. I do not have any contempt for my life; it is all I have known. My mother taught me how to avoid being claimed and to keep under the radar. However, if I am unfortunate enough to be seen, I will do as I am told. That is how life is for a Clone. We do what we are told, no questions asked. The People do what they want, no questions asked.

Other than violence inflicted upon Clones by the People, there is no violence within the city. The People have no reason to fight with one another. They do not have any hierarchy. There are those who have more than others, but if a Person wants more, it is just handed to them. If a Person has some aggression issues, they are easily resolved by utilizing a Clone.

As a Clone, I am nonviolent. We all have any violent traits removed at a cellular level. The only violent Clones are the Police Clones, but they only act in defensive violence. They do not attack anyone with rage or hatred. They are trained to use only enough force to subdue and nothing more.

While I wait for the bus, I look around the lightly trafficked street. There are still not many people bustling around yet this morning, but the bodies are slowly increasing in number, all of them Clones. Small birds of different colors chirp happily in some trees that have bright green leaves and fragrant pink flowers. A slight breeze plays with a loose strand of my hair. I wish my hair were not stiffly pulled back, so it could sway freely in the wind. The air smells so fresh and crisp, and the warm rays of the sun caress my cheeks. I am not too worried about any People wandering around this part of town. It is rare for a Person to have any reason to come to the Clone sector, but when they do, we all steer clear, because they are usually looking for trouble. In areas where People frequent, Clones walk with eyes lowered, but here I can freely admire the beauty surrounding me. There are not as many trees, and the architecture of our dwellings is not as extravagant as found deeper within the city, but there is still beauty and charm to be seen if one is willing to look for it.

Last year I had my first contact with People. Prior to my internship, I had only seen a few People come and go through our school. The first day of my internship was a complete shock. Apart from the soft inhale and exhale of others breathing, the slight ruffle of clothing as someone moves, the annoying sound of food smacking around as it is being chewed, and a single teacher talking, I am accustomed to relative silence. At the hospital, there are People talking freely everywhere. The chatter makes my head hurt and my ears ring. It is so strange to see People touching other People without hesitation or consequence. At first it seemed so wrong, but something deep inside told me that is how it is meant to be. That thought has been eating at me ever since my first day. I have longed for someone to touch me, or even just look at me like the People do with one another.

Imagining what it would be like to feel wanted or loved causes a tightness to pull at my chest. I am excited to start my Essential Function, but I am also looking forward to seeing Boston. We are both assigned to be nurses in the Emergency Room of the only hospital in the city. The last time I felt this sort of tension, it was not even my own. In school a few years ago, we were learning how to properly place an IV line. The teacher paired us off, and I was placed with Boston. Boston was about to insert the needle, but he was concerned he would hurt me. He became so tense that I began to have sympathetic tension in my own body. It just washed over me like the wind is right now. I calmed him down by giving him a reassuring look of confidence, and I gently set my hand on his. I had a funny sensation when my skin touched his. I have never touched someone just to touch them before. Other than my mother of course, but that was different. Boston and I quickly pulled our hands away from the other. I imagine that feeling to be what it feels like every time the People touch one another. Boston proceeded with the IV without tension or hesitation, and placed the line as perfectly as a Clone is designed to.

My hand slightly tingles with the memory of my hand resting on Boston's. Suddenly, I want more, and

I can feel a tight smile trying to tug at my lips. As if by magic, I feel another body brush softly against my back. Goosebumps explode all over my body. The tightness in my chest expands, and the smile tries harder to overcome my self-control. I look out of the corner of my eye to see who I hoped it was. Boston is now standing close enough to create a slight electricity between our barely separated arms. The corner of his lips slightly twitch as he too attempts to conceal a smile. There is a bright twinkle in his caramel eyes. The bright sun causes light to shimmer slightly as it reflects off of his bald head. Boston physically looks exactly like my brother, but at the same time, he looks completely different to me. I always imagine how much easier life would be if I never had to worry about keeping my hair an exact length like Boston's Clone type. They are all as bald as a newborn baby.

My hand, which dangles at my side, keeps brushing against Boston's. He slightly hooks my pinky with his own, and my heart feels like it has swollen so much it will soon explode. I am generally very good at suppressing my feelings, but the tension in my chest cannot be stopped as it spreads and continues to tug at the edges of my lips. I dip my head as I can no longer suppress the smile that has bubbled out from within. I do not want the cameras to take notice. The white and green bus pulls up with a squeal just in time to help me swallow a giggle. I quickly wipe the smile from my face as I casually pull my hand away from Boston's, but I purposefully bump into him as I shift my weight. The bus doors slide open and I climb aboard. This is likely the bus's first stop, as there are no other riders aboard yet. Four other Clones board with us, and other than Boston and me, everyone spreads out in the long bus.

Boston and I stand in the middle of the bus and hold on to a shiny vertical pole. Even though there are vacant seats, Clones are not permitted to sit. People ride this bus as well, and if a Clone is found occupying a seat, there are consequences. Boston stands behind me with his broad shoulder pressed against my back to give me a small amount of stability upon the bumpy ride. The bus is driving much too fast on the uneven pavement. The roads closer to the heart of the city are well manicured, but the roads through the Clone sector are poorly taken care of at best. I find myself fighting an internal battle between my Clone upbringing and my desire for more contact with Boston. This is the longest physical contact I have ever had with him, other than what we were told to do in class. I feel a warmth inside that I have never felt before. I want more, but I know I cannot. I do not understand these feelings, and have no idea where they are coming from.

I should have paid more attention to the bus's route. When we reach the next stop, and the bus abruptly halts, my body is jerked forward then thrown back into Boston's strong chest. I am so close to Boston that I can feel his heartbeat racing against my back. His warm breath on my neck that sends chills down my spine. His hand protectively rests on my hip to steady me. I look up into his startled but pleased eyes. The spark that flies through my body sends my heart aflutter. I bashfully smile back while I regain my balance and again rely on my own feet to hold me upright. We are stopped outside of the Owl, which is a gentlemen's club, where People go to drink liquor and do whatever they wish with Clones specifically created for that purpose. Even though I am not meant to know much about the city, I do know a great deal about the human anatomy and the natural course of propagating the species, due to my medical training.

Several Clones board the bus, as well as a rowdy group of young People that are likely leaving the Owl. I use the addition of bodies as an excuse to grudgingly move to the side so I am no longer making any contact with Boston. I look up into Boston's familiar face. He looks hurt by my repositioning, but I give him a look of caution which he understands. He knows as well as I do the consequence if we are caught. I give him another warm smile as the bus jerks to a start. I am better prepared this time and easily hold my ground.

There is a lot more noise now that there are People on board, intoxicated People at that. I hardly hear them as I keep exchanging glances with Boston. We have always been able to communicate with silent glances. He knows me better than anyone, my mother included.

The ride continues to be bumpy, as we have not yet departed the neglected roads of the Clone sector. The bus hits a bump at the same time as it whips around a corner. I am now regretting my decision to move away from the strong support Boston had given me. I see Boston's face contort with dread as I ungracefully fall into the lap of a young man who is sitting next to me.

"If you wanted a lap dance, I would have ordered one for you last night. After all, it was a celebration in your honor, Cam. It is not every day you turn eighteen." A pudgy young man sputters with a hiccup.

"Since when do I need you to get me some tail, Leroy? I am fully capable of getting my own. In fact, it apparently just falls in my lap as needed," chortled the young man whose lap I landed in.

I quickly stand upright, "Sorry, sir. Please forgive my clumsiness."

I know not to make eye contact, so I lower my eyes to the floor and begin to study my white tennis shoes. How on earth did I get a grass stain? I have not walked through any grass. The young man's shoes are black and very shiny and positioned awfully close to my own.

The young man I landed on is standing in front of me. He uses his hand to gently raise my chin. I allow him as any obedient Clone would. I still keep my eyes lowered as I feel his eyes scouring my face. I feel his soft, but slightly calloused thumb run down my jawbone. His thumb stops at the small L-shaped scar on my chin. I cannot help myself, I look up directly into a pair of stunningly beautiful blue-green eyes. The eyes seem gentle, inviting almost. My eyes have found a will of their own as they search the young man's tan-skinned face. His tussled brown hair has golden highlights, which catch the sun through the large windows of the bus. The movement of the bus causes the young man's long hair to hang over his eyes. The effect makes me think of the sandy beaches with crystalline ocean waters that I once saw on the cover of a magazine a patient at the hospital had. The young man is handsome and looks like no one I have ever seen before. Definitely not a Clone. However, even though I have never seen this stranger before, I somehow feel drawn to him, as if I knew him in a previous life. I should be terrified of the close scrutiny this Person places upon me, but instead, I am elated. Everyone else has vanished from my consciousness.

"Hmm, interesting," the young man murmurs under his breath.

"Leave her, they've got plenty just like her at the Owl," the man Leroy yells over the noise from the bus, bringing me back to reality.

I try to pull away, but the young man grabs my left wrist. My heart begins to pound out of my chest as the man procures his cell phone, which he proceeds to use to scan my barcode. A gasp of fear escapes from my mouth. At this point, I am using all of my willpower to keep tears from escaping. It is all over. My life has not even begun and now it is over. The young man comes closer, too close for my comfort, but I am not allowed to back away, because he did not order me to. His lips are close to the sensitive area of my neck right below my jawline. The smell radiating from the young man is not the rancid smell of alcohol and vomit that I can smell from a distance emanating from his friend Leroy. The young man's smell is intoxicating, invigorating. I try not to breathe it in, but it has already seeped into my veins. Even though I feel my life is over, my stomach churns with butterflies, and the rest of the occupants of the bus again fade away. All that I see are those mesmerizing blue eyes looking at me as if they can see through the mask I wear and into my soul. All that I feel are his fingers twisted gently around my wrist and the soft air he breathes against my skin.

"I think I will save this for later." I shudder as the young man whispers into my ear as he shows me the screen of his phone. My barcode tattoo is brightly displayed on the screen. My chin begins to tremble as I force the tears to stay at bay. The bus stops and Boston uses the opportunity of more bodies boarding to subtly position himself between the young man and me. Boston has his head lowered, but he ever so slightly gives the young man the calloused glare of a rabid dog. The young man either does not notice or does not take the warning seriously, as he sits back down with his friends and starts laughing at whatever comment was just said.

The hospital is the next stop, but before the doors fully close, I quickly escape from my worst nightmare come true, and exit the bus. The morning is still young, but the streets are slowly beginning to bustle with early morning commuters. There are few enough bodies that I am able to take off in a sprint down the road. After I keep up the pace for several blocks, I turn down a darkened alleyway. I quickly check for any cameras. Fortunately there are none here. I curl up behind a dumpster and let my tears fall unabated. I regret my behavior during the interaction with the young man. I feel so foolish for looking him in the eyes. Why did I not listen to my brain when it told me to look away? Why was I so preoccupied with Boston that I did not pay attention to the bus ride and staying upright?

I feel a warm hand wrap around mine. The hand raises me up to stand. I have to slightly crane my neck to look up into the familiar face of Boston. I have never noticed how tall he is until now. Probably because I am positioned much closer to him than ever before. All of my restraint vanishes as I wrap my arms around his waist and burry my face into his chest. I continue to cry softly, but the tears quickly wither away as I am comforted by the rhythmic beating of Boston's heart. At first, Boston becomes tense, and has not a clue how to react. Before this, the most contact we have shared was several minutes ago on the bus when he was standing behind me. Boston slowly relaxes, and he wraps his arms around me. As my sobs soften into a light whimper, Boston bends down and places his cheek close to mine.

"You are okay, Alabaster. That jerk is not going to lay a hand on you again if I can help it. We will likely never see him again anyway." Boston's words are comforting as he whispers them in my ear.

Boston slowly turns his head and caresses my cheek with his lips. I do not understand what is happening, but my head slowly turns toward his as my lips begin searching for his. The search is not a conscious decision, but rather one fueled by pure instinct. It is as if something deeper, something primordial guides my lips, something deeper than genetics. When our lips meet, they move together slowly, as if whispering a dangerous secret. I can taste the sweetness of oranges mixed with the saltiness of skin. The kiss is slow at first, but it quickly progresses from a gentle whisper to something else as lips part and I feel the wetness of another's mouth. I cannot contain the yearning inside as I urge Boston further. Boston slowly moves his hand from around my waist up under my shirt. The warmth of his hand on my back sends a tingle throughout my body. Boston takes a step forward, completely closing the distance between our bodies and pinning my body to the cold cream-colored stucco wall behind me. The cold sensation is a welcome one, as I feel like my body could possibly combust. I pull him closer. My whole body aches to become one with him. The world disappears and all that exists is the two of us. My hand finds its way under Boston's shirt, and now traces the firm muscles of his abdomen.

I am yanked back to reality as a car's horn angrily shouts from the road. Boston and I pull apart as if nothing has happened. We stare down the alley toward the road with expressions reminiscent of a deer caught in the headlights. There is no one there. The car must have been passing by, and no one had witnessed the serious crime just committed. I straighten my clothes and my hair as I head back to the road. I briefly pause to wipe any remaining evidence of tears, before looking back to Boston. He is staring blankly at his hands as if trying to comprehend what they had just done. I am of no help to him because I do not even understand what just happened, and I am still struggling to fight the urge to run back to him to be in his arms once more. I take one last deep breath of air to settle my rampant emotions.

"Come on," I call to him. "We are going to be late."

Chapter 2

Boston finally looks up and joins me. I take one deep breath before stepping out onto the street. No one notices us as we emerge from the dark alley, or at least no one seems to notice. We begin walking faster. Had we stayed on the bus, we would have arrived at the hospital twenty minutes early for our shift. However, our early exit has left us with a ten-minute walk to the hospital. That plus the unknown length of time spent in the alley means we are going to be cutting it pretty close. We have ridden this bus route enough to know where to go. Otherwise we could easily become lost in the labyrinth-like city streets.

Luckily, after a brisk walk, we arrive at the hospital at the same time as the majority of the other Clone nurses. Boston and I are familiar with the hospital after our internship last year. We both head toward the east wing of the hospital where the ER is located. Upon arrival outside of the sliding-glass double doors, I fall into my familiar routine. I hold my wrist under a barcode scanner sitting to the left of the ER's entrance.

A small red line flickers across my tattoo before the machine beeps and my Clone name appears on a small LCD screen. I approach the glass doors which automatically slide open, allowing me to enter. Inside the ER, everyone is bustling. I again recall the first day of my internship a year ago and the overwhelming feeling that weighed me down. I had no idea where to start. Even with all of the rigorous training there is so much to take in all at once, much more than one can be prepared for.

I now know to first approach the electronic LCD board which covers the majority of the wall behind the nurse's station. There are many vertical rows of patient names. Each name has a correlating horizontal row describing their illness, what room they are in, who their doctor is, their current condition, and lastly, who the nurse is. At first, my name is not on the board. Boston's is not there either. For a moment fear darkens my eyesight as I imagine the People knowing what we had done in the alley. I quickly gain my wits back when the current list of Clone names flash out and are replaced with new ones. It is now the start of a new shift, and I find my Clone name, A14B45T3R, pop up on half a dozen patient lines. I quickly memorize my patient names, their illnesses, what room they are in, and their current conditions.

I do not need to write them as this is what I was programmed to do.

I pay no attention to who the doctors are for each of my patients. All I need to know is what each tells me to do. I quickly head to the room of the patient in the most critical condition. As I enter the room, I realize this patient is a Clone. My heart sinks. All of my training tells me to help the People first, and then the Clones if time permits. I am at war within myself again. I cannot turn away. I quickly glance over my shoulder. When I am satisfied that no one is paying attention, I approach the patient. The Clone comes from the other female base type. She looks much different than me. Her hair flows over her shoulder like a river of red and orange flames. It is meant to be pulled back, but due to her current condition, the People are likely letting it slide. The Clone's hazel eyes reveal fear and pain. I hastily take the Clone's vitals. She has a steady beat and strong breathing. There is a large gash on the Clone's forehead, and finger-shaped bruises are growing darker around her throat. The Clone's hazel eyes swim in a sea of crimson. I am unable to determine without an X-ray, but it seems like the Clone's right arm has a displaced fracture. The broken arm along with the gash are not a good sign for a Clone. The broken arm, if not set properly, could mean a useless arm. There is no use for a one-armed Clone. Meaning, the Clone will likely be removed from society. Even if I were able to set the bone, there is still the issue of casting. The arm is not even the worst issue. The gash on the Clone's forehead is deep and wide. The wound is bound to leave a noticeable scar, creating a physically identifiable trait and assured removal. My shoulders slump as I succumb to the hopelessness of the Clone's ultimate fate.

As I turn away, a weak raspy voice gets my attention. "Wait. Please help."

I set my jaw with determination and quickly search a drawer in a nearby cart. My fingers know what they are looking for and soon emerge with a single syringe and a small bottle of clear liquid. I hastily fill the syringe and inject the contents into the broken arm of the Clone. While the lidocaine begins to work its magic on the Clone's arm, I clean and bandage the gash. After I have finished with the gash, I direct my attention back to the arm. I place my hand on either side of the brake. I offer the Clone a foreboding expression. The Clone nods in determination as she prepares herself for the pain that is to come. I apply pressure to both sides of the Clone's displaced fracture. I simultaneously pull the arm apart and slowly slide each end of the bone back into place. A grinding sound like gritting teeth is audible as the ends of the bone rub together. The Clone cringes, but she is able to suppress any screams. She is obviously created to silently take intense pain, probably an Owl Clone. I tightly wrap the arm to suspend the bones so they can fuse properly, if she lives that long.

I lean over the Clone and whisper in her ear, "I cannot do much, but this should ease the pain."

The Clone appreciatively nods and I again turn away and leave the room. I do not look back as I struggle to hold in an intense emotional rollercoaster, which I do not know how to comprehend. Deep down, I know I will never again see that Clone.

Chapter 3

I take a few deep breaths and try to compartmentalize my feelings before moving on to the next patient. Clones are not created to mourn or feel loss. We are designed to be void of emotion, like my father. I should not be feeling this kind of sadness and emotion.

I am busy taking vitals, administering medicines the doctors have ordered, and writing patient notes when he shows up. The handsome young man from the bus is standing at the bedside of my next patient. He is now wearing a white doctor's coat with a black stethoscope around his neck. He has his back turned, but as I am a Clone who can tell identical people apart, I have no problem identifying him from behind. The young doctor is the same height, which is a few inches taller than Boston. The doctor has the same broad shoulders and the same unkempt golden locks. His hair appears cleaner and slightly brushed, but it is still just as unkempt, like he styles it like that on purpose. Cold fear courses through my blood and I slowly back out of the door to escape before the young doctor can turn to see me. However, I may have been genetically engineered to nimbly sew stitches, but stealth is not a strong suit of mine. I back up right into a rolling cart, knocking it over with a loud crash that brings the entire ER to a screeching halt. Everyone stares at me for a few seconds before quickly returning to their duties. I can tell my cheeks are flushed from embarrassment. Boston stands across the lobby from me and he gives me a warm reassuring smile before turning away. I have almost forgotten the reason I was backing up when a voice speaks up behind me.

"Are you trying to wake the entire hospital?"

I turn quickly, too quickly. The cart I knocked over had a tray with many vials with liquid enclosed. The vials all shattered on contact with the hard white tiled floors, leaving a colorful slippery mess. As I turn, I slip and begin to fall with a swallowed yelp. Before I hit the ground, a strong pair of arms catch me around my ribcage. I am lifted and gently set back on my feet. Once I am stable, I look up into the familiar smirk of the handsome young man from the bus. Our faces are only an inch apart. His strong arms are still wrapped around my torso, holding me close and not relenting. I cannot explain why, but I do not mind his closeness as much this time. He feels safe. I feel drawn to him from somewhere deep within. The young doctor studies my face with interest. His eyes are suddenly drawn to the scar on my chin. A look of recognition passes across his face sending my head spinning in terror and my heart aflutter in excitement.

"You again? Didn't we just meet on the bus earlier? You know, if you want me, I am flattered, but next time just try saying 'Hi' or 'Hello.' Stop making such a scene to get my attention." There is humor in his voice, but it still causes me extreme tension.

"I do not know what you are talking about. I have never seen you before," I lie.

I do not know how I managed to lie, as I was created to always tell the truth, especially to the People. The lie came a lot easier than I would have thought. No matter how safe this Person seems, I know to never trust one of the People. The young doctor's arms are still gently wrapped around me, holding me close. So close I can feel his firm stomach muscles and the protruding points of his hips. He smells amazing, like fresh-cut cedar mixed with the first rain of spring. I know what cologne is, but I knew not of the effect it can have until now. I have never been close enough to a Person to smell cologne and Clones do not wear any. It is intoxicating. The smell causes my better judgement to fade into oblivion. I slightly panic as I develop a tightness in my chest that I have only so far associated with Boston. I want to break free, but at the same time, part of me wants more, a lot more. I am so encompassed with his presence, I do not notice his hand reaching for my tattooed wrist. The young doctor releases my body, but I cannot retreat as he now holds my left wrist firmly. He does not hold it in a way to cause pain, but he does not release it as I tug. He casually studies my tattoo.

"Hmm," he begins, "if it was not you on the bus, then the authorities need to be notified, because there are apparently two Clones with the same number. See, I have the proof right here."

I can feel all of the color fade from my cheeks and my jaw drops as the young doctor pulls out his phone, which shows the picture of my wrist that he had taken a few hours earlier on the screen. He begins to call the attention of a security guard when I desperately grab his arm. I pull his waving hand down. It comes easily, but with the size of his bicep, I am sure it would not have were he not willing. His piercing blue eyes meet mine, and I again feel like he is looking into my soul. I reluctantly pull my eyes to the floor, but I keep my hand at rest on his forearm where it seems to fit perfectly. A current of electricity pulsates from the contact. I want to run my hand up his muscular arm, up to his broad shoulders, but I push away the unexplainable desire.

"No, wait, it was me on the bus. I am sorry I lied. I was embarrassed," I say, pleading for his forgiveness.

"A Clone that lies? I didn't know that was possible. Isn't that supposed to be bred out of you?" he inquires skeptically, but still with a playful tone.

I am at a loss. I do not know what to make of this Person. I can feel tears welling up in my eyes again. Without my consent, my lips begin to tremble. A small whimper escapes as I falter at holding the tears at bay.

"No, no, no. Please don't cry. I am only teasing. Come on. Calm down. Take a deep breath. I am Dr. Cameron Staunton. What is your name?"

I look up into his deep blue-green eyes with a questioning look of uncertainty.

"I am Clone number A14B45T3R. You may call me anything you want, as is your right."

"Come on, I know you must give each other names. It would be horrid going around saying, 'Hey, Clone number 185GE9O,' or 'Clone number 50D1PT4, would you please pass the peas.' What a mouthful."

Cameron gives a warm half-smile. His smile is amazing, it lights up his entire face. The scent of his cologne is still having an uncanny effect upon me. It is so intoxicating, it makes my head spin, as does the continued physical contact. The smile reaches his eyes, which are begging me to trust him. I cannot help but to smile back. I feel warmth as blood once again returns to fill my cheeks and I begin to blush again. I feel like such in idiot standing here in the arms of such an attractive Person while blushing like an idiot. Can I trust him with something so personal that only two people in the world know? My brain is yelling at me, telling me no, but my heart is screaming yes. Before I can open my mouth to share the secret, the patient I originally came in to check on lets out an ear-splitting howl.

Dr. Staunton and I both jump out of our binary existence to rush over and help the Person. I recall reading the patient's chart earlier. He was in a car accident and only sustained minor injuries. He should not be howling in agony. I had been coming to do one final check before the patient was cleared to leave. Apparently, something serious had been missed by the admitting staff. Dr. Staunton and I quickly examine the patient, who is holding his stomach. I gently pull his hand away to have a better look, but the patient begins to thrash wildly. I hastily get a syringe and fill it with a sedative. I plunge the needle into the man's bicep. Within seconds the patient is calm once more, but he continues to groan softly. I move the patient's hand away from his stomach and pull the white hospital sheet out of the way. There, in the space between two ribs, runs a small cut. It seems shallow and too small for stitches, so it was left to heal on its own and not bandaged. The patient still moves slightly as the sedative continues to take effect. As he moves, a glimmer from the wound catches my eye. I insert my index fingertip to gently palpate the wound. After a few seconds of prodding, I feel a sharp foreign object. I insert then my thumb and index finger into the opening on either side of the object. Dr. Staunton restrains the patient as he begins to squirm again. I have never suffered a serious injury, but I could imagine the pain this would cause. I tightly pinch the object and pull it out slowly so as to not cause more damage. When the object is fully out, I reveal a shard of glass to Dr. Staunton. It is only an inch wide, but it went in two inches deep. Dr. Staunton nods as he proceeds to insert his own fingers into the incision. His fingers are larger than mine which causes the patient to moan and move slightly. The doctor checks for any remaining fragments as well as any damage done to major organs. We have caused the small incision to grow slightly, so now it merits stitches.

As Dr. Staunton withdraws his fingers, he begins to ask me for a needle and thread. I am already holding a threaded needle out for him with one hand as my other is administering antiseptic to the wound.

"Thank you," Dr. Staunton says as he takes the needle and begins to run the stitches.

When Dr. Staunton is finished tying the last knot, he begins looking for scissors. I am already holding them at the ready. Dr. Staunton gives me another charming half-smile before he cuts the thread. I begin cleaning the area and throwing out bloodied gauze. When I am done with that, I join Dr. Staunton at the sink to scrub the blood from my hands. When I reach for a towel, he takes my hand gently to stop me. I pause and look up at him. I have a sudden urge to throw up from the feeling his touch has sent coursing through me again.

"You did well. You knew what I wanted before I did. It takes most Clones several years to reach that point, and this is your first day, isn't it?"

I nod once and Dr. Staunton releases my hand. We both remain staring at each other in silence. I still do not know if I can trust him. Who am I kidding? I cannot trust him. He is a Person. Regardless of what I may be feeling, I need to follow what I know. I turn to leave, but when I reach the door, I turn back around to him. He has not moved, and he is still staring at me. He is so handsome and he seems to have the same look of confusion on his face as I feel inside. My brain has suddenly forgotten what it knows.

"Alabaster," I whisper before quickly turning back toward the door, minding the slick floor this time.

"Wait, hold on a second. Is that your name?"

I feel Dr. Staunton's warm hand once again encircling my wrist as he stops me. His touch is so electrifying. I inhale swiftly to catch my breath, which has tried to escape.

"May I call you Ally for short?" Dr. Staunton inquires softly.

"As I said before, you may call me whatever you wish."

I do not look back at him as I pull my hand away and leave. He lets it slide out of his grasp freely, but I can feel his reluctance.

"I know, but I would like your permission." Dr. Staunton speaks loud enough for me to hear, as I have created a greater distance between him and myself.

I do not know what to say in response, so I keep going. This is not the way Clones are typically treated by People. He is addressing me as if I were a member of his elite group of People and not a lower being. The tension in my chest returns, and it takes all of my will to suppress a smile, and even more to resist the urge to turn back around.

I force myself to continue down the hallway without a second glance back. I hope he did not notice my moment of hesitation. I know he is still watching because I can feel his eyes on me as I walk the hallway. After I round a corner, I stop and lean my back against the wall. I close my eyes and release a breath of tension and place a hand on my pounding chest in an attempt to calm it. I hope I never see Dr. Staunton again. He is dangerous. The feelings I have for him when I am near him are dangerous.

Chapter 4

Of course I see him again. Dr. Staunton is a doctor, I am a nurse, and we work in the same ER. It is inevitable and, indeed, happens only twenty minutes later. After checking on a few patients, I head down a hallway while writing more notes on a tablet. All of a sudden, I am rammed from the side by another body, causing me to drop the tablet, whose screen cracks on impact. As I do an ungraceful pirouette, I am again caught before an unpleasant meeting with the sterile tile floor.

"We have got to stop meeting like this," croons a deep male voice.

I look up into the striking face of Dr. Staunton smiling down at me. No matter how many times I see his face, there is always a new feature to take in. I hungrily take in every line, every curve, every perfection, and every imperfection. My stomach flops around like a fish out of water. Dr. Staunton gently raises me from the dipped position. Once I am planted on my feet once again, I hurriedly walk away without a word or a second glance.

Chapter 5

Lunchtime arrives quickly. I am starving as I follow behind other lunch breakers. Unlike the cafeteria at my school, this one serves both Clone and Person alike. The two groups do not sit at the same tables together, but they wait in the same lines, are served the same food, and sit in the same dining hall. I smile politely and give a soft "thank you" to the red-haired Clone who loads my tray with chili, cornbread, and a leaf salad. The serving Clone woman brings a flashing memory of my first patient this morning. I again feel sorrow as well as a tinge of regret before I am able to once again regain control of my emotions. I know very well that there will be many an occasion where I will be helpless in my Essential Function. If I let one lost cause affect me this much, I will have a long and depressing life ahead of me.

At the end of the line, I present my barcode tattoo for scanning before I turn to find a seat. I spot Boston sitting with a few other Clones at a table across the room. Boston looks over at me with a smile and he slightly twitches his head, inviting me to join him. I smile slightly and take one step in his direction, but I freeze before the next. There are half a dozen tables between Boston and me. At a table smack dab in the middle sits the charming and attractive Dr. Staunton. He is laughing loudly with some friends, all of whom are People, not Clones. As if he can feel my eyes on him, Dr. Staunton looks back at me. He sees me staring and winks at me before resuming his banter with friends. I get a sick feeling in my stomach and slightly lose my appetite, but I know I need to eat something to keep up my strength for the rest of the day. I carefully navigate through the crowded room, purposefully taking a detour several tables over to avoid the one Dr. Staunton inhabits. I finally make it to Boston, who politely pulls out a neighboring chair for me to take. Boston smiles at me reassuringly. I already feel better, and some of the tension in my stomach releases, but none from my chest. I pull out a small notepad from a pocket in my scrubs and write a quick note under the table.

Please switch a few patients with me. The man from the bus is a doctor here. I do not want to see him again.

I show the note to Boston under the table as I tap his foot to get his attention. Boston is accustomed to this discrete method of attention getting and barely shifts to glimpse the note. He gives a minute nod of his bald head in agreement. We eat in typical silence. Boston slowly scoots his body closer until his side touches mine. I get chills up and down my spine again and can hardly restrain a smile from creeping onto my face. It is a dangerous game Boston and I play, but I cannot help it. I yearn for more. My body desires more. Boston's attentions have become a distraction from this horrendous day of mishaps. However, all good things must come to an end and this is one of those things. Boston arrived before me, so he reluctantly clears up and leaves before I am finished eating. A few minutes pass and it is now time for me to head back. I have not quite finished my entire meal, but my stomach is still on the fritz due to all of the drama. I gather my dishes onto a tray to take over to the dish chute. I stand and turn to dispose of my tray of dirty dishes, but before I make it very far, I am forced to stop abruptly before crashing into a body positioned directly behind me.

"That was a close one. I am glad you have finally broken your clumsy habit. I was a little worried I was going to require a uniform change due to being viciously assaulted with a chili bowl."

Dr. Staunton is flanked by two other young men who all appear to be close in age. They too are doctors and all three are chuckling. The other two are laughing maliciously, but Dr. Staunton laughs with a flirtatious edge. I close my eyes tightly and take a deep breath in.

As I slowly open my steely gray eyes, I dryly apologize. "I am so very sorry again, sir. Please forgive me. If you would be so kind as to please excuse me yet again, I will stay out of your way from now on."

I keep my eyes averted like a good Clone should, but I cannot restrain myself from glaring up at Dr. Staunton for a split second. He backs away and dramatically bows with his arms spread wide, making an aisle for me. Dr. Staunton remains in his prostrate pose as I pass, but he does raise his penetrating eyes to watch me. Across from Dr. Staunton stands one of his friends. From the corner of my eye I recognize him as Leroy from the bus. He sways slightly as if he is still feeling the effects of alcohol and his muddy-brown eyes are bloodshot. The whole effect is reminiscent of bloody stool. Leroy's evil smile makes his red face pudgier than usual. He sticks his foot out just in time to catch my ankle as I pass. There is no hope of catching myself in time, so I instead brace for impact. I crash hard upon my tray with a clatter. The small amount of chili remaining in my bowl smears down the front of my shirt. I sit up quickly and collect the dishes, tossing them onto the tray. I head over to the conveyor belt to discard my tray before leaving the room and the cruelty behind. I am too embarrassed and hurt to hear Dr. Staunton as he yells at Leroy.

I make it to the ladies' locker room reserved for Clones without further embarrassment. I approach the Clone attendant, who is identical to me. She stands outside of the locker room behind the counter. I request a new set of scrubs. The Clone hands me a clean set of light-blue scrubs identical to the ones I currently wear. She scans my barcode while instructing me to bring the dirty set back after I replace it. I nod and head into the room. There are no lockers in the Clone locker room. To require a locker, one must first have personal possessions. There are several concrete benches in rows upon the cold tile floor. There is a wall with four shower heads spaced out evenly on one wall and four toilets without stalls along another. At the far end of the room the wall is lined with a counter that has six round sinks. There is a mirror behind the sinks. There is also a black dome in one corner, which likely conceals a camera or two.

I approach the mirrored sinks quickly. I do not have much time before I will be expected back at the ER. As I look at my reflection in the mirror, I see my gray eyes shimmer due to the crying I have been doing today. There are puffy pink pillows surrounding my eyes as well. My attention then travels down the front of my shirt. The rusty smear caused by the chili contrasts greatly with the sky-blue hue of my top. I take off the top and, in the process, I see the embroidered butterfly my mother had sewn on as a secret gift.

At this point, I am unable to restrain the flood of tears. If I put on the clean top, I will lose the precious gift forever. If I do not replace it, I will have a dirty red stain down my front. In that scenario I will have a shirt that sets me apart from the other Clones. If it brings any attention I will be told to replace the shirt, which could bring attention to the embroidered gift and further, more severe, consequences. I cannot bear to part with the shirt, so I set the dirty shirt into a sink and proceed to scrub. I stand topless with only my skin-colored bra on as I scrub for a good three minutes with little success. The stain goes from a rusty burnt sienna to a light orange, but it remains quite noticeable. Just when I have given up all hope of removing the visible traces of my horrible day, I realize I am not alone. I jump out of my skin when a male voice speaks from behind me. I look up to see Dr. Staunton in the mirror's reflection.

"I am so sorry. I really did not mean for that to happen. I had no idea Leroy was going to trip you." Dr. Staunton sounds sincere as he apologizes. "Why are you attempting to clean that shirt? There is a clean one right there." He points to the clean shirt I left on the counter.

"Oh god! What do you want from me, Dr. Staunton? Why will you not just leave me be?" I cry desperately.

The tears now flow fervently down my cheeks. I do not bother attempting to hold them in, there would be no point. I hug the wet shirt to my bosom, trying unsuccessfully to obscure myself. Dr. Staunton takes two quick strides toward me and produces a towel which he wraps around my shivering body. He momentarily gives what I would consider a gentle hug before releasing me and turning away. Unfortunately, Dr. Staunton does not leave as I hoped he would. I set the hopeless mess of my shirt down on the counter and quickly pick up the clean shirt. I pull it on over my head while using it to dry my tears.

"By the way, you can call me Cameron. Dr. Staunton just sounds too pompous. Are you properly concealing yourself yet?" Dr. Staunton inquires with an unsuccessful attempt at lighthearted humor.

"Yes" is all I can whisper in response.

Dr. Staunton turns around to face me. He wears a look of authentic concern and hurt on his face. I cannot wrap my mind around this man or my feelings for him. How can he be so gentle and caring one second, then so cruel and hurtful the next? I do not understand why I want to wrap my arms around him to comfort him one moment, and then the next I want to punch him in his perfectly symmetrical face. The feelings I have for him are not normal for a Clone. In fact, they are emotions that are meant to be genetically bred out of me, just like lying.

"I think we had better be going, Cameron." I draw out his name. "We will be late. There are patients to tend to."

I begin to walk past Cameron while wiping the last remnants of tears from my eyes. Cameron steps in front of me, impeding my way. I do not look down at my feet as I know I should. Instead, I gaze at Cameron directly in his magnetic azure eyes. I try to convey hate in my glare, but the look in his eyes causes me to shudder slightly. Not with fear, but with something else. I am all he sees.

"They can wait," Cameron whispers as he places a soft kiss on my forehead, and then proceeds to slowly place more across my forehead, down my cheek, and over my jawbone. After each kiss he tentatively meets my softening gaze, as if asking permission, or like he is waiting for me to tell him to stop. I do not want him to stop. He gives a longer kiss atop the faint scar on my chin before stopping. I still do not want him to stop. My whole body trembles as Cameron stares deeply into my eyes. His lips hover over mine with no more distance than a piece of paper separating them. I do not pull away and he moves no further. We are at a standstill. The rise and fall of my chest has increased along with the speed of my pulse. My lips are open loosely, invitingly, welcomingly. The only sounds in the room are our breathing and the annoying buzz of a florescent ceiling light. My entire body trembles with both trepidation and longing. I stare desperately into the deep pools of Cameron's eyes with desire, but also anxiety. Cameron has the same look of desire, but also vulnerability. Just as Cameron has seemingly set his mind on proceeding, I duck away and sprint off before he can stop me.

Chapter 6

When I return to the ER, I see Boston has held to his silent promise. He has switched his name with mine for all of the patients under Cameron's care. I am glad he knew which doctor I meant. I breathe a silent sigh of relief and proceed to take a mental note of the newly configured assignment board. I head back to my rounds of checking vitals and administering medicines ordered by the patient's doctors. Before I know it, the next shift of Clones has arrived and it is time for me to leave. I try to spot Boston in the crowd of bodies coming and going. I hover just a couple inches over five feet, which is the shortest of the five Clone types. This fact makes it difficult to see over the crowd of people leaving.

"Who are you looking for?" inquires a voice that has become all too familiar today. "It, by chance, wouldn't be me, would it?"

I do not think I would be disappointed to never hear Cameron's voice ever again. Part of me knows that is a lie.

"No one," I chide curtly.

I should not be talking to a Person like this. I do not know where my attitude has come from. I do not turn around to see Cameron, even though part of me wants to. Instead, I use my small stature to my advantage as I fluidly wade through the river of traffic. Cameron is much larger and his broad shoulders hold him back. He is tall enough that I am certain he can still see me though.

I am not positive, and I do not look back to confirm, but I faintly hear Cameron yelling over the crowd, "It really was a pleasure running into you all day. I look forward to doing it again tomorrow!"

I quickly get on a bus. It is overflowing with hot, sweaty bodies, but I am able to squeeze in. I hide a few soft sobs in the bevy of bodies. My stop is one of the last on this route. The bus slowly empties until there are only four Clones left, including the driver. Boston is not one of them. I and the two other Clones exit at the last stop. The driver, who resembles Boston, wishes us all a goodnight as he closes the doors and drives off. I head down the street and the two other Clones go in the opposite direction, leaving me alone on an evening lit mostly by the full moon and stars. The street lighting in the Clone sector is not substantive, and of the few light posts, most are not operative. It is a short walk back to my dwelling, but I walk slowly. I need some time to process the day. I know that no one in my family unit will ask how my day was, but I still want to be alone in my thoughts.

I cross in front of the dark opening of an alleyway and begin to scream as a hand grabs my arm, pulling me into the darkness. Another hand clasps over my mouth, stifling the sound of my pleas. I struggle to escape until Boston's familiar face and kindly caramel eyes appear before me.

"It is just me, Alabaster. Calm down. I could not stop thinking about you today. Each time I saw you, my knees began to buckle and my heart would race."

Boston runs his warm hand down my cheek, where it rests, cupping my face. I press my face into his palm, absorbing the warmth it has to offer. The soft skin of Boston's hand soothes the mild burn of my cheek as the result of the tears that have flowed across it today. I look up at him. I am comforted by the warmth of his familiar light-brown eyes. I notice the difference between his and Cameron's eyes, other than the color. Boston's are warm and inviting, whereas Cameron's are deep and piercing. Boston's invite me in, but Cameron's pursue my soul, drawing me deeper into the depths of his own, with or without my consent.

"At lunch, it took all of my energy to restrain myself from continuing where we left off. I need you, Alabaster. I cannot explain what I am feeling, but I realized today, I have always felt it for you."

I gently kiss the palm of Boston's hand as his other hand finds my waist. The distance between our bodies becomes microscopic as he pulls me closer. Boston's lips find my neck and leave butterfly-soft kisses down to my collarbone. The hand on my waist sneaks under my shirt and around to the middle of my back. Boston slowly walks me backward until he has me pinned against the cold stucco of the Clone dwelling behind. I shudder as his kisses intensify, leaving behind a hot tingling sensation in their wake. I somehow manage to weave my hands into the elastic drawstring waist of Boston's light-blue scrubs that match my own. I slowly work my fingers between bare skin and fabric, making Boston gasp. Boston's free hand is pressing firmly against the stucco façade behind me, seemingly supporting his weight. The other hand remains on my mid-back, holding me close. Boston brings his lips back up my neck until they rest upon my lips. The fiery burn throughout my body ignites as our mouths open and close as one. I tug at the waist of his pants, urging him closer.

Barong! Barong! Barong! The sound of the curfew bell rings loud and clear. It is the first warning, signaling five minutes until all Clones must be home with lights out, unless they work the night shift. Boston and I pause momentarily and look at one another. When the bells stop, Boston attempts to return to my lips, but I turn away from his advance.

"We need to go home. If we get caught--"

"Let them catch us," Boston whispers between kisses on my neck.

"You do not know what you are saying, Boston. You know the punishment for being out after curfew, and the punishment for doing what we are doing is far worse." I fill my voice with an urgent, pleading tone.

"Fine."

Boston angrily pushes away from the wall and jogs off without another look back. I watch Boston's figure fade into the distance before I leave the scene of yet another crime. My dwelling is two houses down from the alley, but I run swiftly to get there. When I enter my dwelling I barely have enough time to quickly grab an orange someone neglected to dispose of before crawling into bed. It is illegal for us to save any food from a meal, but at the moment I do not

care. I have larger offenses to worry about than a
member of my family unit not properly disposing
of food. It was likely my mother, as she would not
want me to go hungry after a long day of work. As I
head down the hallway, the last and final procession
of curfew bells toll. All of the lights in the house
are extinguished as soon as the last bell rings. The
hallway is pitch black, so I do not bother trying to get
a nightgown from the laundry chute. I resolve to sleep
in my uniform. I lie in my bed atop the covers and eat
the orange in darkness.

Chapter 7

Sleep is a stranger to me tonight. I lay awake staring up at the ceiling. Every time I close my eyes, I relive the burning touch of Boston, or I fall into the endless blue-green depths of Cameron's eyes. I feel as if the tension in my chest is going to make my heart explode at any second. I have no desire to return to the ER tomorrow. I want to avoid any potential contact with Cameron. I feel sick to my stomach just thinking about him, but he is all I think about. The thought of another encounter with Cameron makes me want to punch something, but it is all I seem to want. I am not meant to feel these violent tendencies, but I am also not meant to feel these emotions either. What is going on with me?

I have always been fond of Boston, but I find myself yearning for Cameron. Every part of my body feels like it is reaching out to him. I am angry at myself for wishing that what had almost happened in the alley had been with Cameron rather than Boston. These feelings are making me hate Dr. Staunton passionately. I can't be calling him Cameron. It is not my place as a Clone, and it makes him feel so much closer to me. On the other hand, he told me to call him Cameron. If I were to call him Dr. Staunton it would be a direct violation of the laws set before me. What if I ask the hospital director for another assignment in the hospital? No, I can't do that. I do not want to be separated from Boston. Maybe he could switch too? But that will not work either because there is no guarantee we will be assigned to the same post again. And what would I tell the director? That I had somehow fallen in love with a Person? Or a Person is harassing me? There would be no excuse for my desire to transfer, and it would only bring unnecessary questions. Besides, it is difficult to imagine life without Boston in it. He has always been a major part of my life. It would be like removing my mother or my lungs or my heart. I could not possibly live without any of those and I can't possibly live without Boston. I have a bond with Boston that surpasses even that of my mother and me. If we were no longer at the same assignment, I would likely never see Boston again, and that I cannot bear. I will have to grit my teeth and risk bumping into Cameron again, literally.

Sometime in my tossing and turning, the Sandman finally finds me. He does not bring any dreams with him, but the sleep he brings is a more-than-welcome gift. Dawn comes too soon. The brilliant rays of the sun pound upon the window pane, rudely waking me up. My head throbs as if an earthquake is occurring within, splitting my skull into pieces. I drag myself out of bed, feeling like I had somehow gained a hundred pounds during the night. I spend more time in the cold shower than I should. When I get out, I dry off and dress in my newly provided light-blue scrubs, which are neatly folded upon my bed. The set I wore yesterday has vanished, likely my mother's doing. I hope she did not notice the missing embroidered butterfly. My heart breaks a little more, if at all possible, at the thought of losing that gift. After I am dressed, I sit on my bed and place my hand on my soft porcelain cheek. I close my eyes and imagine Cameron's touch rather than my own. In the almost-privacy of my room I do not attempt to hide the smile that forms from my thoughts. The camera in my bedroom is at my back anyhow. I look at the time on my small alarm clock. I begin to panic as I realize I need to hurry or I will be late. My fingers nimbly put my hair into a braid as I hurry down the hallway.

Everyone else has already left for work or school, but a cold cup of black coffee, a cold bowl of oatmeal, and an apple still sit on a plate on the table at my seat. I stand behind my chair and hurriedly inhale the food, which hits my empty stomach hard. I finish quickly and add my dishes to the rest of my family unit's. I then proceed to send my family unit's dishes through the chute. I leave the house and run at full speed to the bus. I make it onto the bus just before the bifold doors close. The next bus is in twenty minutes, which would have delivered me late for work. I look at the passengers of the bus with disappointment. Boston must have boarded the earlier bus. As it is, I barely make it to the ER before the patient screen flickers and the nurse names change, signaling the next shift. Too late to talk to the director now.

I take note of my patients. My shoulders relax with relief as I notice I do not have any of Cameron's patients. Boston must have already switched our assignments around. I am also comforted by the fact that Boston is not mad at me after last night. I was uncertain if he would forgive me for pushing him away. I make a mental note to thank him for the switch later.

Today I begin with the first patient on my list and continue from there. I do not want another hopeless

case to start my day. Lunchtime arrives faster than
I had anticipated. I head to the cafeteria with a few
other Clones. When I arrive at the cafeteria, I take
a quick look for Boston. He must have gone much
earlier today because he is again nowhere in sight.
To my relief, neither is Cameron. After I get a tray of
food, I find a nearby seat at a table with Clones. Three
of them look exactly like me, two look like my father,
although a lot less spiteful, and one, like Boston. We
all eat in silence, as is customary. I clear my dishes
and take them to the chute. After yesterday, today is
relatively uneventful. It is perfect. I finish the rest of
my shift in peace as well. My headache from sleep
deprivation has softened to a gentle lull. I can almost
hear my peaceful bed calling my name from here. I
enter the last of my patient notes into a tablet which
I hand off to the next shift's nurse, scan my barcode,
and head down the hall with the other commuters.
I leave the hospital doors and follow the foot traffic
toward the bus stop. As I round a corner, a forgotten
voice stops me in my tracks. The sound warms my
heart as it sends chills up my spine.

"I feel as if you have been avoiding me."

I turn to see Cameron leaning against the
building's white stone wall. He pushes off and saunters
toward me. There are so many People and Clones

around. I bump into a few passing bystanders as I back away while Cameron approaches me.

"That was because I was avoiding you, and still am."

I turn around to continue on to the bus. I feel fingers wrap lightly around my bicep as Cameron spins me around and pulls me closer to his body. My head is sent aflutter both from the speed with which he spins me and the involuntary feeling my body experiences from contact with Cameron. My brain is trying to tell me to run, but the gravitational pull my soul feels toward his silences my better judgement. Cameron holds me by both of my shoulders while he steers me backward until my back touches the cold wall he was previously leaning against. Cameron releases me and raises both of his arms, placing his palms against the wall to support his weight as he leans into me without touching me. I have an urge to grab him and pull him closer like I did with Boston last night, but I restrain myself. The intoxicating smell of Cameron's cologne fills my nostrils and makes my knees weak. I begin to tremble with both longing for him to touch me and the fear of someone witnessing. Cameron slowly dips his face into the curvature of my neck. He still does not touch me, but his warm gentle breath causes the migration of goosebumps all over my body as it hits my skin. I cannot suppress a soft moan of my desire for more. My pulse increases as does the pull I feel toward Cameron, which I am still unable to explain.

"Alabaster," Cameron whispers in my ear, too softly for anyone besides me to hear.

His words trigger a cacophony of feelings, most of which are effecting the private area between my legs. I can barely hold myself up any longer. I feel my knees begin to buckle from their trembling. My face turns up toward Cameron's of its own freewill. I close my eyes so that I do not become a witness to my own crimes. My lips know what they are searching for without my eyes telling them. A hot fire spreads from my lips and erupts into my chest, sending electrifying tingles throughout my body as my lips find their prey. My palms are against the wall, and I scratch at the brick with the loss of my last ounce of restraint. Cameron seems taken aback at first from the fury in my kiss, but then he urges me on by gently biting my lower lip. I again release a pleasurable moan. Our lips are the only part of our bodies touching, but the sensation I receive far surpasses any feeling I ever had with Boston. Kissing Boston caused a small flickering fire from a single match. Kissing Cameron causes my entire body and soul to erupt in an all-engulfing forest fire that refuses to be quenched until it has devoured everything.

Without warning, Cameron's lips are ripped away from mine as another body plows into him. I hear the sickening sound of bones cracking as a fist makes contact with Cameron's nose. I am still in too much of a daze from the kiss to sort out what is happening. More People appear seemingly out of nowhere as Clones make themselves scarce. Clones are programmed to be nonviolent, so much so that they do not even wish to witness it. Before the attack commences into a full on brawl, the figure who attacked Cameron is restrained by four extremely large Clones. These Clones are the third male type, the Police Clones, and it takes all four of them to restrain the attacker. The presence of the intimidating Police Clones pulls me out of my stupor. When I finally get my wits about me, the world around me becomes clear once more, and I realize Cameron's accoster is Boston. An icy weight fills my chest at the horror of what I am witnessing. A single tear runs down my cheek as Boston looks at me with shame in his eyes, but also great sadness. Boston looks away from me. I quickly wipe the lone tear on my shoulder before anyone notices my sorrow. One of the monstrous Police Clones releases the subdued Boston and he begins to grab my arm to take me in for questioning. Cameron quickly steps in between the behemoth and me. Cameron's face is covered in blood and his once perfectly straight nose is slightly pointing to the right.

"She is with me. You leave her here."

The monstrous Police Clone grunts and stalks off with the other three Police Clones and Boston. The excitement from the street fight soon wears off and onlookers continue on their way. Cameron turns back to me.

"You look terrible," I say flatly. "Come on, let's go back into the hospital and clean you up."

I turn and walk toward the hospital, but when I do not hear any footsteps following, I turn around. Cameron remains where he is, looking beyond me toward the hospital with indecision written on his face.

"Are you coming? You need to get that nose taken care of. Please come with me, sir."

Cameron looks at me and slowly shakes his head causing his hair to bounce happily despite the eventful tone of the evening.

"No, I'm not going back in there. Not like this."

"Fine, where do you propose we go? You need to have that nose fixed before we can stop the bleeding."

"You can do it. Go ahead. I have seen you snap several bones back into place over the past two days."

A jolt of fear courses through me as I remember the red-haired Clone I illegally assisted on my first day yesterday. Cameron says nothing further about that incident or any other. He turns and walks over to a nearby green wood-slat bench where he lies down on his back. I pause and look around for witnesses before I follow after him. The commuters have all vanished from the street. I sink down on my knees next to Cameron. The cobblestones of the sidewalk are abrasive on my knees. I can feel my skin splitting slightly through my thin cotton pants. I have felt greater pain in my life, so I pay it no mind to focus on my current patient. I examine Cameron's nose and palpate the once perfect feature. He flinches slightly, but he holds mostly still.

"All right, but this is going to hurt." I position my hands on his nose.

"On the count of three. One, two"--*crack*--"three."

Cameron releases a holler, "Ouch, goddamn it. I thought you were going on three. Son of a bitch that hurt more than the fist."

I smile smugly while Cameron's eyes well up and he releases a few additional choice words. I rip off one of my shirt sleeves and pour some water on it from a water bottle someone left abandoned under the bench. A few ice cubes accompany the icy liquid, which I bundle into the sleeve. I then press it firmly against Cameron's nose. As I hold the bundle,

Cameron places his hand atop my own and strokes it with his thumb.

Cameron and I sit in silence while the bleeding slows. The air has a slightly cool tinge tonight. I shiver and I wish I had something more than thin cotton scrubs on. Cameron has his eyes closed from the pain. He does not notice the look of worry and concern plastered on my face while I distractedly stare off in the direction the Police Clones took Boston. Although I am worried about Cameron, most of my worry is for Boston and his wellbeing, since Cameron's predicament is not quite as life threatening. When Cameron's pain has dwindled to a mild throb, he finally looks up at me. I am a split second slow in hiding the look of despair in my eyes.

"Don't worry about me. I'll be fine. I've had worse. One time I crashed my motorcycle and I had the wickedest road rash down my side and leg. I will survive."

Cameron places his hand that is not holding mine around my back. Only his fingertips make contact with my lower back, sending electrified tingles up and down my spine, causing me to gasp.

"As for that Clone who attacked me, well, he probably won't be so well off."

I can no longer hold in the welling emotional turmoil from the past twenty-four hours. If the hospital parking lot were as packed as it had been earlier, heads would have turned in our direction due to the loud cry I unwillingly release. I pull my hand away from Cameron's, stand and proceed to run away. I have no idea where I will go––I just know I need to get away. Unfortunately, I only make it a few paces before the grief causes me to crumble to the cobblestone sidewalk. I am certain my connection with the hard unforgiving cobblestones will leave me bruised and sore, but I do not even care. The pain from the fall is small in comparison to the anguish inside. I am briefly shaken from my despair when I feel the strong arms of Cameron wrap around me, pulling me into his lap, and holding me in his lap in the middle of the sidewalk. I attempt to pull away, but Cameron holds me firmly to his chest as he rocks me. When I stop resisting his embrace, Cameron comfortingly rubs my back. His touch is so soothing.

"Shshshsh. You are okay, don't worry, calm down, it is all going to be fine," Cameron says while trying to calm me. "I take it you know the Clone. Who is he? Why did he attack me? Aren't you all meant to be genetically incapable of violence?"

I struggle to respond, as my breathing is labored from my crying.

"He is my best friend, my only friend." I manage through my whimpers. "We are genetically not prone to violence, but that obviously does not mean we are incapable of it. I do not know what came over him. Maybe he saw you and me together. He likely thought you were taking advantage of me and reacted with violence to protect me. Oh, what have I done?"

I hold my face in my hand while grabbing my chest in pain, as if my heart has spilt open. I release another agonizing cry before I become silent. Cameron and I sit for another few minutes in silence, aside from my intermittent soft whimpers.

Barong! Barong! Barong! The first set of curfew bells toll, breaking the silence. Fear grips me, causing my vision to darken. I sit upright and attempt to stand.

"Oh no, oh dear, curfew. I will never make it home in time." I begin to take a step away, but Cameron has his fingers held fast around my wrist.

"No, let me go, I need to hurry," I shout at Cameron in protest while I try to shake his hold on me.

"You said it yourself, you will never make it. Think about it." I pause my struggle for release and fall into the depths of Cameron's blue eyes. "There is a twenty-minute bus ride to the border line of the Clone dwellings. I got on the bus yesterday morning at the Owl, which is another fifteen beyond that. You were already on the bus by that point, which adds at least another five to ten before there is another stop, which may or may not be yours. There is no way you will make that entire distance on foot in five minutes. You are safer with me. After all, I am one of the People."

I stop my futile fight to run and resume crying. I know he is right, but I hate the fact. His smile is so smug and full of himself. How could I ever have felt anything but hate for him? He is not selfless or caring like a Clone. All he can think about is himself. I want to put an immeasurable distance between this Person and myself, but I feel so weak from all of the crying, and my entire body aches, and it is unresponsive to my commands. I begin trembling again, but this time from grief, not from the cold air, nor from the heated pleasure I experienced earlier. Cameron holds me closer. He must think the chill in the air is causing me to shiver. My knees finally give out completely, but Cameron catches me and sweeps an arm under my knees, lifting me off of the ground.

"Where are you taking me?" I inquire with little interest.

I do not care, not really. I just want to crawl into a hole and die. I bury my face into Cameron's chest to hide my sorrows. I am done crying, for the sole reason that I have run out of tears. I slip into a calmer state as I inhale Cameron's cologne and feel his steady heartbeat.

"To my house, I live not far from here."

I can tell Cameron is talking, but I am slowly slipping away from consciousness.

"I think I can do something about your friend too."

At this point, Cameron's words are lost upon dead ears. Shortly after he is finished speaking, I have completely succumbed to my exhaustion. I am certain I dream the tender kiss upon my head as Cameron proceeds down the vacant street. At least, I think I am dreaming. Why would a Person ever tenderly kiss a Clone?

Chapter 8

I wake up in the most luxurious room I have ever seen. My eyes are in wonder at all of the colors and the sheer size of the room. I have been in rooms this large and larger on previous occasions, such as the school cafeteria and the one at the hospital. Neither of those are so extravagantly decorated. Every wall is adorned with massive paintings, each one framed in reflective gold trim. A massive golden chandelier with crystals dangling every inch or two hangs luminously above me. When the morning sunshine hits the crystals, it sends little rainbows dancing upon the walls, floor, and ceiling. I begin to move, trying to sit up. I am amazed by the cloudlike softness upon which I am lying. It is a milk-chocolate-toned couch with too many throw pillows to count and a fluffy cream-colored sheep skin draped over the back. I have seen many couches, mostly in the many waiting rooms of the hospital. Never have I once thought they were this comfortable. I have to admit, it is not bad. This room is full of so many things, but I do notice there is something missing. Cameras. There is not a single camera in this room.

I am alone and silence surrounds me. Someone had placed a light-weight fleece blanket on me at some point last night. I am still wearing the same torn and dirty clothes I had on yesterday. I notice the blood splotches on the front of my light-blue shirt and the frayed fabric that serves as a reminder of the torn sleeve used for Cameron's nose. I am once again gripped by the pain of grief as I recall the events of the previous evening. I had hoped it was all a horrid nightmare. I quickly get up and head for the door, running scenarios of ways to save Boston through my head. However, I do not get too far. After only one step away from the couch I trip over an obstruction on the floor and fall to the fine wood-grained floor. There comes a loud grunt which did not originate from my own mouth. I roll over to see Cameron lying on the floor holding his stomach in pain.

"Why are you so accident prone? I need to write a letter to the genetic sequencing director to tell him to find the gene for clumsiness and remove it henceforth. Unless you were meaning to kick me, in which case I should call the police instead."

Cameron stops whining as he sits up and looks at me with a flirtatious smile. I am too stunned to move, but I find the motivation to roll back over onto my stomach where I landed in an attempt to hide my shame. After a few seconds of recovering from utter embarrassment again, I sit up on my elbow and look back at Cameron once more. He is so handsome and the morning sunshine emerging from the overly ornate window behind him creates a soft angelic halo surrounding him. I know Cameron well enough to see the deceitfulness of the image. He is no angel.

"Were you going to leave without a goodbye?" Cameron inquires as he ruffles his messy bedhead.

Even with his golden-brown hair in shambles, Cameron is still capable of melting my heart. I try to shake away the flutters increasing in my stomach. I am not falling for his antics any longer.

"I need to get home. I need to get ready for work. My family unit is likely concerned about me not returning home last night."

Lying was easy the first time, but it only seems to get easier as I continue to do it. My family unit would be unconcerned with my absence. They know and understand the demands placed upon Clones. My mother is likely curious, but probably not worried. Apart from her, it is likely no one else even noticed my absence.

I sit up and once again prepare to stand. Cameron grabs my hand and pulls me toward him. I land on the carpet he slept on. The dark-brown shag is so soft, it puts my mattress to shame. I remain lying on my back where I landed, and Cameron leans over me. I feel vulnerable and my pulse begins to increase in rate. We stay here in a motionless standoff for a few moments. I take in every feature that I apparently missed last time. I can feel heat radiating from every point of contact with his body, even with the thin clothing separating us. Every time I attempt to hate Cameron, I seem to desire him more. One corner of Cameron's full, rosy lips curls up into a half-smile, which causes my heart to rapidly attempt escape from its ribcage prison. The prisms from the crystals make Cameron's eyes sparkle as they look bluer one second, then a deep green the next. I can feel something drawing me closer to him without my conscious consent. Before I have closed a noticeable distance, Cameron pops up to his feet without warning and with ease. Once standing, he extends a hand down to me. Should I take it? Should I trust this Person? My hand raises out of its own desire, and, before I can pull it back, Cameron's hand is already encircling it, and I am on my feet. What is the point of having a brain when my body is driven by something else?

"Well, then, I will drive you. It will be faster than the bus."

"No, I couldn't. You have already done too much for me. I will take the bus. Thank you for your kindness last night. I am sorry for all of the inconvenience and troubles I have caused you."

I pull my hand away which I can tell Cameron is reluctantly releasing. There is a significant amount of effort needed to pull my eyes away from their invisible connection to Cameron's, but I somehow manage to turn away. I carefully navigate through an obstacle course involving several tables topped with ornate cases and more oversized couches like the one I woke up on. More furniture than I could imagine to be functional or even necessary. I am finally close to the door, but Cameron makes it there before me. He proceeds to open the hard redwood barrier for me. I force my eyes to stay away from Cameron's captivating blues as I pass by him.

On the other side of the door my jaw drops and I lose my breath at the sight of the grand hallway. It is floor to ceiling white marble laced with golden swirls. From the ceiling hangs another chandelier so magnificent, it makes the last one seem like a worthless trinket. The beauty is astounding. I hesitate entering the room, as I feel unfit to be amongst such splendor. A tonal sound echoes through the room and breaks my wonder.

"Ah, perfect timing," Cameron says as he squeezes by me through the doorway. I am sure he had enough room to pass without making contact with me, but he somehow did not manage it.

Cameron turns back to me with that cocky half-smile as he heads to a large set of mahogany double doors at the far end of the hall. The doors are each three-people wide and at least two-people tall. Cameron opens them both simultaneously, revealing three figures.

"Come in, come in, gentlemen," Cameron says in the most charming of voices as he welcomes his guests inside.

One visitor is obviously a Police Clone, due to his enormous stature. The second visitor is an older man with gray eyes, and hair that was once black but is now salted with gray. He wears a long chestnut trench coat and dark-brown slacks. He is one of the People. My heart rate beats in double time as my eyes fall upon the third visitor. I grasp the door frame, both to keep from falling and to prevent myself from running over to the four men. The last visitor is Boston.

"Thank you, Constable, for bringing my Clone home to me. I am sorry for the misunderstanding," Cameron continues on, flaunting his charming smile.

"Not a bother, sir. I did, however, have a difficult time finding your ownership documents," the constable, the man with the salt-and-pepper hair, replies politely with a slight bow.

The visitors all remain outside of the house.

"Oh, yes, I have them right here."

Cameron produces a white envelope from the pocket of his jacket, which is hanging from an ornate cast-iron coat tree near the enormous double doors. I can't help but wonder why one would need doors so large they could easily fit one of the city's buses.

"I have been meaning to turn them in for ages now. Would you be so kind as to take them in for me?"

Cameron presents the envelope to the constable, who accepts it with suspicion in his steely blue eyes.

"Yes, I would be happy to deliver the documents for you. However, would you again explain to me why on God's green earth you would instruct your Clone to assault you? Seems foolish to me. You know what they say about dogs who get a taste for blood."

"Ah, yes, I do indeed know what they say. But do you know what they say about the cat with too much curiosity?" Cameron gives the constable a stern look before he continues on, "Anyhow, it may have been a tad foolhardy of me to give such an order. After all of the pain and discomfort of having my nose broken, I doubt I shall ever do it again, sir. To summarize the account, which I already gave to the officials in your office over the phone last night, I told the Clone to attack me to impress a young lady, whom I have had my eyes on for some time now. I thought it would be quite the dramatic show if I were caught in the midst of a fight over her. But alas, I was both injured and alone, for she ran away with fright."

The constable nods with a "humph" of disbelief but seemingly accepts the lie. A burst of excitement fills my heart. Cameron told a lie to rescue Boston. I do not know why he would risk so much to save the life of a single Clone, but maybe he is not as evil as I had suspected. I smile slightly, but my concern for Boston and myself soon overtakes the hopeful feeling about Cameron's intentions.

"How about that one?" The constable nods toward me while pointing a bony arthritic finger in my direction.

My stomach churns violently as fear embraces me.

"Do you have her papers?"

Boston finally looks up and sees me. It is the first time he has raised his bowed head since the doors opened.

"Oh, heavens no. She does not belong to me. I don't believe she belongs to anyone, actually. I just brought her home last night for a little, you know, fun." Cameron winks at the constable. "After all, the girl I had my eyes on was gone, remember?"

Boston's eyes become fiery as he glowers at Cameron. I can see his shoulders rise and fall more rapidly as he begins breathing harder. Hopefully Boston can contain himself because I am sure the Police Clone would not hesitate to smash him.

"Well then, I would be more than happy to return her to the Owl for you, sir," The constable adds helpfully, but with a chess player's subtle smile.

"That will not be necessary. I had planned another go with her before I head out to work. But thank you ever so kindly for the offer, sir. Now, if you will excuse me, I must be getting ready. Have a splendid day, sir."

The constable's smile falters slightly as I watch the men from my standpoint. No one seems to notice Boston's upper lip curling slightly into a snarl, his muscles tensing, and his hands balling into fists.

"You as well, sir." The constable bows before turning away to leave.

The Clone Police officer shoves Boston through the doorway. Boston is unable to divert his attention from Cameron to the ground in time, and his body makes a heavy thud as it hits the floor. Cameron closes the gigantic double doors, causing an echo to fill the lavish hallway.

Chapter 9

I run over to the two young men as Boston pushes up off the floor and resumes the interaction he began with Cameron last night. Cameron apparently had noticed Boston's increasing rage, as he is prepared for the attack this time. Cameron successfully ducks under a few swings. When I am finally close enough, I grab Boston's arm in an attempt to stop him. However, Boston is so full of rage, he does not realize it is me. He throws me off so he can continue assaulting Cameron. I hit the unforgivingly hard white marble floor with a soft cry. I am sure the impact will leave a bruise on my hip and my elbow, which took the brunt of the force.

I raise my voice at Boston, finally getting his attention. "Boston, stop. What are you doing? He just saved your life!"

I have never yelled at someone before. It feels strange, but somewhat enjoyable. Boston stares down at me, and the hate in his eyes is rapidly replaced with deep remorse. Cameron hurries over to me, concern written all over his face, to help me. Cameron cautiously helps me stand. He holds one of my hands and has his other arm wrapped gently around my back. His touch makes me forget about the pain I feel emanating from my hip. I really wish I did not become distracted every time Cameron touches me, because he is touching me everywhere right now, making sure I am not broken. Boston is no longer full of rage, but he does become aggravated once again while Cameron tends to my wellbeing.

"Why do you let him touch you, Alabaster? He is nothing more than a dirty piece of shit. I saw what he was doing to you last night. It is the same thing he does to every Clone he meets." Boston spits at Cameron's feet, leaving a bloody pink splotch.

"Boston, you are hurt. Come sit down. Let me help you, please."

I take my hand away from Cameron's and leave the comfort of having his arm around me so I can approach Boston. I take Boston's hand and urge him to follow me toward the room I woke up in. Boston does not budge as I gently pull his arm. He stands facing Cameron with a hateful look in his swollen eyes. Boston's face is caked in blood from his nose and several cuts, including a large gash above his eye. I do not remember Cameron getting in any punches last night, meaning Boston was likely brutally beaten while incarcerated. I give Boston's hand another tug and he finally breaks his glare and follows me. As he walks, Boston holds his ribs and winces with every limping step he takes.

"You are welcome!" Cameron shouts from the front door.

Boston does not acknowledge him, but I turn and give Cameron a shaming look before closing the room's door. I guide Boston to the first chair we come to and sit him down. I spot a bowl filled with water and a few towels on a table in the middle of the room. I navigate around the superfluous amount of furnishings toward the bowl. The water has a pink tint, and there is blood on one of the white towels resting in a heap next to the bowl. Cameron must have used this last night to clean his face. There is another small stack of clean white towels on the other side of the bowl. I wet one and take it back over to Boston. He is leaning back in the chair, somehow already fast asleep. Due to being bludgeoned last night, Boston likely received little to no sleep. I gently dab at the deep gash above his eye. Boston will need stitches. He will also not be able to leave this house again if it scars, which it will. When the gash is clean, I continue on to the dried blood covering his swollen face. I press as softly as possible, trying not to wake him, but he doesn't so much as flinch. Soon Boston's face is clean and, other than the swollen eye and the gash, he looks normal again. I leave the room to find Cameron. I need to stitch the gash on Boston's brow as soon as possible, otherwise the scar will be much worse.

After walking through many doors and into many rooms, each equally as extravagant as the last, and down several long hallways, I finally find Cameron in the kitchen eating at a table. The table is loaded with decadent foods of all types. Much more than one man could possibly eat. A pile of toast-colored flat disks covered in some kind of dark-brown liquid, a large slab of meat incrusted with breading and smothered with coagulated white gravy, and eggs in several different shapes and forms are only a small portion of the spread lain out for Cameron. There is no oatmeal in sight. The smell emanating from the table is so sweet, it is almost sickening. I can smell the familiar rich aroma of coffee somewhere in this room, which is enticing, but I have more important things to tend to. As a Clone, I am designed not to put my own needs and desires before those of others, and it is about time I start acting like a Clone again.

Cameron has already showered and is now wearing a maroon T-shirt which makes his eyes stand out like emeralds. His hair looks clean and it still looks slightly wet and a few shades darker, but it is still unkempt. Every time I see him, my heart flutters, my knees begin to knock, and I am forced to use all my willpower not to run to him. I have always felt so in control of myself, and this is a new, unwelcome experience for me. Cameron looks up at me and smiles. His whole face lights up. A good sick feeling erupts in my stomach, and I momentarily forget why I was looking for him in the first place.

"Well, hello. How is your friend?" Cameron's words are difficult to make out through the mass of food in his mouth. "Boston, right?"

I falter. I cannot believe I said Boston's name aloud. It is bad enough I told Cameron my own name, but to endanger Boston by foolishly sharing his name. The good sick feeling transforms into just a sick feeling. I somehow manage to find my voice after a moment of awkward silence.

"He is sleeping. Would you have a needle and thread I may use please, sir?"

"Yes, I'll get it for you."

Cameron stands and struts toward me. With every step closer, my heartbeat quickens and my eyes widen. I am still standing in the doorway, and even though there is plenty of room to pass by without contact, Cameron's body touches mine. I lock my knees to prevent myself from crumpling as Cameron's cologne clouds my senses. He pauses ever so slightly as he presses his body against mine. How does he affect me so?

"Pardon me, my lady," Cameron says with a smile pulling up only one corner of his enticing lips.

I am torn between love and hate with the effect Cameron has upon me. Cameron leisurely walks down the hall to another door I somehow managed to pass without opening. He opens it and reveals a closet full of medical supplies. Cameron looks at everything and taps his foot. He seems to be putting on a show.

"Ah, here it is."

Cameron stands on the tips of his toes and stretches to reach something on a shelf high up. I look away when his shirt rises, revealing chiseled abs and the hollow craters underneath created by his hip bones. I do not need any further reason to feel so uncontrollably drawn to this man, but I do sneak another peek. He is still stretched and riffling through the top shelf, but he is looking out of the corner of his eye back at me. I turn away with a blush again. When I no longer hear the sound of Cameron shifting things in the closet, I look back toward him. He is already standing inches away from me again. He holds a plastic sleeve with a sterile needle and thread in the small space between our bodies.

"Here you are. Why are you blushing?" Cameron's smile grows with his amusement.

I tilt my head down and away from his staring eyes. Not because I want to be a good Clone, but because I am embarrassed as I realize Cameron knows the effect he has upon me and he is utilizing it.

"Thank you, sir."

I snatch the sleeve and hurry down the hallway. I reach the halfway point of the hallway and open the door I think is the room I need.

"That is the bathroom. Unless you need to make use of it, you want to be two more doors down." Cameron can't suppress a laugh as I feel my cheeks burn with intensified blushing.

I shut the bathroom door and continue down the hallway until I reach the correct door, all without looking back at Cameron. I open the door and enter before slamming it closed. I momentarily lean against the door and close my eyes in frustration. Why can't I get it together around this man? I have always had a photographic memory, and I have never gotten so turned around like that. I knock the back of my head lightly on the door. A groan comes from Boston. He is still sleeping despite the noise I caused slamming the door. His body leans sideways and is dangerously close to falling out of the chair. I stop feeling sorry for myself and walk over to him. I set my hands on his falling shoulder and gently pull to straighten him. Boston groans again as he obediently rolls over. Unfortunately, he keeps rolling toward me. I try to stop him, but his momentum is too much. Boston falls out of the chair on top of me. I am unable to get out of the way in time and Boston's mass takes me down with him. The union of his body with the ground does not even startle Boston, let alone wake him, but the impact does knock my breath out. The sound of the impact does spark the curiosity of Cameron, and he quickly appears in the room. I am pinned to the ground under Boston's unconscious mass. I futilely try to push him off so I can wriggle free.

"My, my, my. I am really starting to believe if something bad can happen, it will happen to you. You have a gift, love." Cameron leans against the doorframe in a spectator pose as he sports an amused smile.

"You could help, you know. It is hard to breath."

Cameron gives another laugh as I continue to squirm for escape. He finally leaves his post with a sigh and a roll of his eyes before walking over to where I lie trapped. He then bends over and unceremoniously rolls Boston over, removing the burdensome weight from me seemingly without any concern for Boston. Cameron then stands back as I scramble to my feet out of breath.

"Would you require my services any further, ma'am?" Cameron says rather cockily.

I think for half a second before replying, "Can you help me get him to the couch?"

Cameron sighs and again rolls his eyes as he easily pulls Boston's arm up over his shoulder. I hurry over to Boston's other arm to help support some of the weight, although it doesn't seem like Cameron needs my help. Cameron must be in really good shape because he does not break a sweat as he deals with Boston's dead weight. Boston still does not wake, but he groans with every step closer to the couch. Once at the couch, Cameron releases Boston's arm and lets his body fall limply onto the couch. I do not anticipate the sudden increase of weight I am now responsible for. Subsequently, I am unable to remain standing very long before Boston's body weight brings me down once again. I move as fast as I can so that I do not get pinned again, but Boston still lands on me enough for Cameron to find humor in it. At least I landed on the cushy couch and not the hard floor this time, and with a little shuffling, I am able to stand again. Cameron dramatically wipes his hands together, and his cocky smiles remains as annoyingly handsome as ever.

"Well, there you are. Anything else my lady?"

I glower at him. "No, thank you."

Cameron bows before turning away to leave the room. Before he exits completely, Cameron adds, "Oh, and you may want to hurry up. Your shift starts in twenty minutes, and there is an eight minute walk to the hospital. I'm heading over now."

I nod at Cameron before he disappears through the door with a cheeky smile that somehow causes my body's eager response. I hear the echoing sound of the large entry door closing. Now I am stressing. I take a deep breath as I try to center myself again. This is enough foolery for one day and I need to get to work before there is any more trouble. I also need to tend to Boston, so I quickly clean Boston's wound again before setting a few sutures. Boston does not even flinch as the needle pulls the thin black thread through his skin. He continues to sleep on. When I am finished, I look at the clock on the wall. It is difficult to tell the time on it because there are so many jewels sparkling, thus creating a glare. From what I can tell, I now only have seven minutes before the start of my shift and Cameron said the hospital is eight minutes away. I apply a gentle kiss upon Boston's forehead.

"I will be back. I promise."
I then quickly leave.

Chapter 10

After closing one of the heavy mahogany front doors, I am clueless which way to go. I was already asleep in Cameron's arms before we were too far from the hospital last night, so I have no idea what direction we went. The streets are bustling with People, but I am not allowed to address any of them. Only speak when spoken to. I stand on my tippy-toes to look over the tall heads of the People. In the distance, I can make out what I hope is the tall cream-colored stone of the hospital, but I can't risk going that way and it not being the hospital, and me being that much farther from the hospital.

"Psst." I hear a sound emanating from the grand doors of Cameron's house behind me. When I look back, a man resembling my father is smiling in the open doorway pointing in the direction of the cream-colored building I suspected was the hospital. My shoulders relax slightly as I smile back in appreciation.

I take off at a sprint in that direction. I make it to the hospital just in time, and I am completely out of breath as I scan my tattoo. I smell funny and I still have blood from Cameron and now Boston as well on my light-blue scrubs that I have been wearing since yesterday. I am still missing a sleeve as well. My hair is a complete mess, but I quickly disentangle the chaos and work my fingers harder than ever to create a quick fishtail braid as I look at the patient board. By the time the braid is complete, I am already heading to my first patient.

When I reach the room, I am shocked to see Cameron. It did not occur to me that if Boston was not here to swap patients out, I would have to work alongside Cameron. My heart gives an unprovoked skip.

"I am glad to see you made it on time. This patient needs her IV changed every hour," Cameron states with indifference before he leaves without giving me a second glance.

Before he is completely gone, I find my voice through the shock. "Camer––I mean, Dr. Staunton. Thank you."

I do not dare use his first name with so many People around to witness. Even if he instructed me to. It is just improper.

"For what?" Cameron replies without turning, and he does not stay for an answer.

I am filled with a new emotion that I am unable to describe. The only way I can try to start is anger laced with sorrow, which is soaked in confusion, with a sprinkling of hurt to top it all off. I come full circle back to anger because I do not like the other feelings Cameron has put me through. He is definitely broadening my emotional horizons. I feel foolish for ever thinking there was more to Cameron than the rest of the People.

I only see him in passing from that point on, even though I have several patients who are under his care. Cameron does not acknowledge my presence for a second longer than the length of time it takes him to tell me his patient care instructions, but most of the time, he sends me his instructions via the tablet I carry for patient notes. By the time lunch arrives, I feel sick to my stomach. Mostly from the disinterest Cameron has provided me thus far, but also from the lack of food. I had no dinner last night due to all of the drama, and this morning I was helping Boston rather than enjoying the overly large spread Cameron had. I am not confident I can stomach eating anything, but I know my body needs sustenance. My shoulders slump as I shuffle toward the cafeteria. I go through the food line with my eyes as good as closed. I do not even look at what is placed on my tray or know how the tray ended up in my hands to begin with. I get my tattoo scanned and sit at the first table I come to before spooning something into my mouth. Unfortunately, I do not notice this particular table is occupied by People, not Clones.

"Excuse me, can we help you?" inquires a woman with hair so deeply black, her unblemished white skin pops into focus.

The only thing betraying the woman's angelic beauty are the two soulless blue eyes she uses to bore a hole through me. I look up with a panicked expression frozen on my face. I am surprised the food I just place in my mouth does not fall out while my jaw drops in shock.

"Oh, forgive me. I am so sorry for intruding," I murmur through the food stuffed in my mouth.

I quickly pick up my tray and move over another two tables before I find a seat at a Clone table. I do not dare look back at the table I had unfortunately sat at, but I can still feel those cold blue eyes burning through me from where that woman sits. Even though I am filled with terror from my mistake, my body begins working on its own to fill my needs. My food disappears from my plate faster than a vacuum could have managed. All I want to do is to get out of here. Not just the cafeteria, but the hospital.

I dispose of my tray and head back to the ER. Although I am no longer starving, I still feel weak. Right now I am so glad I am a Clone and not a Person. If these are the kinds of emotions they feel on a daily basis, then I am lucky to have them bred out of me. But then why am I feeling them now? The taupe walls help support my weight as I lean against them whilst I walk down the hallway. I finally stop and lean my back against a wall and I briefly close my eyes in exhausted despair. How could my simplistic life change so drastically in only two and a half days?

I push off the wall with determination and head to the Clone locker room. I acquire a clean light-blue uniform from the front desk before entering the room. The same girl who is identical to me tends the desk. She does not ask any questions, but she again tells me to return the dirty uniform once I change. I head straight to the bay of sinks at the far end of the locker room. I stand in front of a sink and splash cold water on my face and the back of my neck. It is so refreshing and rejuvenating. I notice how dirty the water is as it drips off of my nose and into the sink. Even though I am meant to head back to the ER immediately after lunch, Clones generally have twenty minutes for lunch. Seeing I have only been gone for about eight minutes, I figure I have enough time for a quick five-minute shower. I hastily turn a shower head on and disrobe. The water is as cold as it usually is for Clones. I let the icy droplets hit my face, hoping they will wash away the memory of tears from my cheeks. I grab an ivory bar of soap that was left on a small shelf and scrub my body raw in an attempt to wash away the memory of both Cameron's and Boston's hands upon my skin. My plan does not work as the memory rests far deeper than the skin itself.

The soap has no scent, but as I rinse off, the soap takes the smell of body odor down the drain in a frothy spiral. When all of the soap suds have vanished, I get out and dry in a hurry. I pull some clean white underwear up over my derriere. I then pull up my cotton pants and tie the drawstring a little tighter than I normal like. I insert both arms through the straps of my brassiere and I stand with my hands behind my back in an attempt to clasp the garment. I jump as two warm, large hands take the clasps from my cold, numb fingers. The intruding hands latch my bra in place and disappear. I grab my shirt and hastily pull it over my head before turning to see who is there, even though I suspect, or maybe hope. I am not disappointed. Cameron stands a few feet away in the middle of the room.

"Hello." He greets me candidly with his self-assured half-smile.

"Is that all you have to say?" My blood boils over as I begin yelling at him. "I don't understand you. You are so hot and cold, sometimes simultaneously. You are cruel and hurtful one moment, then in a blink of an eye, you are kind and considerate. I am through with you and your silly games. Please just leave me be."

I walk past him to go back to the ER before someone notices I have not yet returned. I quickly pull on my socks and shoes as I walk. I am surprised that I do not fall on my face.

"I could say the same about you."

I stop a few feet from the door and whirl around on Cameron.

"Me? Cruel? How so?" My voice has somehow gained an octave as I squeak the words out.

Cameron has already turned around to face me and is sauntering casually closer. I try to back away, but my legs do not want to listen, in fact, I think my legs want to walk towards him. So instead of backing up, I stand my ground and glare at him.

"Well, for starters, you are continuously running into me. I am beginning to think it is on purpose. Yesterday you went out of your way to avoid me, depriving me of the only beauty I look forward to since I met you. You had one of your Clone groupies accost me last night so you could take advantage of me. You are also inconsiderately walking around the ER being all hot and sexy-like. It makes the other nurses jealous and all I hear is their complaining."

"What do you mean? A quarter of them look exactly like me! Why not bother one of them? What makes me so special? "

My emotions are being pulled in so many directions. I feel as though I will shatter into a million pieces like a fragile porcelain doll. I can feel the sting of tears trying to break free from my eyes, so I turn away and head for the door again. I cannot allow him to see me cry again. When my hand is on the knob, I feel Cameron's breath on my neck near my ear. His hands hover around my shoulders, but he does not touch me.

Cameron leans in closer to my ear as he whispers, "You make you special, Alabaster."

The tears win their fight for freedom as I rip the door open and sprint down the hall back to the ER without a glance back. Before entering the sliding doors of the ER, I dry the remaining tears and take a deep breath. I again study the patient chart as I braid my wet hair into a simpler braid. I finish reading the board and turn to begin my tasks when I realize

Cameron's name is missing from the doctors' column. I turn back towards the screen to double check, and yes, his name is absent. I assume, and hope, he has left for the day. Good riddance is what my sensible side says, but the thought does not seem to fill the void in my heart. Another part of me prays he is not headed to city hall to report my misconduct.

The rest of the afternoon passes in an uneventful flash. As the evening wears on, the next shift arrives. I prepare to leave, but I now have a dilemma. Should I go home like a good little Clone? Or should I go to Cameron's house to check on Boston, and see Cameron again? I did promise Boston I would return to him, but going to the private residence of one of the People without a direct order is a violation of the Clone laws. And if Cameron is not home or if he sends me away, I will never make it to my own home before curfew sets in. I ultimately determine that going to Cameron's is too much of a risk, so I head home instead. Even though it is the sensible thing to do, part of me refutes the decision.

Chapter 11

I drag myself out to the bus as I silence the last of my indecision. I climb aboard and stand zombielike, holding a rail. I am exhausted mostly due to the emotional rollercoaster I involuntarily rode on today. The bus ride passes in a blur. I am at my stop before I realize I was ever moving.

"Last stop, hon," announces the driver.

I wake from my stupor and exit. I have taken this bus many times before, so my feet know the way home on their own. When I enter the house, my family unit has just started eating dinner. My mother's eyes light up at the sight of me, but a worried crease forms across her forehead. My mother knows not to ask what is wrong in front of my father, but her eyes implore. I slump in my chair and barely touch my food. My stomach is too twisted to consider putting anything inside, which is a shame because this is one of my favorite meals, consisting of half a boneless, skinless, flavorless chicken breast and steamed broccoli. As the rest of my family unit clears the table,

I stand and join, even though I have hardly eaten
a thing. I then head straight to bed, where I do not
bother changing into my night dress. I feel weak and
have no more reserved energy for such frivolity. I do
not remember my head hitting the pillow because I
fall asleep on the way down.

The needy cry of the alarm demands my
immediate attention. My mother must have snuck
in and set the alarm because I cannot recall doing so
myself. I turn it off and head to the bathroom to get
cleaned up and ready for the day. How I wish I could
call in sick. The icy water from the shower wakes me
up and I begin to regain some stamina. I scan my
barcode in the hallway and a few seconds later a clean
set of light-blue scrubs appears before me. I head to
my room to get dressed, after which I again scan my
barcode and toss my used clothing into the chute
on my way to the kitchen. A member of my family
unit has already laid out our breakfast because the
table sits ready with four bowls of oatmeal and four
bananas today. I can almost hear the hot cup of black
coffee calling my name like a siren in the night. The
pot is full, so I fill a cup with the energy-giving liquid
before I take a seat. The table is so bare in comparison
to the one Cameron sat at yesterday morning. Why
anyone would order so much food, let alone need so

much food, I cannot fathom. I drink my black coffee before anything else. It is a little too hot to chug, but I do it anyway. The burn of my throat helps to rouse me. As I eagerly spoon my oatmeal, my mother appears and refills my coffee. It is days like this that make me appreciate the coffee pot being one of the only appliances we can have. My mother gives me a concerned look of interest about my wellbeing. After last night's satisfying sleep and this second cup of coffee, I feel like a new Clone, and I give my mother an expression as such. My mother opens her mouth to ask me what was wrong last night, but she quickly clams up because my father walks in. I give her another look of reassurance and a smile.

I finish my breakfast and finally feel ready for the day, which I did not believe to be achievable. My father and brother depart for their daily duties, leaving my mother and me alone together. We both know there is no time to talk, so my mother gives me a casual caress on my arm. It may appear casual, but I know the true meaning of reassurance and love she is providing.

"I love you, my sweet Alabaster. Be safe," my mother whispers at a barely audible level.

Love? Did she just say she loves me or am I just hearing things? I thought we are designed to be unable to love. I definitely do not feel I deserve it, but her words somehow fully lift my spirits. We both leave the house and walk to the bus stop like we did on my first day. She gives me one last look of encouragement before she leaves and heads away. Once the bus arrives, I board and find a place to stand inside the almost-empty bus. The ride is as bumpy as usual, but I sturdily cling to the rail. I feel rather odd falling into routine so easily. It is not really the same routine, because Boston is not here. Sadness begins to creep in to my upbeat feeling due to his absence.

I do not have much time to fret over Boston because Cameron's awful friend Leroy boards at the stop near the Owl. I dip my head as low as possible, hoping he does not notice me amongst the throng of other Clones who have boarded since my stop. Leroy seems extra pudgy today as he is sloshed and, apparently, the alcohol forbids him from concealing the extra weight. His dirty-blond hair is in an extra messy form of disarray. Whereas Cameron seems more attractive the messier his hair is, Leroy's has the opposite effect. I imagine the severity of Leroy's bloodshot eyes to be rather painful. Unfortunately, Leroy does see me and he smiles dangerously. He comes and stands near enough that I can smell the sweet stink of liquor on his breath.

"You're that one Cameron keeps staring at, aren't you?"

Leroy's words are slurred, which makes it hard to understand what he is saying, but I get the gist. It is a dangerous thing to be recognized by any Person, especially one like Leroy.

"No sir, I do not know anyone by that name," I lie as I keep my eyes to the ground.

Before I know what has happened, my cheek is on fire. Leroy has slapped me. I did not think it was possible, but Leroy's eyes have become a darker shade of red while they blaze with an insatiable rage.

"Don't you lie to me, you dirty little Clone whore."

I feel droplets of eighty-proof liquor hit my face as Leroy spits the words out. His face has also become red in his fury, almost as red as his eyes. One of the other young men who entered the bus with him grabs Leroy by the arm and pulls him over to sit with them. He follows obediently as he laughs hysterically. Leroy occasionally looks at me and blows me drunken kisses. I use all of my focus on remaining calm, but on the inside, I feel broken. I have never been hit before. I almost feel like I should turn myself in for voluntary removal, if there is such a thing. I do not see how I can fall back into my Essential Function with two different People capable of recognizing me, as well as all of the drama it has caused. I am beginning to understand why we Clones are all created equal.

The hospital stop does not arrive soon enough. I depart the bus and hurry inside. I melt into the crowds in an attempt to disappear. I can hear Leroy and his friends disembarking behind me, but I do not look back. I weave through the crowd to get into the relative safety of the hospital. I do not understand why Leroy would get off rather than go home to sleep off the aftermath of his night at the Owl. He is a doctor and has a lot of responsibility while at work. I do not see how he will be able to make the tough decisions necessary.

I erase Leroy and the bus ride from my mind as I scan my tattoo at the ER entrance. After entering the sliding glass doors, I wait for the assignment board to change. When it finally does, I instantly notice something amiss. Not only is Cameron's name still not on the board, but neither is my Clone number. I hurry over to the nurse's desk to inquire the issue of my missing number with the head nurse.

"Good morning, ma'am. I am having trouble finding my name on the board. Have I been reassigned?"

The head nurse, who looks much like my mother, but less warm and caring, rolls her eyes at me as she yields a scanning gun.

"Your tattoo please?" the Clone asks with little enthusiasm.

I hold out my left arm and the Clone scans my tattoo. The scanner beeps as the red line reads my tattoo, but several seconds pass as the woman reads the screen. She finally perks up and looks at me.

"Oh, you have been sent for. There seems to be some need for your temporary services at this address." The Clone writes down the address and draws a quick map before handing a small sheet of light pink paper to me. "You must hurry. The note says immediately."

I find it funny that even though her hand is identical to my own, our handwriting could not be more different. After looking at the note I realize I did not need the map drawn out––the address is Cameron's. I briefly feel a little faint, but I quickly get my wits about me as I leave the ER.

Once I am out of the hospital building, I set off at a full run. My body is fueled by excitement, but I clear my mind of what Cameron may need me for as my shoes hit the uneven cobblestones. I reach the house slightly out of breath and ring the doorbell. As I wait patiently outside in the crisp morning air, I hear a loud commotion from within. Even through the thick mahogany, I can hear a tremendous racket. A man resembling my father soon answers the door. It is the same man who pointed me in the right direction yesterday. Even though he shares the same face with my father, I know instantly that he is not my father. He is smiling warmly and has a caring sparkle in his eye. His hair is longer than his Clone type is allowed to wear it in public, but it is combed neatly. Clones who are claimed by one of the People are allowed to look different, but only within the confines of the Person's home. This Clone wears a finely tailored black tailcoat suit with black reptilian designer shoes and a black tie with a gray paisley pattern.

"Please come in, miss. They have been expecting you." The Clone speaks with a charming English accent, also an anomaly for Clones.

The Clone steps aside and leads me into the grandiose white marble hallway. The clamor is even louder inside. It sounds like there is a tornado located in the massive room where I awoke yesterday. The crash of glass breaking follows the thud of a large object hitting the wall. The door to the room opens and Cameron's figure backs slowly out of the room.

"Calm down, Boston. We are going to get this all sorted out."

Cameron speaks slow and soothing, as if addressing a stalking tiger. He is bent over slightly in a stance prepared to dodge an attack. He quickly ducks lower when a vase is flung over his head, sending porcelain shrapnel in every direction as it makes impact with the opposite wall.

"Hey, that was from the Ming dynasty! It's irreplaceable!" Cameron stands upright as he yells in protest.

He hastily slams the door with a resounding echo, immediately followed by another shattering crash against the door. Cameron glares at the closed door with his hands on his hips shaking his head back and forth with a frown. He is in blue pinstriped pajamas and has a pair of black slippers on his feet. Cameron runs his hand through his mess of hair and my fingers twitch with envy.

"Our guest has arrived, sir," states the kindly Clone who answered the door.

Cameron turns towards the Clone and me at the front door. Cameron's face instantly fades from an expression of annoyance to one of extreme joy as his eyes come to rest on me. His nose is still swollen and one of his eyes is sporting a shiner. He is down the hallway in a blink of an eye wrapping me in a suffocating hug that I am unprepared for. We stumble back a couple steps, but we do not fall. All of the tension in my body vanishes at Cameron's touch.

When he releases me, he cups my face in his large warm hands. His thumb caresses the scar on my chin softly as he gently holds my face. His bright smile causes my heart to melt into a soupy mess. Cameron then remembers there is another person in the entry hall with us. He quickly removes his hand from my face and turns to address the Clone who let me in, who still has a bright welcoming aura. I notice the way he looks at Cameron. It is a look similar to the ones my mother gives me. There is a deep love that is beyond blood, beyond genetics, that only a parent could possess. Both my mother and this Clone possess that quality.

"You are excused, Dimitri. I can handle things from here."

The Clone bows before he heads up the stairs. When the sound of a door softly closing reaches his ears, Cameron resumes where he left off. He places his hand back on my cheek and I lean into it. His hands are slightly rough, but the touch of his skin sends a wave of warmth through my body. I did not realize how much I missed his touch until now. Cameron's other hand sits lightly on my hip, but heavy enough to make its presence known. I place one of my small hands atop his hand on my face. I hold his hand there as I turn my lips to kiss the palm, close to his thumb. I remove his hand from my face, but I keep ahold of it. Cameron's other hand remains on my waist where it continues to send electrified signals to all of my nerve endings. I continue to hold his hand as I look up into his deeply penetrating eyes. I can tell that I am all those pensive eyes see. Our fingers intertwine. I feel like I belong here. This must have been my intended Essential Function. It is as if I were designed to be his. My delicately small fingers fit perfectly within his large hand as if they were built explicitly for one another.

I turn my face away as I feel my cheeks beginning to blush. Cameron releases my hand suddenly and brings his face closer to mine. Both of his hands cup my chin as he examines my cheek where Leroy slapped me on the bus earlier. It is the same cheek Cameron was gently holding in his hand only moments ago.

"What happened here? Who did this?" Cameron sounds irate and his eyes have gone from loving to ruthless.

I place my own hand over the palm-printed cheek and turn away to conceal my embarrassment.

"Nothing. No one. I'm fine." I do not know why, but I am unable to tell on Leroy. Probably my Clone training finally bringing some sense back to me, reminding me who I really am. "Why did you summon me?"

Cameron gently sets his hand back upon my waist and turns me back toward him. He hugs me and kisses the top of my head, so I cannot raise my eyes to face him. He allows my change of subject, which causes me immeasurable relief. I never want to see him that angry again.

"Your friend is not very fond of my decorator's work, so he has taken it upon himself to remodel my living room. He also does not believe I am as chivalrous as I paint myself to be. He refuses to take my word that I did not, in fact, take advantage of you and by no means believes it was you who took advantage of me. He almost had me convinced that I am a being, how did he phrase it exactly? 'A being lower than the shit he scrapes out of bedpans.' I think that was how he put it. Your friend has a way with words. He is gifted." Cameron has somehow found a stray strand of my hair and he curls his finger in it as he speaks.

"I missed the part about why you called for me," I say as I attempt to stifle a light laugh into Cameron's chest as another crash comes from the room. "I have no skills in decorating, and in fact find all of your decorations a bit frivolous myself."

"Please, go calm him down. Tell him you are safe, he is safe. That way he will calm down and I will be safe, and my priceless possessions for that matter."

I look up into Cameron's softened eyes and he smiles gently down at me. I cannot help the smile that spreads over my face.

"I will see what I can do. I make no promises about your safety, but I will try my best to save the antiques."

Cameron takes my hand and kisses the back of it.

"I would ask nothing less."

He leads me to the door and gently knocks.

Chapter 12

"You have a guest, my friend. Please refrain from whirling any objects momentarily as she enters. I rest assured you desire her face smashed as little as I." Cameron calls through the closed door.

Silence emanates from the other side. Cameron opens the door and moves aside for me to enter. When I am safely across the threshold, Cameron closes the door behind me. Boston is in the center of the room holding a large colorful egg in his hand and the look of a maniac in his normally calm eyes. Boston carelessly drops the egg, which luckily lands on the overly plush carpet, as he runs to me. He protectively wraps me in his arms and lifts me off my feet. Boston holds me and spins around in a circle laughing and smiling once again. He is now the Boston I know and love. He finally sets me down and begins to look me over. He too notices the fading red marks on my cheek left as a gift from Leroy.

"Did he do this to you? He is going to pay for it. I knew he was lying. Bastard!"

Boston releases me as he heads toward the door, but I clasp my small hand around his, causing him to cease.

"He did not do this. Cameron has not laid a violent hand on me. Come sit down and talk to me, Boston. You have torn the stitches I made on that gash above your eye. Let me mend it, please. You know what will happen if that scars poorly."

Boston lets me lead him to a couch, where I set him down. Someone has replaced the pinkly tinted water in the bowl I used yesterday, so I dip a clean towel in the water to once again clean Boston's face. Boston places his hand on my hips and tries to pull me closer. I swat his hands away gently. He persistently sets his hands back on my hips and pulls a little harder. I again swat his hands away.

"Would you stop. I am trying to get this clean so I can gauge the damage you have done to my work, and it is difficult when you keep moving."

I give him an agitated look of disapproval before I proceed again. I bend over him again to determine if any stitches are salvageable. Boston takes advantage of the situation as he wraps his muscular arms around my waist and pulls me closer. My body lands in his lap with my legs straddling him. His hands behind my back pull me closer to him. I try to wiggle out of Boston's viselike grasp without success. For whatever reason, this does not feel right to me anymore. Sometime in the last day any feelings I had for Boston have become purely those of a best friend or a brother. No remaining passion or desire pulls me to want more from him. However, Boston apparently still has those desires because he becomes more persistent. His hands try to work up under my shirt, and I fight them off. I do not know how to decipher these feelings I had for Boston and now do not. How could those feelings just vanish? Were they ever really there at all? All I know is that when Boston used to touch me, it warmed my heart, but when Cameron touches me, it electrifies my soul, engulfing my entire body in flames. When Boston touches me now, it feels so wrong.

"Boston, stop. Let me go please." My voice is full of urgency as I push against Boston's chest.

"Come on, you know you want this. You know you want me."

Boston's strength overpowers me, causing my arms to give way. His lips begin savagely attacking mine. Boston's hands pull my body closer as he roughly pulls at my clothing. All of the gentleness I once enjoyed from Boston is gone. It is as if this is a different man, but sadly it is not. I reach my hand up to Boston's face and firmly press my thumb into his swollen eye. He releases me with a surprised groan of pain, giving me enough time to stand quickly and back away. Boston looks up at my appalled expression before burying his face into his hands, ashamed.

"What has come over you, Boston? This is not like you." I ask softly.

"Let's face it, Alabaster. I'm a dead man. I just wanted, I just want you. I want to know what it feels like to give yourself to someone completely and have them give themselves in return. I want to know that when I am gone, someone will remember me."

"You are going to be fine. Cameron will protect you. He is a better man than you believe. He is, you will see. You are not going anywhere."

Boston looks up at me with tear-streaked cheeks.

"You love him, don't you? I have known you long enough. I can tell. You love him. You know he feels nothing for you, don't you? He sees you exactly as he sees every other Clone. An object. A thing he can use and own. When you are all used up, you know what will happen? Do you? He will throw you out on the street and the Police Clones will pick you up and you will be removed from society. In other words, you die, Alabaster. Please don't fall for his ruse. Have me, love me. I will give you more love than he ever could. I will devote my life to you, Alabaster. If you will not have me, then let them kill me, because I would die anyway."

As Boston speaks, he leaves the couch and cautiously closes the distance between us. I bow my head and tear droplets begin to extend from my long lashes. I know what he says about Cameron is probably true, but I just can't believe it--I don't believe it. Boston grabs my hands and holds them to his chest.

"My heart beats for you and you alone. It is yours forever. Don't die a fool. Live as a part of the greatest love ever known."

Boston lifts my chin until our lips meet. He is gentler this time, timid even. At first, I accept the affection. But, I slowly lower my lips from his until Boston's lips rest upon my forehead. Kissing Boston feels like a betrayal. A betrayal to Cameron, but more than anything, a betrayal to myself.

"I understand. I wish you all the best." Boston's voice is defeated.

We are still in a friendly embrace when Cameron walks in. Boston and I spring apart faster than a bullet leaving the barrel of a gun. We both have an expression like a deer caught in the headlights. A look of realization spreads across Cameron's face.

He looks at me with an expression of both hurt and betrayal before it fades away into an eerily calm look of disinterest.

"I see what's going on. Please, forgive my intrusion. You may continue. I shall not interrupt again. Oh, and you are free to leave my house anytime now, ma'am. But you, sir, are now my ward, so why don't you find something to do around here. Maybe start by cleaning this mess you made."

Cameron gestures to the toppled furniture and the fragments of once-beautiful vases before leaving quickly. He slams the door shut behind him. A look of utter despair clings to my face and weighs my heart down into my stomach. I quickly leave Boston without another look to follow after Cameron.

"No, Cameron, wait. You don't understand. Come back. That was not what you think. Please!"

I pursue Cameron up the stairs and down another corridor. He does not stop with my pleas, but continues down to the last door of the tunnel-like hallway. Cameron disappears through the door, slamming it shut behind him. When I reach the door I try the knob, but it is locked. I begin to rap lightly upon the red hardwood, but to no avail. I knock harder, louder, as I call Cameron's name. Still no response. I commence to pound on the door so hard my knuckles split and begin to bleed. It hurts, but I can barely feel it over the throbbing pain in my chest.

"Please, Cameron. Open the door. I need to talk to you. Let me explain."

Tears have formed a river system over the smooth skin of my cheeks and down to my jaw, where they slowly drip off. I crumple to the floor in tears, but I still persistently rap gently upon the door.

Chapter 13

It feels as if an eternity passes before I awaken, falling backwards when Cameron finally opens the door. Life returns to me as I look up and see him there. Cameron has showered and gotten dressed since the last time I saw him. He now wears a tightly fitting black T-shirt and faded blue jeans with studs on the seams. How much time has passed? Minutes, hours?

"You're still here? I had hoped you had gone. If you will excuse me, I have some People to rendezvous with, and possibly some new friends to meet at the Owl."

Cameron pulls me up off the ground, turns me in the direction of the exit, and gives a gentle nudge.

"You need to go that direction, down the stairs, and out the big doors at the bottom. You can't miss them. It is getting fairly late. Maybe you can make it home before curfew sets in."

Cameron turns back into his room, but instead of leaving, I turn back around to face him.

"I don't love him. I don't want him. I don't need him. I need you, want you. Every part of my very core, my very being, aches for you and you alone. I love you. Do you not see that? Do you not feel it?"

Cameron stands there with his back turned to me for what feels like another eternity. When he finally turns around, the look upon his face is a little softer than it was when he first opened the door, but he does not move and does not speak. He just stands there staring at me with a blank expression.

"Say something, dammit!" I punch Cameron's chest with my cracked knuckles, but Cameron grabs my wrist before my fist makes contact. His expression is unreadable while he studies the crimson-covered curves of my knuckles.

"You really are an accident waiting to happen, aren't you?" Cameron inquires, but I feel it is a rhetorical question. He turns back toward his bedroom and walks forward, leading me by the wrist behind him. He takes me through the previously impenetrable door. The room behind the door is massive and majestic. There is a darkly laid bed which could potentially sleep five people without touching. A large couch sits at the end of the bed with fathomless pillows. The wide ominous jaws of a Siberian-tiger-skin rug threaten to devour any feet who may venture too close. Red, yellow, and orange flames dance provocatively in a black marble fireplace.

A grand window takes up the majority of the far wall. Through it come the vibrant reds, violets, oranges, and yellows of the setting sun. My gauge of beauty has forever been altered as I take in the awe-inspiring splendor of Cameron's bedroom. Never have I seen such marvels. Cameron continues to lead me over to the couch at the end of the bed.

"Sit." I obey the command and sink into the plush cushions of the smooth black leather couch.

Cameron releases my wrist and he leaves me here. He walks to the other side of the room and my eyes follow intently. Cameron passes beneath an archway into what must be a bathroom. I am uncertain because it is unlike any I have seen before. I am accustomed to closet-sized bathrooms where the toilet sits against the shower, which is only large enough for one standing body and the small sink is practically built into the shower wall. I could stand in the middle of my bathroom and touch all four walls. This is no closet. At the far end, the shower sits behind a wall made of glass that looks like water is raining down it. I estimate the capacity of the shower to be at least six bodies, standing with arms open wide, not making any contact whatsoever. There is a decadent vanity with two identical black marble bowls, each with a continuous fountain flowing from the mouth of a golden dolphin statue. They must function as sinks. On the opposite side of the chamber is a large hot tub like the one at the hospital that is used for physical therapy. This one is not a stained fiberglass tub, but rather a beautiful dark granite with flecks of mica catching the light and sparkling like diamonds. And the light, it is indeed another chandelier. Who would put a magnificent chandelier in a bathroom?

Cameron is crouching over an open cupboard under the vanity. The pure beauty of the room draws me in like a moth to a flame. I am soon standing in the middle, turning in slow circles trying to take in all of the beauty as if I were in the Sistine Chapel and not a bathroom.

"What are you doing?"

Cameron has stopped digging in the cupboard and is standing next to me looking where I look, trying to figure out what it is I am so enthralled with.

"It is so magnificent!" I am so awestruck.

"It is a bathroom."

"I know that, but it is heavenly."

"Okay? Come on."

Cameron takes my hand and tenderly leads me back to the couch. I follow willingly as I continue to look back over my shoulder at the bathroom. Cameron sits on the couch and pulls me down next to himself. He begins to dab my hand with a cloth soaked in peroxide. The sharp sting finally brings my attention away from the bathroom.

"Ouch."

I attempt to pull my hand away from the sting. Cameron holds firmly enough to prevent the hand's escape, but gentle enough not to hurt me. He is looking down at my hand, but his eyes are raised enough to meet my own. My heart flutters as he soothingly blows on the sores without breaking eye contact. Cameron sets my hand on his knee as he unscrews the cap on a tube of antiseptic. A small amount of foggy cream extrudes from the nozzle as Cameron squeezes a portion of the contents upon my middle knuckle. He then takes my hand in his and the experienced tips of his fingers massage the cream across the hill-like joints of my hand. Cameron then sets a square of gauze atop the hill line and wraps dressing around my hand to keep the gauze in place. Once his work is complete, Cameron seals it with a strip of white tape and a light kiss. He lowers my hand back onto his lap but does not release it. The crackle of the fire is the only sound as we sit and look at each other. I have a shy, timid expression as I search Cameron's blank canvas for any signs betraying what he is thinking or feeling. The agony of this standoff is slowly driving me mad. When Cameron finally speaks, I wince ever so slightly as if preparing for a blow to the face.

"So, you think you love me? Does a Clone even know what love is, let alone how to love?"

For being an expert at reading expressions and emotions, I am at a loss as to what Cameron is thinking.

"I may be ignorant of many things, but love is not one of them. I have felt love. My mother loves me. She risked punishment by giving me my name. Naming your child makes them a part of you. She also risked punishment by saving a simple orange from a meal I missed so I would not go hungry. She has even gone as far as presenting me with an occasional forbidden gift because she loves me so much.

"Boston has sacrificed so much for the love he has for me. Clones have every violent tendency removed and programmed out at a genetic level. Boston loves me so much he attacked you when he thought I was in danger, signing his own death warrant. He loves me so much, he would forgo his wants and desires so I may be happy.

"I feel all of that and more for you. Love is the ever constant pull on every fiber of my being to be near you. I do not feel this way because I am created to serve you as a part of the People, but because I choose to, my soul chooses to. I love you."

Tears lightly streak my face and my body begins to tremble while I speak. As I say the words, I know they are true, no matter how much I have tried to convince myself otherwise. While I sit facing Cameron, I slowly lose any hope that he feels the same for me. Cameron's face has remained void of emotion, but it has softened a little more. All at once, and without warning, Cameron is holding my trembling body close to his, kissing my lips passionately, caressing my back, and lifting me off of the couch in his arms. A myriad of emotions flood through his lips into me. My arms wrap tightly around his neck and I am eating up every kiss, every emotion he presents. My legs are twined around his waist, holding him close. My hands lightly pull the hair at the base of his skull. As Cameron lays me gently on the bed, our lips do not break contact. He looms above me and reaches one hand slowly under my shirt. I give a whimper as Cameron's warm fingers crawl across my stomach and beyond to where they softly dance upon my breast. My hands migrate down his rippled sides where they fumble with the button of his jeans. After an unsuccessful mission, my hands slide back up and under his shirt to study and memorize every hollow and every bulge of his abdomen. Cameron's shirt has worked up far enough that it no longer bears a purpose, so he uses his free hand to gracefully remove the snug black shirt over his head in a single fluid motion. The half second pause I suffer from the depravation of his lips upon mine causes me to moan as I reach behind his neck to pull him back down to me. With one hand, I entwine my fingers into his golden-brown locks. I gently pull his hair as I simultaneously pull his head closer. My other hand has returned to its studies of the landscape of Cameron's chest. Cameron's lips press against mine and our tongues stroke one another. He gently bites my lower lip before his kisses traverse down my chin to my jawline and, from there, down my throat to the crevasse created by my collarbone. I, in turn, nibble his earlobe and place kisses along the side of his neck. Cameron releases a groan of pleasure as my explorative hand has found a weak spot in the impenetrable fortress created by the stubborn button of his jeans and now rests upon the hard protuberance hidden therein.

There comes a loud, resounding knock from the bedroom door followed by an English accent. "Please forgive me, sir, but some people have come to call."

The magnetic force pulling Cameron and me together is momentarily severed. Cameron rests his forehead on mine and we stare into each other's eyes smiling.

"Tell them to come again another time, Dimitri. I am too busy to be bothered. Even better, tell them to schedule an appointment."

Cameron turns his head to speak toward the closed door, but returns his attentions to me after he is finished. I flirtatiously bite my lip and Cameron moves in for another kiss, but Dimitri's voice comes through the door once more.

"I have already done that, sir, but they are being rather persistent. That new boy you have is attempting to stall them, however, I think I hear them coming up the stairs now."

"Aw shit."

The words escape Cameron's lips more to himself than to either Dimitri, on the other side of the door, or me, lying beneath him. Cameron gives me another passionate kiss before springing off the bed and heading for the door. I get out of the bed and straighten my clothes and hair out. I am unsure what to do with myself and feel rather awkward. I decide to stand here with my head bowed in submission. I hold my hands together in front of my body, trying to look as inconspicuous as possible.

Cameron makes it to the door just in time to open it for the unexpected guests. Leroy is standing in the doorway with a fist raised to knock on the now-open door. There are several other young men and women standing behind him, including both Dimitri and Boston.

"Well good evening, Leroy. What a lovely surprise." Cameron courteously greets his guests.

"Surprise? You told us you wanted to go out and party. You told us to swing by and take you out for a night filled with debauchery and frivolity."

Leroy seems both enthusiastic and irritated as he speaks. I note how he and his horde sway unsteadily. They must have already started the debauchery and frivolity without Cameron. Leroy has just noticed Cameron's bare chest. He looks around Cameron's shoulder directly at me, where I still stand near the bed.

"I see you have already started the night without us, Cam." Leroy gives me a dirty smile and a wink. "Invite us in and we can all have a go on that one before leaving to make this night legendary!"

There are calls of agreement from both the men and the women alike at Leroy's proposition. Leroy has definitely started without Cameron, as he is already intoxicated and slurring his speech. I wonder if he has even sobered up from the last run in I had with him. In the rear of the crowd, I can see Dimitri attempting to restrain Boston, who has murder in his eyes as Leroy speaks. Dimitri slowly gains control of the younger, stronger Boston. It takes great effort, but Dimitri successfully hauls Boston down the hallway and away from the group.

"You know, even though that does sound like some fantastic entertainment, I think I have changed my mind and will now politely bow out. Now, if you will please, see yourselves out. Oh, and feel free to raid the liquor cabinet on your way out. Enjoy, my friends, and goodnight."

Everyone else seems elated at Cameron's generous offer. Everyone aside from Leroy, whose chubby foot halts the procession of the door as Cameron attempts to close it.

"What is with you lately, Cam? You have never put a piece of Clone tail ahead of your friends before. What is so special about this one? Does she have a cherry-flavored pussy?"

Leroy falls back into the arms of the group after receiving a blow to his face from the fist of Cameron.

"Get the hell out of my house."

Cameron slams the door and locks it.

"You are going to regret this, Cameron. Mark my words, you bastard."

The solid-wood blockade muffles Leroy's drunken threat, and the sound of footsteps fade down the hallway until they disappear completely. After a few minutes pause, the grand doors of the house entrance slam with a resounding echo along with a slight rattle of the walls, causing me to flinch slightly.

I leave my post and cautiously approach Cameron. Once at his side, I take Cameron's hand to examine the damage done by his volatile reaction. The knuckles already show signs of swelling from the punch he administered. A trickle of blood meanders down the back of his hand from a split knuckle. Cameron is still tensely staring at the door like it may open at any second and he will be forced to defend what is his.

Chapter 14

"We need to get some ice on this." My voice snaps Cameron out of his trance.

"Huh? Oh, yeah, I guess so." Cameron turns his hand around and flexes then extends his fingers while examining it. At least he is able to move the already-swelling knuckles.

Cameron takes my hand in his undamaged one and he leads me out into the hall. We head down the stairs and go to the kitchen. I still marvel at the extravagance, but I am becoming desensitized to it. Once in the kitchen, Cameron opens a door, which I assume is another closet. However, when he opens the door, a gust of frigid air escapes in a rush with a frosty mist licking everything within reach. The inside of the door is lined with colorful boxes, each with a picture of various foods. Bottles of dark liquid are numerous, and there is also a box filled with little glistening ice cubes. I stand amazed in front of the massive food supply as Cameron grabs a few ice cubes, wraps them in a towel, and places the bundle on the knuckles of his hand. Cameron begins to walk away when he notices the freezer is still open and I remain starting inside it blankly.

"It's called a freezer. It keeps things cold. You must be starving. With all of the happenings today you have missed both lunch and dinner. Let me get you something."

Cameron closes the freezer and leads me to a chair at the table I remember overflowing with food yesterday. Cameron sits me down before walking over to a phone on the counter. He lifts the phone and dials a number. The phone rings a few times before someone answers.

"Hello, I would like my dinner sent out now, there are two of us dining this evening. Thank you." Cameron hangs up the phone and turns back to me. "Dinner should be here shortly."

Cameron leans against the minibar near the wall, where he smiles at me.

"I am sorry about Leroy and those guys. I have known Leroy since we were toddlers. Our mothers were best friends, so we grew up together. I know he has been getting out of hand, but that was over the top, even for him."

"It was nothing I am not accustomed to. He was actually acting mildly from some accounts I have been told of," I respond absentmindedly while taking in some of the splendor of the kitchen that I missed yesterday. Instead of the marble prevalent in the entryway, this room is homelier. The floor is laid with golden wood planks, the cabinets are a warm redwood, and the countertops are topped with speckled grey granite. The lighting is warm, causing the whole atmosphere to be rather cozy. I recognize a coffee pot, but there are a handful of other appliances that I could never begin to comprehend. Some are small, but others are large. There are two square objects so large, they are not on the counter, but rather part of the counters. One is covered by the granite top and has a few buttons, but the other has a flat surface with plate-sized circles upon it and a myriad of dials and buttons.

I can feel Cameron's eyes on me, so I look back at him. He is deep in disturbed contemplation. His brow is furrowed in concern as he stares at me.

"What is the matter, Cameron?"

Cameron looks away from me as he begins speaking. "I've always known the way Clones are treated is unfair, but I guess I never realized the extent. It's not only unfair it's wrong."

"It is not that bad, the life of a Clone. I mean, we are always fed. There is comfort in always knowing what is expected of me. I am never forced to decide anything. There is peace in that. And not all Clones are treated poorly."

Cameron's face is slightly red and he is staring off into the distance. I can see that his jaws are clenched tightly and his knuckles have turned white due to his tight grip on the minibar's granite countertop. Cameron opens his mouth to say something, but the conversation is silenced by the resounding sound of a buzzer. The sliding door of a food chute, similar to the one in my own home, opens, revealing two sparkling silver domes within. Cameron pops out of his reverie like the conversation never happened. His expression is once again soft. He removes both of the domes and brings them over to the table. He sets one down across the table from me and the other in front of me. He then lifts the reflective silver dome, releasing a most pleasant aroma. There is such a massive pile of food on the plate, I struggle to decide what to eat first. There is a cloudlike substance with white chunky pieces, a pile of glistening golden corn, and a large slab of pinkly tinted meat. There is also a salad on the side, but instead of just the leafy greens, there is cheese, tomatoes, and cucumbers mixed in, and a whitish creamy substance on top with small toasted cubes on top of that. Cameron is already eating the food from his plate without indecision. I decide to start at the top and work my way around. My first bite is from the cloudlike substance. A smile takes over my face as my taste buds explode from the delicious flavors. The food I am accustomed to is bland and textureless. Even the food at the hospital cafeteria does not compare to the rich flavor of the first bite from this plate. Cameron lets out a chuckle as I eat bite after bite with hardly a breath in between.

"Slow down there or you'll choke."

I look up at Cameron and I can feel not only my cheeks, but also my ears turn red with embarrassment. I continue on with the meal at a slower speed, but I still finish before him. When my plate is basically licked clean, so not a single remnant of the delicious food has been neglected, I begin collecting my dishes to dispose of as usual.

"You don't have to do that. Dimitri will take care of it. Why don't you and I go back upstairs?"

Cameron is now standing next to me, holding my hand to his lips, placing a seductive line of kisses from the back of my hand slowly up to my wrist, and continuing on up my arm. I set the plate down and allow Cameron to lure me out of the kitchen. As we begin to round the banister of the stairs, I pause.

"What about Boston? Where is he? Is he going to be all right?" My brow is furrowed with concern for my best friend.

"Don't worry about him. Dimitri is already showing him the new duties for which he is responsible. He probably already has a temporary cot set up in the Clone living quarters down in the basement."

Cameron points his finger to a door we already passed a few feet before, which leads under the staircase. He gives one of his charming half-smiles as he tugs insistently on my hand. I smile up at him and follow, reluctantly at first, but willingly soon after. By the time we reach the landing at the top of the stairs, we are racing down the long hallway. I am rarely surefooted, but I am faster than most when I am not falling over my own feet. At the moment, my feet stay true to me and I beat Cameron to the door of his bedroom. I stand with my back against the door, blocking the knob when Cameron arrives seconds after, out of breath.

"How can you not walk across a room without falling, and yet run like the wind without as much as a stumble?"

As Cameron moves in for a kiss, a cocky smile spreads across my face as I stealthily turn the knob hidden behind my back. After quickly opening the door, I dodge his advance and slink into the room. Cameron almost falls, but he catches himself and follows after, grinning, and continues the chase. He fails to catch me as I again dodge his attempts. We are both smiling and laughing wildly while we dance around a couch in the middle of the room. After Cameron's many unsuccessful attempts, I stand behind the couch laughing, and he seems too worn out to continue. It was a ruse. He uses one final burst of reserved energy to lunge over the couch and tackle me. We land gently on a plush white carpet that has cloudlike softness. The laughing slows to a halt and we stare into each other's eyes, breathing heavily to fill our deprived lungs with oxygen, but also with anticipation. Cameron brushes some loose strands of hair out of my face, tucking them neatly behind my ear. I take his hand and kiss the meaty muscle of his thumb.

"You can call me Ally if you would still like to." I stare up at Cameron to see his response.

"Thank you for the offer, but I don't think I will." He pauses and I can feel the light fade from my eyes.

When my smile falters ever so slightly, Cameron continues on, "Only because 'Alabaster' has kind of grown on me."

Cameron smiles victoriously, and I playfully punch his shoulder. I throw Cameron off balance long enough to slip out from under him. I head in the direction of the bed. Cameron recovers quickly and follows at my heels. We meet up at the bed and both of us flop down into the sea of blankets and pillows. We lie side by side with our fingers intertwined. I move in for a kiss, but Cameron stops me.

"Wait a second, I don't want to do this."

My smile is stripped from my face and an intense pain rips through my heart like a knife. I quickly sit up and pull myself away from Cameron.

"I understand. I had better find myself a cot in the basement with the other Clones for the night. I think curfew has already set in. Unless you would rather I leave immediately." I begin to wiggle to the side of the bed, but Cameron catches me before I reach the edge.

"That's not what I meant."

"Is it not?"

Cameron smiles at me with loving adoration. The agony in my heart dissipates like a thunder cloud that's run out of steam. An uncertain smile works its way back to my lips.

"No, of course not. I just meant, I want to know more about you before we do anything. I want to know what has happened in your life to make you *you*. You are so different from any Clone I have ever met. I knew it the first time I saw you in the bus. I could tell you were putting a great deal of effort into blending in, whereas other Clones just blend. You had such courage to look me in the eye like you did. Your first day at the hospital I saw you give that Clone woman enough morphine to ease her pain, even though you knew her life was over, and if you were caught, yours would be also. The patient that was in the car accident, you helped me with him as if you were a fellow doctor, not a Clone nurse. The first time I moved in to kiss you, you did not pull away. Even the Clones at the Owl turn their heads away when someone tries to kiss them, but you never have. You never even broke eye contact. You act so differently than any Clone I have ever known, witnessed, or heard tell of. I just want to try to understand you. Tell me, please. And that is not an order."

Cameron releases my hand after he kisses it. He then scoots himself back into the middle of the massive bed and up to the pillows, where he props himself up. He pats the vacant spot beside him, inviting me to join.

I slowly crawl closer with a playful smile. Cameron grows impatient and lunges forward, tackling me and pulling me closer. I squirm and giggle as his fingers dance upon my ribs as if they are playing upon the ivory keys of a piano. When I finally give in, Cameron lays me beside him with one of his arms around me, where it softly strokes my arm. His other arm lies across his body, where he holds both of my delicate hands. My hands fidget within his while I speak softly with a self-conscious tone.

"I do not know what there is to tell. I was raised the same as every other Clone, had the same rules, same instruction. I have always seemed more curious than my counterparts, as if in search of a part of me I felt was missing. My mother encouraged my behavior, although she cautioned me to be wary of the People. To be wary of you."

I tap the tip of Cameron's still-swollen red nose.

"Even Boston has never been as curious as me, and often he discouraged my behaviors. Now, you tell me something."

I change the subject off of myself. I am not comfortable or accustomed to talking about myself.

"How did you already have the document to claim Boston? I have been told it takes at least twenty-four hours to get the papers, because they want each Person to think about it before claiming. There is a lot of responsibility. After all, it's essentially claiming responsibility of a life."

Cameron contemplates his answer for a moment. I can't tell if he is thinking of an answer or if he is trying to decide if he should tell me the answer or not.

"Yes, it does take twenty-four hours and yes it does require some responsibility. Truth be told, I had already filed for the papers after bumping into a unique specimen. However, after getting to know said Clone, I came upon the conclusion that she is fully capable of finding her own place to belong. So, after you were so concerned about your friend's wellbeing, I had the papers changed slightly. It is usually an equally long process, but it does help to have a father who is a high-ranking government official."

"You can still claim me, you know. I would let you."

"Ay, yes. I would love to, but unfortunately, I am now unable to do so. We are only allowed to claim one Clone in a twelve-month period of time. I will still be able to call on you daily, but not indefinitely." Cameron places a kiss on my forehead. "Someone else could claim you and steal you away from me."

My eyes begin to grow heavy, so I barely hear him whisper.

"You're not going anywhere. I will not allow it. I would die first. I love you."

Cameron reaches down and pulls the heavy blanket up over us. I roll over onto my side and bury myself into the safety of his embrace.

Chapter 15

I am accustomed to waking before the sun, but Cameron apparently is not. He is still peacefully sleeping as I carefully duck under his arm. I sneak out of bed, which is easier said than done. There is so much cushion and fluff that I keep sinking in deeper. I freeze as Cameron gives a slight groan. When he does not wake, I continue my escape from the bed. I head to the Sistine bathroom for a quick shower.

I remove my scrubs, which I slept in once again. For whatever reason I always feel dirty when I sleep in my uniform. It just does not feel the same as a nightgown. I am not sure where to put my clothes, so I leave them on the counter before heading toward the massive shower.

There are so many bronze knobs and dispensers that I do not know where to start. I pick one at random and turn it. A tranquil waterfall comes to life and cascades down the ridged back wall. It is beautiful, but not functional. I decide to leave it on, as it is lovely to watch. I try another lever and it emits a cold spray from one of the three shower heads above. There are still other levers, but I do not risk discovering what they may bring. Besides, this is not my first icy shower. My teeth chatter slightly as I investigate the many colorful dispensers. I sing a silent thank you, as the dispensers are each labeled. I get a good lather from the shampoo in my silky brown hair. I am enthralled by the fragrant smell it possesses. After rinsing the shampoo, I use a liberal amount of conditioner. It too has an amazing scent. Every product I, along with every other Clone, have used is unscented.

As I reach for a bright-green bar of soap, another hand appears out of nowhere, beating me to it. I slip and begin to fall because I am startled by the intruder. I do not make it far before I am caught by the very ripped, very naked Cameron. He lifts me up and makes sure I am standing steadily on my own two feet before releasing me.

"My God, Alabaster! This water is freezing!" Cameron reaches around me for one of the unknown levers I had not braved turning.

The stream of water instantly becomes hot and steam rises all around us. It is not burning hot, but it is hot enough that it turns my skin pink where it hits. I have never felt the incredible power of a hot shower.

The hot water seems to relieve all of my stress as it pelts my skin. The aches and pains of my muscles are washed away. As I thaw, Cameron uses the green soap to build up a good lather, which he then massages all over my body. The scent of the soap is not a disappointment either. It smells like fresh-cut grass. Cameron begins at my shoulders and works his way down to my back toward my buttock. I have never had another's hands touching my bare skin so freely, and never did I think it would be as enjoyable as this.

The incredible hot water easily washes away the soapy suds as fast as they are applied. Cameron kisses and nibbles my neck as his hands roam around my body and begin to wash my stomach. The soap has gone missing in action as Cameron's hands go in separate directions from there. One hand scours up to my breasts and the other migrates south, where it stays between my legs. I gasp desperately as Cameron's southern hand applies firm pressure against my flesh and his fingers trace small circles. My knees grow weak, so I place both hands against the shower wall. Cameron is practically holding me while he presses harder against me, his hips grinding at my back. Every one of my nerve endings has been awakened and electrifying tingles encompass my body, cumulating where Cameron's hand moves between my legs. I spin around and pull him closer into my body. Even though I am clueless as to what I am supposed to do, my body seems to know. Our lips make contact, each attacking the other as if fighting for air. We moan and groan as we bite and pull the other's lips. My arm is over Cameron's shoulder and behind his neck drawing him in closer yet. My other hand has found its way down to Cameron's erection, caressing and stoking it. Cameron's hips thrust against me. He grabs my rump with both hands and lifts me off the ground. I wrap my legs around him and he presses me against the ridged waterfall wall. I now understand the functionality of the ridges as I receive a back massage from the pressure Cameron applies.

Our mouths have been connected for so long that we are both running short of air, but we refuse to allow our lips to part. I use Cameron's shoulders to pull myself higher up his torso. I then direct the tip of his long shaft to help it find its target as Cameron thrusts. When it finds its home, I lower myself down. Both Cameron and I release a gasp of both pleasure and the need for air. The tightness I feel inside is overwhelming. There is slight pain, but it is enticing, and it soon fades into ecstasy. We move slowly at first with Cameron grinding back and forth and me using his broad shoulders as leverage to pull myself up and down until we fall into a fast-paced rhythm. The kisses lessen as both Cameron and I begin breathing harder. A cry escapes my lips as the pleasure intensifies. A warm flood of euphoria flows through my body, causing my toes to tingle and all of my muscles to slightly convulse. Cameron gives two final hard thrusts before releasing a loud groan. We rest our foreheads together with our eyes closed as we both gasp to catch our breath.

After simultaneously opening our eyes, Cameron and I stare deeply into each other's eyes. We share a few more pecks. I unwrap my legs and Cameron lowers me to my feet. My legs still feel a little numb and unsteady, but I manage to hold myself upright. Neither one of us can wipe the smiles from our faces. I cannot help but giggle from the joy trying to burst forth from within. I turn the water off and Cameron grabs a fluffy white robe hanging from a hook for me. He drapes the robe around my shoulders from behind whilst kissing my neck. Cameron reaches the robe's sash around my waist and ties it off. Both Cameron and I step out of the shower and Cameron procures his own identical white robe. We both keep looking at each other and smiling. The giddy joy I feel is overflowing, and my legs still maintain a slight tremble.

As I dry off, I notice a clean set of clothing for us both next to the sink. I have no clue how the clothing got here. Hopefully Cameron got it before joining me. I shudder to think Dimitri brought them in, or worse, Boston. I don't know how Boston would handle witnessing what just happened, but I can assume it would not be as happy an ending. I drop the robe and proceed to clothe myself in a clean set of my usual light-blue scrubs. I use a hand towel to dry my brown hair before I pull it back into a braid. I am very impressed at the effect Cameron's shampoo and conditioner have had on my hair. It seems so much fuller and smoother than normal. Cameron is also dressing, but he dawns a dark-blue pair of jeans and a dark-green button-up shirt, which makes his eyes appear emerald green rather than a light-blue green. His messy golden hair is much darker when wet. Cameron soon is at my back with his arms wrapped around me again.

"Shall we go eat some breakfast before getting ready for work?" Cameron inquires.

"No, I need to go tell my mother where I have been. She must be worried. I will return shortly, that is, if you will have me."

"I would have you now and forever more," Cameron whispers into my ear, then tickles my neck with his lips.

"I will need to leave soon or she will have left for work already."

Cameron nibbles my ear and gives an unhappy whine.

"Really? You can't wait another ten minutes? Twenty tops. What if I drive you?" Cameron begs imploringly as his hands begin wandering again.

I chase down his hands and detain them. I turn toward Cameron and shake my head back and forth in a sad but playful *no*. I cup Cameron's face in both of my small hands. I bring his face down to my level for another soft kiss. Cameron's kiss intensifies in an attempt to keep me here, but I pull away and turn to leave. Cameron follows after and catches my hand. He does not stop me. He just follows me out of the room, down the hallway, and the stairs. He walks with me all the way to the great mahogany double doors of the entrance. Cameron stops me again and gives me one final kiss. I momentarily have second thoughts about leaving when Cameron finally, reluctantly pulls away.

"I will need to head into work today, so you should probably head there after your visit. I look forward to working with you."

I nod in concession with a smile. Cameron opens one of the large doors for me. He gives me a wink and watches from the doorway as I walk down the street. He does not go back into the house until I turn the corner and am out of sight.

Chapter 16

I am struggling to keep the energy coursing through every fiber of my body contained while I walk down the uneven cobblestones. I want to laugh, scream, cry, and run yelling through the streets, but I know I can't. If I were to do as such, I would be arrested and removed from society indefinitely. Especially seeing Cameron would not be able to intervene and claim me. I keep my head down lower than necessary to try to conceal the smile I am unable to suppress. I reach the bus stop just as the bus pulls up. It is the first bus of the morning and very vacant, and the sun has barely risen. The trip takes no time at all, and I disembark at my usual stop in the Clone sector of the city.

I remain oblivious to my surroundings, so I do not notice that I am being followed until it is too late. Out of the blue, I am shoved into a wall by a large object. I let out a small cry of pain as my body is smashed against the wall by the repulsive body of Leroy.

"I don't know what Cam sees in you, but I intend to find out." Leroy slurs the words as he begins to rifle with his belt. I remain trapped by his mass, unable to move. Leroy licks my face. His breath is revolting and he still reeks of alcohol. I gag from the repulsive smell. I need to get away, but I feel so helpless. The Clone part of me is already submitting, but something else is alive and ready to go down with a fight. I knee Leroy as hard as I can in the groin. Leroy recoils enough for me to slip out of my prison. However, he recovers quicker than I planned. He dives to grab my ankle, causing me to fall to the ground. My knees and elbows open in scarlet ribbons as they carry the brunt of my fall. I struggle to escape, but Leroy still holds my ankle. I kick at him and crack Leroy directly in the nose, causing blood to spray. Leroy releases his hold with a yelp as he grasps at his busted nose. I swiftly gather myself and make a run for it. I am not too far from my dwelling now. I know I can make it, but what then? I reach my front door and am inside before Leroy regains his footing or vision. I can barely breathe and am crying hysterically as I enter my dwelling. It is still quite early and my father and brother are apparently still asleep. My mother has set the delivered breakfast on the table and is now making coffee, which she immediately abandons to come to my aid. She strokes my soft brown hair as she wraps both arms securely around me in a full and complete hug. There is no way a Person on the other end of the kitchen camera would mistake it for anything else.

"Calm down, darling, what happened? Come sit down, have some coffee."

My mother tries to lead me over to a chair at the square kitchen table, but I refuse to follow.

"I have made a grave mistake, Mother. I can't stay. I need to run. I need somewhere to hide. I need to get back to him. Mother, I, I, I, I."

I hyperventilate as I break down in tears again.

"What has happened? You're bleeding, Alabaster."

My mother has noticed the open skin of my elbows and knees. The thin material of my pants are in tatters around my knees and blood soaks through.

"I was attacked by a man, one of the People. I should have let him do what he wanted with me, but I fought back, Mother. I kicked him. Twice! Oh, how could this have happened? How could everything go so wrong when it was finally starting to go right?"

My mother changes her tone of voice immediately as well as her overall demeanor. It is as if she has become another person. She no longer holds the submissive aura of a Clone, but rather the power and authority of a member of the People."

"You are right, you need to run. I know where you need to go. Follow me."

My mother snatches two apples from the breakfast table before she grabs my hand and leads me out the front door of our dwelling. It is the only door. I look around and I do not see Leroy or any of the massive Police Clones, but I am certain they are on their way. We briskly walk around to the back side of our dwelling where the dirt alley runs. Once behind the dwellings, my mother hurries me over to the tall grass of the field that surrounds the entire city. She points me out into a direction deep in the yellowing green grass. The wind blows through the tall grass malevolently as I stare out into the forbidden expanse.

"Run straight in that direction. Do not stop until you reach a meadow. At the meadow turn right forty-five degrees and then keep running your fastest. Again, do not stop. You are to keep running until you are found by the rebels. You need not search for them, they will find you. When they find you, ask for Anton, and tell him Eliana has sent you in search of his aid."

My mother places both apples in my hands as she pushes me forward, urging me to hurry.

"Wait, who is Anton and who is Eliana?" I turn back to my mother, tears blurring her shape as they cloud my vision.

I am frightened to go.

"I am Eliana, and Anton is the only one who can help you at this point. Go now. Run!"

I turn, take two steps forward, but pause and turn back around to my mother.

"Mother, please go to the hospital and tell Dr. Staunton I had to leave. Tell him I, tell him I love him, I will always love him. Please, Mother, please."

The tears now streak my cheeks and my mother takes the two steps to me and we again embrace each other. She releases me and urges me to go with haste.

"I will do as you beseech, but you must go. Go now. Do not look back just keep going!" My mother cries after me as I turn and run.

There are heavy footsteps and loud voices coming from the city and the life I have left behind me. I dare not look back. My feet stay true as I swiftly glide through the waist-high grass. Each blade is sharper than the last and as they hit my legs, they cut through the thin fabric and bite at my skin. I push through the pain and press on through the grass.

There is still no end to the green expanse in sight when I become winded. The edges of my sight are fading into darkness, but my legs keep moving, propelling me forward. When I finally make it to what I assume is a meadow, I stop. The grass here is only tall enough to rise above the sole of my white shoe. I take a few bites of an apple as I walk toward the center of the meadow. My chest aches from the exertion placed upon my lungs. My vision begins to clear as I am able to catch a few breaths, but small stars twinkle at the edges of my sight. The legs of my cotton scrubs are in tatters. In the center of the clearing, I see a pink flowering tree. I walk to the tree and following my mother's instructions, I turn right. I drop both apples as my hands are no longer able to hold them. I only ate half of the one. The juice was rejuvenating, but if I eat more, I will likely throw up. I begin running again. Before I reach the tall grass again, a sharp pain reaches my side like a hot poker. I don't let it slow me down. The short pause at the meadow momentarily cleared my tunnel vision, but another five minutes of my insane pace has brought it back. I keep pushing through the pain and the darkness that is closing in as my vision goes from tunnel to pinhole.

I can tell I am out of the tall grass now, because my feet fall hard onto dirt and rocks, and my legs are relieved from the sting of the grass cutting into my flesh. These shoes are not made for running and the soles are not thick. I can feel the sharp points of rocks bruising my feet as they fall on them with great force. The rocky ground is not as forgiving of the impact my feet make as was the grassy field, and now each step is causing my shins to shoot pain up my leg.

I feel slightly cooler, like I am sheltered from the beating sun. I look up to see green blurs above me. Trees perhaps? I keep pushing my legs, but they do not respond as willingly as they should, slowing my stride. I begin wheezing because my lungs ache to be properly filled with oxygen. My feet finally give way, sending my body careening to the ground. I had more momentum than I thought because my body slides on the rough forest floor. Sharp rocks tear at my flesh, but thankfully I don't feel any of it. Apparently, my body has become numb. The darkness of my vision recedes momentarily, but it is blurry at best. I roll over onto my back and look up to see a man's familiar face staring down on me.

"Anton, Eliana." These are the only two words I am able to force out as a whisper. I hope these are the rebels. The last thing I remember are hands on my shoulders and a man's voice barking orders before the darkness returns, swallowing me into unconsciousness.

Chapter 17

Sleep is not gentle to me. I am bombarded by violent dreams. In the first nightmare, I am a beautiful silver fish swimming in crystalline waters as beautiful as the blue-green pools of Cameron's eyes. The water soon turns black with oil, cutting out the dancing rays of the sun. I am suffocating, so I swim to the surface in a futile attempt to escape. The oil covers my body, weighing me down as it fills my lungs and making the oil impossible to swim through. I can't breathe, but that is of little concern because, at that moment, the oil ignites. Red and orange flames begin to dance on the water's surface. They do not dance playfully like the sun's rays, but aggressive and full of passion and hunger. I am suspended, trapped within the thick oil, watching as the flames dance closer. Fear begins to grip me, but I do not allow it to have control over me. With one final surge of willpower, I escape the fiery inferno and I am flying above the surface of the water. My fish body does not stay airborne for long and I fall back toward the water and flames. When I pass through the flames, I am stripped of the diamond-like fish scales by the hungry flames licking my body, and I continue to fall.

I land into my next dream with a hard thump against a wood-grained cutting board. The board is stained red, a red so dark, it is almost black. I am now a powerful hawk. My stripped scales have revealed a body covered with shimmering chestnut brown and golden feathers. I cannot move. A large, red stained hand holds me firmly against the board. I look around to see my brown-feathered brethren aimlessly walking around, wingless and void of their former regality. This butcher has taken the only thing that makes a bird a bird. He has taken away the beauty nature had once bestowed on them. I close my black eyes in an attempt to shut out the sight of the merciless mutilation. I feel one of my magnificent wings being pulled to its full extension and immobilized. There is little light in this hell, but there is enough for a large knife to catch on the sharp edge of its razor-like blade as it is raised high above me. I hear the twang of the sharp blade cutting through the air. I release my fears, my anxieties, my worries. I will not die with those diminutive feelings weighing me down. All at once, the grace, freedom, and power of soaring high above the clouds fills my spirit.

Suddenly, there are no hands holding me captive, binding me to an involuntary fate. I no longer feel any pain or terror. All I feel is freedom as I spread my mighty wings. I feel the air flow around my body as it raises me higher into the azure skies. I turn my head to the side to see the beautiful emerald-green and ebony wings of a butterfly rather than the powerful brown-feathered wings of a hawk. I have morphed into an enchantingly beautiful butterfly. I soar with as much pride as a mighty hawk.

My attention is captured by the distinct cry of a newborn baby. I flutter down to the tree tops in search of the desperate pleading of the helpless babe. The clear skies fill with dark angry clouds set on destruction. A strong wind beats at my fragile wings. Feral gusts of wind push and pull my delicate body wherever they wish. They try to pull my fragile body to shreds. My eyes have finally zeroed in on the baby's cradle located high up in a tree. Pink little hands and feet peek out above the edge of the teetering cradle. Due to the lack of results with their efforts of tearing me apart, I can see the winds leave me for a new victim of their wrath. They approach the precarious cradle with the same hungry vigilance of a wolf pack.

I attempt to grab the wisps to stop them, without success. I try to fly faster, to head them off and stop their prowl, but the winds flow fluidly around my useless efforts. The winds laugh at my futile attempts with thunderous cackles. The baby releases a playful giggle while the deadly winds rock the cradle back and forth. The chubby pink fists grab at the wisps of wind, who slip smoothly away. The winds knock the cradle harder and harder in an attempt to knock it out of the tree, but to no avail. The cradle is lodged securely in a fork of the tree's bough. I increase my efforts to reach the baby when the winds give up their assault upon the cradle and turn their attention to the vulnerable tree bough. They each take turns pummeling the thick tree branch. The air vibrates as lighting crashes against the base of the tree, igniting the bark in eager flames. I reach the cradle just when the bough breaks. I try to push the cradle from underneath, attempting to at least slow the baby's descent to the ground, but I am so small, and the cradle so large. Before the cradle hits the jagged rocks below, smashing me beneath it, I wake up.

Chapter 18

I am lying on my back, staring up into the florescent glare of ceiling lights. I squint my eyes at the unwelcome brightness and I attempt to move my arm to shield my eyes. My arm only makes a few inches of progress before a tightness around my wrist halts the movement. I try my other am with the same result. I move to roll over but pressure across my sternum prevents me. I look down my body and panic ensues as I realize I am strapped down to a hard table. I am filled with the same panic I had in my dream, but it is more powerful because I know this is real. My legs are also restrained at both my thighs and my ankles. I begin to thrash wildly, trying to break free from my bonds, even though I know all of my attempts are futile. I release a ferocious scream like a feral cat and continue to thrash.

The sound of a buzzer demands my attention. It signals the unlocking of a large metal door. The door opens with a screeching cry that causes me to wince as it pierces my eardrum. I try to turn in my bindings to look back over my shoulder toward the nose coming from the door. The restraints are too restrictive for me to move enough, but the three figures who enter the room are soon standing at my bedside where I can see them clearly. Two of the strangers are Clones and one is a Person. A dark-haired man with a dark beard and equally dark skin stands next to a redheaded Clone woman with a bandage on her forehead and an arm in a sling. They are both standing behind a man with the face of my father who possesses the same look of bitter disdain that my father has trademarked. I did not think it possible for another to hold so much contempt as my father. I don't know if I should be impressed or worried. I choose to go with impassive.

"Who are you people? Where am I? Let me go, I demand to be released."

I have no idea where my defiance has come from. It goes against everything I was taught, everything I was created for. It goes against my very nature. The three strangers are slightly taken aback before the leading man, the one who resembles my father, chuckles. The other two take his reaction as their cue and follow in suit. The Clone woman has a melodic laugh void of worry, but the Person's throaty laugh is filled with a malicious tang.

"We are wondering the same thing about you. And seeing that we are the ones in charge here, our questions shall be answered first. Starting with who you are, and how did you find us?" The Clone with my father's face asks with an all-too-familiar stern look upon his face.

I struggle for freedom again, but to no avail. Pain from the cuts I have already sustained today are making their presence known as I try to kick and move, adding new pains. Someone changed me out of the tattered remnants of my light-blue uniform, because I have a clean set of emerald-green scrubs on now. However, these new clothes no longer remain clean, because the blood from my sores is beginning to seep through as I reopen the wounds with my struggling.

"Feisty, aren't you?" the man with the beard says with a jeering chuckle.

I glare at the man and spit in his leather-like face. His dark-brown eyes are set ablaze with fury. The Clone woman places her unslung hand on the enraged man's chest, stopping him as he moves forward to backhand me. The man resembling my father looks back at the bearded man reprovingly before he turns his attention back to me. The man who looks like my father has replaced his sour look of disdain with a fake smile of gentleness as he continues to interrogate me. As if I would trust him. He may be able to change his facial expression, but not what lies behind those brown eyes. I find it curious how my father and this man share the same eyes as Dimitri, but when I look at Dimitri, all I see in his eyes is genuine kindness and loyalty. Whereas this Clone and my father are full of hate behind the surface.

"When we found you, you said two names. Who are they?" My father's Clone type inquires.

I stop struggling as I try to remember anything before I woke up here. It all seems like a blur. I start from the last thing I remember and work my way back. I remember running, a pink tree, the sharp cutting of tall grass on my legs, my mother's forbidden hug, fighting an attacker, and Cameron. A flood of both joy and sorrow overwhelms me. Tears burn as they begin pouring out from of my soul and out of my eyes. I try to focus on the names my mother told me to use, but they are blurred by my grief. What names had I uttered to these people? My mother had told me to run, to run and not look back. She had told me to ask for Andrew? No, not Andrew. Come on, Alabaster, what was the name? For Anton, Anton was the first name. I force myself to focus more. My head hurts. What was the other name? It was a woman's name. Eleanor or Ann or Amy? No, it was Eliana. I face the man in charge and force out the words my mother instructed me to deliver.

"I was told to come here and ask for Anton, and to tell him Eliana had sent me. I do not know who Anton is, but Eliana is my mother."

The man in charge smiles a little more authentically, but he still has a pompous look about him.

"And who are you?"

"I am Clone number A14B45T3R. I was created to serve in the Essential Function of nursing."

"Do you have a real name, Clone A14B45T3R?"

"No, I am a Clone. I am not allowed to have a name."

"Well, Clones are also not allowed to be defiant, rude, or demanding. But you seem to have no trouble at all manifesting those qualities."

I turn my head away from the stranger who looks like my father. He is the only one of my visitors talking. This stranger carries himself with finesse and authority uncommon to a Clone. I give him as much trust as I would Leroy, maybe less.

"I like you. Eliana always said you were coming along just as we had planned, but I never imagined you would be so perfect, Alabaster."

I whip my head back to the man with confusion written all over my face. The man is smiling down on me with satisfaction written on his face.

"Clones are also not permitted to lie." The man gives me a wink as he proceeds to loosen my bonds.

The red-haired Clone goes to my other side to assist. It is a bit harder for her because she only has one arm to use. I am uncertain, but I think she is the clone I helped a few days ago in the hospital. If it is that Clone, she seems slightly different. I can't put my finger on it, but there is definitely something different about this Clone. It cannot be her; I know it is impossible. That Clone has most certainly been removed from society by now.

"I am Anton, leader of the rebels." I am distracted from my thoughts by the Clone who looks like my father. "It is a pleasure to finally meet you. This here is Steven," He points to the bearded man who obviously does not like me. "And you have already met Octavius once before. Seems she owes you a debt of gratitude from what she has told me."

Steven continues to glare at me dangerously, but Octavius cancels out his anger with an equal amount of compassion. So Octavius is the Clone I helped. But how did she end up here, and why does she seem so fundamentally different? Anton takes my hand to help me sit up and gives it a firm hand shake.

"Welcome to the rebellion."

Chapter 19

I stop my avid pacing when I hear footsteps out in the hall. It has been two weeks since I came to the compound, and two weeks since I earned myself this luxury prison suite equipped with one of the finest concrete-slab beds I have ever had the opportunity to rest upon. How did I earn this royal treatment? After being welcomed to the Clone rebellion with open hands, I rejected the offer with a closed fist. A closed fist right into the nose of Anton, followed by my knee to his groin. Then Steven came at me with open arms, which I ducked under. I somehow caught his arm and pinned it behind his back while I slammed him into the wall. He hit hard because his momentum was already moving that direction and he didn't have time to react. His head made contact first and he crumpled to the ground in a pathetic heap. Octavius looked alert, but with her injured arm she did not attack. When Anton finally recovered his dignity, the door burst open to be filled by a mountain of a man, a Police Clone. He came at me, so I swung my still-fisted hand at him. He dodged and I swung my other arm, which he dodged again. I then gave him all I had, but every throw was parried. I have no idea how a massive sinewy thing like that could move as fast as he did, but his motions were like a blur, but so were mine. I finally made contact with his face and we both stopped suddenly with puzzled looks of surprise on our faces. He recovered quicker than me and he took hold of my arms, and then I was once again restrained on the table.

Looking back, I have no idea how I was able to fight like that. My whole life I was raised to be submissive. I never had any combat training or self-defense instruction. During the fight, I felt in control of myself, but completely out of control. It was as if someone else had taken over my body like a master puppeteer. I keep wondering how it was all possible. Why couldn't I do that when Leroy attacked me? Why did I freeze up when Cameron was attacked by Boston? Cameron. I miss him so much. No, I cannot think about him right now. Cameron's deep blue eyes, and his honey-wheat hair flowing through my fingers. Stop, I need to focus.

The footsteps beyond the door are getting closer. It is not meal time, so someone is coming to visit. I quickly lie on my bed and try to act bored. Well, more bored with the whole situation in general, not just bored because there is nothing to do. The door opens with squeaky hinges. The large Police Clone enters first, followed by Anton. The Police Clone moves off to the side and stands comfortably with his hands held behind his back. Anton sleeks toward me. I casually pick at some debris caught under my middle finger which stands proudly at attention at Anton's presence. I have no idea where my rebellious attitude is coming from, but at this point it does not matter. I am dead if I go back to the city and I am dead if I join their insane rebellion.

"Hello, Alabaster. How are you liking your stay here so far?" Anton asks with acidic sarcasm.

I clinch my jaws tight to prevent a retort from escaping and I force myself to ignore his foul presence.

"I was very impressed with your display the other day. I have arranged for you to hone those raw skills. This here is the captain of my rebel guard. He oversees all of the training of new recruits." My gaze lingers to the massive Police Clone. I do not think he should be called a Police Clone now that he is a defector. He is huge in comparison to me. My waist is about the same diameter as his thigh. He stands at least a foot and a half taller than me, perhaps two feet. The top of his head is mere inches from the ceiling. His eyes are as blue as the evening sky and under the left one, a nice-sized scar runs along his strong cheekbone. The captain is missing a portion of his left ear as well. The worst scar is one that runs across his neck at a diagonal. The scaring is jagged, and whatever happened to him likely had him near death. It is amazing he survived. When our eyes meet, I feel a dagger of ice pierce my gut from his gaze. The look Rhino gives me is not really malicious, but more calculating.

I know Anton has been talking the entire time I have been analyzing the captain, but I only notice when the room is filled with silence and the captain's eyes are not the only eyes burning into me. I finally turn my attention back to Anton while I try to recall anything he said.

"So now's the time for you to make a choice, Alabaster. Stay in this room and rot, or go with Rhino now and train to fight for freedom," Anton says with a tone that I am sure means he has already had to repeat himself at least twice.

I turn my attention back to the captain, who must be Rhino, because there is no one else here. I catch only a moment's glimpse of what looks to me like pleading in the captain's eyes, but it is gone, replaced with calculation before I can be sure, or perhaps before Anton can take note. I cannot explain why, but I have a feeling I can trust this ex-Police Clone. I stand up and lazily stretch my neck.

I glare at Anton and give him my decision: "I will train, but only to fight for freedom from you."

I hear Rhino cover a burst of laughter with a cough, but I do not break my staredown with Anton. Anton's face turns red, and I somehow hold my resolve together when his eyes slightly bulge. His fist is clenched at his side, and I can tell there is a war going on somewhere within about whether or not he wants to hit me. The restrained side seems to have won, for now.

Anton calms himself and turns to address Rhino. "Well, I will leave her to your devices. Feel free to beat her and that loose mouth if you must. We need her alive, not pretty."

Chapter 20

Rhino nods to his commander, who does not give me a second glance before exiting my cell and stomping down the hallway. When I do not hear Anton's pounding footsteps anymore, I turn my attention back to Rhino with a smile, which I quickly wipe away. Rhino's blue eyes are looking me up and down with the calculation of a seasoned warrior. He seems to be looking for both weakness and strength. I unconsciously stand a little taller with tension. Rhino proceeds to circle me. The cell is not very large, but his massive body manages a full circle around me in the small space without touching me. I sense the hit coming before I see it, and I duck just before his fist makes full contact with my jaw, but he still clips it hard enough to make me spin. I lose balance and land hard on the concrete bed. I catch the edge of the slab with my nose and crimson warmth trickles down over my lip. I don't have time to wipe the blood away before I sense another attack coming. I roll out of the way just as Rhino's massive boot lands where my head was moments ago on the concrete. When Rhino begins to pull his foot back, I grab the boot and twist Rhino's foot with all my strength. He is off balance for just a second and that is all I need. I lift the leg up and the giant falls down. I hear the crack of bone when his nose makes contact with the metal toilet bowl.

I drop the heavy foot and I prepare for another attack. Rhino stands up and wipes his nose. He looks at his hand and starts laughing. I do not know what to make of it. I remain poised for action, but he looks at me, still smiling.

"It's been a long time since someone got the better of me. I promise it won't happen again," Rhino states. His voice is deep, gravelly and full of a playfulness that does not fit the situation. His face is angry, but his eyes are smiling.

I can't get a read on this Clone. I have always been able to gauge what a person is feeling, or sometimes what they are thinking, but Rhino leaves me with more questions than answers. He takes a step closer to me, and I flinch and step back.

"Steady there, sport. I'm not coming at you." There is a raspy lilt to Rhino's voice, like it pains him to speak. Possibly from the injury that left that vicious scar.

He takes another step and I don't move this time except to tighten my defensive crouch. Rhino leans in and lifts my left elbow slightly so my fist is closer to my face.

"Keep your hands higher. Good." Rhino starts pulling and pushing my shoulders, arms, and legs while giving me one- to two-word direction along the way. He finally stands back and grunts with satisfaction. Apparently, he is a man of few words. "That's enough for today, clean up and meet me in the catacombs tomorrow at sunrise."

Rhino walks out of my cell before I can ask him where exactly are the catacombs. "Where are the catacombs?" I yell at his broad back, which is already more than halfway down the long corridor. He does not acknowledge me. Great, now I am due for a meeting at an unknown location at a time I have no way of knowing, seeing my suite of a cell has no window and no alarm clock. At least he left my door open.

I look in the small tarnished mirror above my sink at my swollen nose. The blood has already dried and crusted on my lips. I wash it off with the frigid sink water. I soak a washcloth in the water and place it on my nose after wringing the extra water off. I rotate my jaw to test it out and, sure enough, it hurts. After using the cold washcloth to ice my face, I tentatively touch my nose. It does not seem to be broken, so that is a plus. I run the cloth under the cold water once more before lying on my bed and placing it back on my nose.

Before I know it, I have drifted away into dreamless sleep only to wake up who knows how much later. I hurriedly get off the concrete bed and run through the still-open door of my cell. I never closed it for fear that it may not open again for a long time. I look up and down the hallway and, to my chagrin, there is no one in sight for me to ask what time it is or where the catacombs are. I set off at a sprint in the direction Rhino went when he'd left. I make turn after turn without finding anyone or stumbling upon my destination. Winded, I stop to take a breath. I hear voices somewhere nearby, so I walk toward them. After two more turns and another long hallway, I finally find who the voices belong to. In a large room, there are five or six people sitting in some comfy-looking couches, talking and laughing and seeming to be having an all-around good time. To my surprise, there are People and Clones talking freely and interacting together like I have never seen before.

"Hello," I say in barely more than a whisper. All of the faces turn to me with smiles.

"Welcome, you must be new," A middle-aged man with a combover says with a genuine smile. "Come have a seat and join us. We were just hanging out until breakfast is ready. What's your name?"

"Uh, thank you for the offer, but I need to be at the catacombs, but I do not know where they are."

A Clone who looks like me, but several years younger than me, jumps up. "I'll show you. Come on."

She heads for another door of the room and waves for me to follow. She leaves the room, but pops her head back in when she realizes I am not hot on her trail. She gives another reassuring smile. "I don't bite. Come on already. I'm sure if you're headed to the catacombs you're going to meet Rhino, and he doesn't fancy being made to wait."

This girl is probably right. I can imagine Rhino pacing the floor or tapping his toe impatiently and the thought makes me smile. The girl takes it as a smile for her, and she seems to become even more eager to be my escort. I quickly replace the smile with a neutral expression and I follow the child.

I discover the girl's name is Agatha, but everyone calls her Aggie, and boy is she a chatter box. I can't repeat anything she has said because she says way too much way too fast for me to even keep track. To be polite, I just keep nodding and giving the occasional 'um hmm' when she leaves a pause to breathe, which is rare. While she walks, I notice she has a slight limp, barely noticeable, but it is noticeable enough to seal her removal if she were in the city. Finally, we enter a cavernous chamber where the temperature feels like it has dropped ten degrees and the only sound is the intermittent drop of water from the pointy formations that dot the ceiling. The room is mostly empty, aside from large black mats in the middle, and a row of menacing weapons on a rack along the wall.

"Well, here we are." Aggie's voice slices through the evanescent silence of the room, making me jump.

Rhino rounds a corner at the far end of the cavern and Aggie backs up slightly. "Good luck, looks like you'll need it."

At first, I do not know what she means, but then I see the expression on Rhino's face. Shit, I must be late. I smile unsteadily, but it soon falters when Rhino grabs a wooden staff and begins twirling it with precision and malice. I find myself crouching into the same defensive position Rhino taught me last night when he is only a few feet away. I'm ready when he swings the staff directly at my head. I duck and roll a few feet to my left, but I'm not ready for the next swing he takes and I barely raise my arm in time to block the hit meant for my head. He hits my right forearm hard enough to leave an immediate bruise, and my hand now refuses to work. Before I can accept the pain of my arm, I fall to my knees from the impact of Rhino's next hit to my lower back. A small cry escapes when I hit the ground. Before I have time to blink, Rhino brings the staff down on my head, but I don't feel the impact. I open my eyes to see the staff just centimeters above my face with Rhino looking down the wood sternly.

"Next time you're late, I won't stop," he growls before extending his hand to help me up.

I take the offered hand and Rhino lifts me to my feet like I weigh nothing. I glare at him while I brush myself off. I can move my fingers again, but I have developed a knot where he hit my arm, and it is tender. Rhino is smirking at me, but before I can say anything to wipe the smirk away, I am again ducking another attack. I duck and roll away again, but this time I am ready for his second attack. I'm quick enough to glide under his second swing, the one that hit my arm last time, then I'm off in a sprint. I head for the weapons to get something to protect myself. I grab a staff like Rhino's and I turn in time to hold the staff in both hands and block Rhino's skull-splitting attack. With a grunt, Rhino nods in approval. He then proceeds to go full-throttle. I can barely keep up, but I manage to parry each attack. Soon enough, my strength begins to ebb, and his shows no limit. A merciless hit makes contact with my thigh, which brings me to one knee, but I suddenly see an opportunity. When he swings for my head, he places too much weight on his front leg. I drop under the forceful swing, and I use Rhino's forward momentum against him by hitting him right behind the kneecap. He goes down like a bag of sand. I still have no idea how I have been able to keep up with Rhino or how I seem to know these fighting techniques. I have only ever seen one fight in my life, and Boston was no trained killer, neither was Cameron. My heart sinks a little from thinking about Cameron again.

Rhino doesn't give me much time to contemplate what Cameron may be doing right now or to wonder if he misses me. Rhino rolls onto his back and hops up to his feet with the agility of a cat. I'm astounded by the nimble agility displayed by this massive Clone. I catch another grin of approval, but it is quickly replaced by a devilish grin, and I am back on the defensive. I'm much slower this time around and he lands too many blows for me to count. He swipes both my feet out from under me and I land on my back hard enough to be winded. Rhino laughs while I struggle for breath, but not in a malicious way. He extends a hand out to help me up and I reach for it, but instead of letting him help me up, I swing myself under his prostrate form, place my legs on his stomach and use his weight to leverage him up and over me. He flips over and lands on his back hard enough to be winded in return. I jump up and swing my staff at his face, but stop mere centimeters from making contact. At first, he is startled, but then Rhino laughs some more.

"Tell me, sir, how is it I can fight like this?" I inquire.

Rhino stops laughing and his face becomes stoic. "Not my place to say. You'll find out soon enough. I think that's enough for today. Go to the mess hall and get some breakfast." Rhino stands and takes my staff and proceeds to put both his and mine back on the racks.

I want to push further, but I know it will be fruitless, and I am starving. "Where is the mess hall?"

Rhino does not look back at me, he just says, "Your little friend there can show you the way."

Puzzled, I look around. In the doorway, I see the little face of Aggie peeking around the edge of the doorframe. She smiles and waves at me. I give a polite wave back and limp toward her.

Before I leave the room, I hear Rhino bark, "Same place, same time, tomorrow." I turn to confirm, but Rhino has already disappeared.

Aggie takes my hand and pulls me along. "Wow, you really were something. I knew I should go do my chores, but I figured I could stay and watch for a few minutes. I mean I have all day to do chores anyway."

I know Aggie keeps talking, but I find it even more difficult than before to focus on her words. I begin to feel aches and pains all over. My eyelids steadily grow heavy. Seeing Aggie still has my hand, I let her lead me down the hallway blindly. Soon, I can tell we are in possibly the only well-lit room within the rebel complex, so I open my eyes to see a room full of tables and chairs full of babbling People and Clones. The cafeteria is roughly the same size as the hospital's cafeteria and, like the hospital's, there are both People and Clones dining together. The major difference that makes me do a double take, is Clones reside at the same table as People. People are talking to Clones as equals. They joke, they laugh, they console, they show affection, and they do not seem to notice the oddity of it all. I take one step back because I don't really want to be around so many people at the moment, but then I catch a whiff of food. Aggie pulls me to the back of a lineup of people waiting for a plate of food. I soon have a plate with my usual porridge and fruit, but I also have two slices of bacon! I don't believe I have ever had bacon before, but it smells amazing.

Aggie leads me to a table where a bunch of other girls her age are chatting incoherently. There are a couple of Clones, one that looks like Aggie and I and one that is the redhead type. The other four girls are obviously not Clones, seeing as one is as dark-skinned as Boston, another is blonde haired, and the other two have fair skin, but hair of ebony. The girls sound like a bunch of little birds chirping after a spring rainstorm. The chatter stops when the girls notice my presence.

Aggie stands taller and proudly puffs out her chest. "This is my new friend, uh…" She pauses with a puzzled look on her face. "Um, I'm sorry, but I don't remember your name."

I do not want to become part of this world of rebels and I do not want to become attached, so I lie: "I don't have one."

I hear all the girls gasp in unison with equal parts shock and disapproval. Aggie pulls me down into the seat next to her and says, as a matter of fact, "Well then, we will have to give you a name." All of the little birds chatter in agreement with eagerly nodding heads. All at once, the girls start throwing names out as suggestions. Aggie contemplates each name, but authoritatively dismisses each one decisively with a shake of her head.

Aggie snaps her fingers with a grin. "I've got it! Porsche." All of the other girls smile approvingly and Aggie smiles victoriously. She looks to me and asks, "I mean, that is, if you like it."

I smile and nod politely. I find them sweet, but I tell myself not to get attached because I won't be here long. I need to get back to Cameron. After eating my breakfast and heavenly bacon, I excuse myself and head to my room.

"Wait, I can show you the way," Aggie says before jumping out of her seat.

I smile kindly at her. "You have not finished your meal yet. I am certain I will find the way."

I remember the paths I stumbled around this morning, so I am certain I can navigate back without a guide. Aggie looks sad, but she gets over it quickly, and sits back into her seat.

Chapter 21

As I lie on my bed, I do not try to stop the tears. I cry because I miss Cameron, but I am also crying because I hurt everywhere. How does Rhino consider beating me teaching me? I suppose I did somehow start to anticipate his next move because of other moves before it, but he barely said a full sentence. One thing is for sure, this hard concrete slab is doing nothing to comfort my bruised body. I haven't a clue how I will fall asleep while I shift uncomfortably. My mind is reeling nonstop and I can't clear it enough to close my eyes. With an exasperated sigh, I get out of bed and get dressed in the simple cream-colored scrubs I have been provided at the rebel compound. One thing I learned from Aggie is there is a curfew with a mandatory lights-out rule at nine every night, and anyone found outside of their designated room after that time is severely punished. Sounds familiar to the city that they are fighting so hard against to me. Hypocrites. I have too much on my mind to stay cooped up in this little room another second. Even though the concrete floor is freezing cold, I do not put my shoes on. If Aggie was telling the truth about the curfew, then I want to be as quiet as possible, and my tennis shoes squeak too much. I peek around the corner of my door into the hallway. When I hear and see nothing, I tiptoe out and down the hall. I do not know where I am going, but I know I can't stay here. Perhaps I can find the exit to this ridiculous bunker and escape back to Cameron.

I remember the halls I took early this morning and nothing stood out as being an exit, so I take a different turn to find uncharted hallways. After countless hours pass, I am about to give up when I hear voices. I follow the hushed voices to a dimly illuminated room. I am not brave enough to peek around the corner to see who the voices belong to, but I listen intently when I hear my name.

"How is Alabaster's training?" I hear a voice I know belongs to Anton from the hatred he seems to be able to fill the simplest words with; my name holds the most venom for him.

"She is very advanced. The genetic manipulation seems to have worked better than on my type." Rhino's gravelly voice is unmistakable.

"Will she be ready soon?" I can hear the blood-thirsty tone in Anton's voice, and I can imagine the hunger in his eyes.

"Soon enough." Rhino's short response is true to form.

I've had enough. Enough lies, enough manipulation, enough being used. Unfortunately, I've also had enough aimless wandering of these dark halls. I trace my steps back to my cell. I am going to escape this place, but first I will need to find the exit and devise a plan of action. For now, I will play their little game. I do not know if it's quite safe enough to return to the city yet anyhow. I curl up on my bed and close my eyes.

Chapter 22

"Porsche, you need to wake up. Rhino told you to meet him at sunrise again so that means you only have ten minutes to make it. Come on come on come on come on." I wake up to Aggie shaking one of my bruised shoulders.

I try to sit up, but my whole body feels like a rubber band pulled too tight. I can barely move anything and my skull is splitting. Aggie's words finally settle into my muddied head and I jump out of bed. She helps me tie my shoes, then we are running down the empty halls. Aggie is laughing like it's all a game, and she is having so much fun I can't help but laugh too. We are both out of breath when we finally make it to the catacombs. We fall to the floor laughing hysterically. When I finally catch my breath enough, I open my tear-filled eyes to see the face of Rhino staring angrily down at me.

His attention turns to Aggie. "Out!" He points a finger to the door and Aggie scampers to the exit.

When Rhino turns away, I peek back to see Aggie peeking around the doorframe, stifling a giggle. I am more adept at hiding my emotions, so holding my bubbling laughter within is child's play. I stop paying attention to Aggie right when I see a fist coming at my face from the corner of my eye. I dodge Rhino's fist and let instinct take over. Somehow I already know Rhino is going to bring his knee up, so I slide to the side and insert my elbow into his ribs. The force I used wasn't enough to affect him, but his own body weight works against him, and he is winded from the impact. I take the opportunity to slug him along his scarred cheek. I don't hold back, and I am sure I have broken a knuckle from the impact, but the pained grunt from Rhino is well worth it. I hear several sets of hands clapping and I look back to see Aggie with a gaggle of the girls we ate with yesterday. My spirit is lifted with the support.

Rhino and I resume our fight stance and circle one another, looking for weaknesses, gauging our opponent. He feints and I sidestep, I feint and he backs up half a step. When we seem to be at an impasse, I find my chance and I make my move. I slide under his legs, and when he tries to turn around to face me, I snake his ankle and bring him down with a thud. I know that won't keep him down, so I drive my elbow down on his gut and throw a few good facial blows in before he throws me off. I hit the rack of weapons with a clatter and barely dodge a falling sword aimed for my decapitation. Rhino still lies prone where I left him, but he lifts his head to make sure I'm not advancing on him again. After a couple minutes of catching our breath, we are at it again. There are a few more bodies added to our crowd of fans, but they are not all girls Aggie's age. There are some adults, and I swear I spotted Anton, but he is gone before I can be sure.

Rhino and I battle for a few hours before we call it quits. It wasn't soon enough. I'm starving. Aggie and her friends walk with me to the mess hall. They are all talking the entire way about how well I fought and how they want to be like me when they grow up. They all want me to teach them how to fight too. I nod here and there, but I'm still trying not to commit to anything with the rebels here. After lunch, I pull Aggie aside.

"Hey, do you think you could give me the full tour?" I ask her.

Aggie's eyes light up. "Of course I can. You know, I'm the best person to ask, because I know everything about, well, about everything here!" She keeps on rambling, but it's too fast for me to keep up with, so I just smile and nod as she takes my hand and begins my tour.

After what seems like three hours of hallway after hallway of uninteresting facts, Aggie finally give me some helpful information. We are standing in front of the massive exit doors. There are two guards stationed there right now, but the doors are wide open, a warm spring breeze flittering in. I inhale the fresh air deeply.

"The doors are open all day." I finally tune in to what Aggie is saying. "And to leave, you have to have a clearance card signed by Anton or one of his generals, but at night, they close the doors, and they are locked by Anton. He's the only one with keys. No one is allowed to come or go at night, and the doors have to be closed so no one on the outside can see any light from inside. I think that's silly, because no one is meant to have any lights on after curfew anyway, but that's the rules I guess."

"So, at night, no one guards the doors? They're just locked?"

Aggie rolls her eyes at me. "Duh, why would someone guard a locked door, silly?"

When I don't respond, Aggie continues on her tirade about the everything of everything, and leads me on. I look over my shoulder at the doors until we round a corner and they are out of sight. Aggie's tour goes on until we once again convene at the mess hall for dinner. I eat as much as possible, and I sneak an extra piece of fruit or two before I excuse myself from the table.

"Do you want me to accompany you, Porsche?" Aggie asks.

"I would love you to accompany me, Aggie, but you haven't finished eating yet."

Aggie looks both guilty because she has spent the last ten minutes pushing her vegetables around the plate, and hurt that I don't want her to be my escort.

"Hey, I'll tell you what. Why don't you come wake me up again tomorrow? You were so helpful this morning and I'm sure I can count on you," I say with a flourish.

Aggie beams proudly and nods enthusiastically. "Yeah! You can count on me, Porsche. You sleep like a log, but I'll make sure you're up on time."

I smile at the girl's enthusiasm, and I kiss the top of her head before I realize what I'm doing. No matter how hard I try, Aggie keeps growing on me.

Chapter 23

On the way back to my room, I decide I am not escaping tonight. I keep telling myself it's because I want to have a little bit more food to take with me, but I know it's because I don't want to let Aggie down by not being here for her to wake up tomorrow. I wash up at my small sink and crawl under my light blanket. I suppose I'm too worn out and in pain to run away tonight anyhow. Before I've counted a single sheep, I'm out for the count.

True to her word, Aggie wakes me up at the crack of dawn. "It's time to get up, it's time to get up, it's time to get up in the morning! It's time to get up, it's time to get up, it's time to get up right now. Rise and shine, sleepy head," Aggie chants until I pull myself out of bed with an exasperated grunt.

Boy, how I miss my simple alarm clock with the simple good-morning beep-beep-beep. I wonder how much of my soul I would need to sell to Anton to get an alarm clock. Once again, Aggie helps with my shoes and drags me out at a sprint. We are not as giggly today, mostly because I'm still groggy, but also because my ribs hurt too much to laugh. When we get to the catacombs, we are faced with a small crowd lined up along the walls. Apparently, Rhino and I have an audience today. I spot Anton off to the side with Octavius and Stephen. Octavius gives me a thumbs up, and Stephen gives me the bird. The crowd hushes down when we enter. Rhino is already waiting on the center mat with a come-and-get-it grin on his face. I always thought I'd be the type of person to walk away from a fight, but something inside me responds to his taunt with a vengeance. We both fall into our technique of circling the opponent, assessing the weaknesses and looking for an advantage. While we circle, Rhino grabs a small blade from one of the weapons racks, so I chose one of my own. Rhino charges me with knife in hand and, before I know it, my knife has left my hand, and I watch helplessly as it sails toward Rhino and sinks hilt deep into his shoulder. The impact sends Rhino to the ground, where he proceeds to remove the blade.

"No, do remove it!" I scream, but the crimson blade clatters to the mat.

I run over to Rhino, where I'm joined by Anton. I tear Rhino's shirt away from the wound and my nurse's training takes hold while I assess the damage.

There is a lot of blood and my first instinct says he hit a vein. I palpate inside and when I feel the broken vein, I apply pressure.

"What do you need, Alabaster?" Anton asks without looking at me or Rhino, and especially not the blood.

"I need clean hot water, towels, and gauze. Then I'll need a suture kit."

Rhino is conscious, but he hasn't made a sound. He is clenching his jaw and staring up at the ceiling. "You heard the woman, get to it." Anton commands the bystanders.

"Hold on a sec," I say when one of my fingers brushes against something hard inside the wound. I get my fingers around a bullet-shaped object, but when I gently pull, it doesn't budge, and Rhino hisses through his teeth. I'm guessing that's the closest sign he'll give that something hurts. "There's something in here and I can't get it out. Do you have a medical facility in this place?" I rack my brain through Aggie's tour yesterday, but I don't remember seeing anything resembling a medical facility, which either means they don't have one, which is unlikely, seeing how many people live here, or that this place is larger than a half-day tour could reveal.

"Someone get a gurney. We need to take him to the medical wing." Anton barks.

The look on Anton's face reveals both anger and consternation.

"He's not going to die if that's what you're worried about. A doctor can easily remove whatever that is and sew him up without a hitch," I say with assurance.

Anton's jaw clenches. "I'm sure you're correct, but we don't have a doctor anymore. He was on a reconnaissance mission to collect more medical supplies and was caught. My sources tell me he was removed immediately, without a trial. That means all we have is you."

Before I can question further, four large men come over with the gurney. Even though they are large, they are still not Police-Clone large. When two of them try to lift Rhino onto the gurney, they fail miserably. Rhino is just too big, and the one closest to Rhino's head drops his wounded shoulder. Rhino's jaw draws tight from the pain, and then he punches the man straight in the face with his good arm. The man is out for the count.

"Dammit, I can walk, you idiots," Rhino growls while he gingerly begins to stand.

Seeing as I'm the one staunching the blood flow with my fingers, Rhino picks me up with his good arm, because there is no way I would be able to reach his shoulder with him standing at full height. He carries me with one arm like I weigh nothing at all. All of a sudden I feel like one of those annoying toy dogs I see some of the better-off People carry under an arm or in a purse.

"Everyone, back to work already!" Anton yells as he leads the way. A few people, including Aggie, trail behind us, but the majority of the others go their own ways.

True to form, Aggie starts talking and Rhino rolls his eyes. He is walking slowly to keep me from jostling my fingers, but it happens now and again, and when it does, he pauses for a split second and his face tightens before he moves on with greater care. I'm too busy trying not to move to watch the route we are taking, but soon enough we are in a brightly lit sterile room with shiny cupboards full of medical supplies lining the walls and a patient bed in the middle. Rhino goes to the bed and carefully lies down. I stay seated on his chest, because I'm positive I won't be able to see the wound from the floor.

"Anton, go look over in those drawers for a scalpel." I nod at a stainless-steel rolling drawer cart. "And I need more gauze."

Anton does not do a good job of keeping his cool in a stressful situation. He is all thumbs, and a tray of tools clatters to the ground with a crash. He finally brings a scalpel over, and Aggie's little hands are overflowing with white gauze. I smile at her before taking the gauze.

"Aggie, sweetheart, thank you for your help, but I think it would be better if you left the room." Aggie's sad face breaks my heart a little, so I add, "Well, I meant so you could stand guard, you know. Make sure no one comes in to bother us?" She then stands tall and puffs out her chest with pride before giving me a salute and marching toward the door.

"Okay, Anton, I need you to find where my fingers are and apply pressure. I'll need both hands to remove the object."

Anton's face pales. "What? But there's so much blood. You're not a doctor. How do you expect to remove it without damaging or killing him!"

Rhino and I both give Anton a look that says, "Seriously?"

"Fine, but if he dies, his blood is on your hands," Anton states with a matter-of-fact tone, but when his fingers get close to the crimson mess, his face turns green and he starts to gag.

"For fuck's sake," Rhino grumbles before placing his own finger into the cavity.

Rhino follows my fingers and resumes pressure so I can slide my fingers away. He only used one finger, but his finger is so big, I'll have to widen the opening some. I clean away as much blood as possible so I can see what I'm dealing with. I then cut an extra inch so I can probe to find the cylindrical piece of metal. Rhino remains stoic, making not a noise, but his jaws are clenched tight enough to break bone. When I have my fingers on the foreign object, I carefully cut it out of the muscle that has grown around it. It must have been placed in there when Rhino was only a baby. I'm careful of any major veins and arteries as I work my way through.

After what was only an hour, but felt more like five, I hold the small capsule in the palm of my hand. It's half the length of my pinky and the color of gangrene. I set the capsule on a metal tray for later examination, then I proceed to finalize Rhino's stitching. When I'm finally ready for Rhino to remove his finger, he releases a huge sigh of relief that makes me lose my balance momentarily. Rhino tenses up again. He gives me a look of scorn, but as he relaxes it turns into his usual grin. I am soon finished with the suture, and I seal everything over with a clean gauze.

"Keep it clean, change the bandage a couple times a day, and no physical activity for two weeks," I say with a light tap atop the gauze that makes Rhino flinch ever so slightly.

I smile knowing if he can't do physical activity, then I don't have to either.

As if he can read my mind, Rhino responds, "If that's what the doctor orders, then I guess I'll have to find someone else to do your training."

My smile fades away and Rhino's grin returns with short-lived laughter and another wince. I carefully climb down before helping Rhino sit back up. He probably doesn't need my help, but I give it anyway. I dig around the drawers and cupboards in the room until I find a sling. I try to set Rhino's arm in it, but the sling is made for someone a third his size. Instead, I grab a clean sheet, and tear a strip of the fabric to create my own sling. I then turn my attention back to the mysterious cylinder, but it has gone missing, and so has Anton. Before I can voice my anger, there comes a commotion from out in the hallway. I can hear Aggie yelling at someone, telling them they are not allowed to enter. Aggie comes in with an exasperated look and throws her hands in the air. "I told them you were busy, but they insisted they see the doctor."

Entering behind Aggie is a couple with a child who looks very ill. I shoo Rhino off the bed, replace the sheet, and have the couple lay the little boy down. I am covered to the elbow in Rhino's blood and my once-cream-colored scrubs are spackled with blood. I find a change of clothes and scrub up before taking the boy's temperature and checking his vitals. Aggie is very helpful and intuitive. I wonder to myself if she was designed to be a nurse as well. By the time I am done figuring out what ails the boy, another patient arrives and I can hear more from out in the hall. It seems the rebel doctor has been sorely missed. Rhino assumes Aggie's roll of bouncer, but he does a better job of it. I see patient after patient, but soon, the hallway grows quiet and the last patient leaves for the night. Aggie and I sit up on the bed and lean against each other with a sigh. Rhino looks in and motions for us to leave with a tug of his head. Aggie and I follow his lead. Rhino breaks off and Aggie and I head to the dormitory section of the compound. Aggie surprises me with a tight hug around my waist before scampering off to her own room. Her limp is more noticeable right now. Perhaps a long day of working in the infirmary made whatever causes it worse? I suddenly feel protective of her. Does she have a parental unit assigned to her? Who watches out for her? She is already out of sight before I can catch her to ask. I'll have to remember tomorrow.

I drag myself down the silent hall and crawl into bed. On the plus side, I'm not in severe pain from fighting Rhino, but I am possibly more exhausted. I don't get a chance to talk myself out of escaping tonight because I fall asleep too fast. It would have been a short argument anyhow. These rebels need someone trained in the medical field, and even though I am not a doctor, I am better than nothing. Aggie needs me too. If I could get word to Cameron, he could come and work the rebel infirmary with me. I dream about Cameron and working side by side with him. Treating the rebels by day and making love by night.

Today, I wake up before Aggie comes, but when I hear the pitter-patter of her little feet I pretend to be sleeping. When Aggie is close enough, I wrap my arms around her in a hug. She squeals with surprise and then we are both laughing. After we settle down, I get dressed in my creamy scrubs and we leave my little room that has somehow grown warmer over the past few days. Aggie and I keep up light conversation while we head for the infirmary, and when I say we kept up the conversation, I really mean Aggie kept up the conversation and I followed along as best as possible.

There is already a line outside of the infirmary and Rhino is already ordering people around. He has put some thought into the order of the line. The people at the front are in worse shape than the people at the end. When everyone notices my presence, they begin to tell me their ailments and they beg for my help. I smile to each and assure them I will do my best, but I begin to feel overwhelmed. Aggie squeezes my hand reassuringly and we make it through the throng and into the infirmary. Rhino closes the door behind us, wrapping us in silence. I release the breath I hadn't realized I was holding. Rhino hands me a clipboard with a list of my patients, but my attention is drawn to the smell of coffee. Rhino had apparently done more than categorizing the patients of the day this morning.

After I fill a cup, I check my first patient of the day, but this patient is not on the list. Rhino's arm is in the makeshift sling still, but it doesn't seem to bother him. He tries to shoo me away, but I give him a stern expression and he submits to my examination of the injury.

I take a look over the list I had discarded in my acquisition of coffee and chuckle at the descriptions of the issues some of the patients are suffering. One of my favorites was: *Patient has a sizeable concussion on his elbow.* I may not be a doctor, but I think I can handle a concussed elbow.

"All right, bring the first one in," I say with an attempt at enthusiasm. I know it's going to be a long day, but luckily, that's what I was designed for.

The days of Rhino's recovery went by in a blur. I treated many of the rebels, with ailments from small contusions (or concussions as Rhino would say) to an emergency kidney removal. I don't know who was more excited about getting back to training, Rhino or me. I was still expected to spend a few hours after training and lunch in the infirmary. It turns out Aggie does not have a parental unit, none of the Clone children do, so I had Aggie throw a bunch of blankets on the ground in my room as a makeshift bed so she could stay with me. Aggie knows my real name now. At first, she was hurt that I didn't share it with her, but she decided it suits me better than Porsche.

I enter the catacombs to find Rhino standing behind a table. The table has a set of black cargo pants, a black shirt, and some lightweight black body armor. It's the same wardrobe Rhino wears daily, but it is all in my size. Rhino gives me one of his signature grins before leaving the room for me to change into it. I wasn't surprised to find everything fit perfectly. Anything tailored for my Clone type always does fit perfectly. My movements are restricted slightly by the armor, but it is surprisingly lightweight. Rhino comes back in a moment after I am finished dressing and gives a nod of approval before commencing his "training." Today, we are learning the fine art of swordsmanship. As if the last time we had trained with a small blade wasn't enough torment for him, now Rhino has me with a full-length sword. At least I can't throw a sword at him the same way I did the dagger. I've never held a sword in my life, but my body feels like it is just an extension of my arms and I am able to wield it like I have used it every day of my life. An audience forms while we train. Do these people not realize they are supposed to be preparing for their great and righteous rebellion?

After hours of parrying and attacking, we finally break for lunch before anything eventful can happen. My arms are leaden and my new clothing is saturated with perspiration. I head back to my room to change before lunch. I don't want to wear these clothes in the infirmary anyway.

Aggie begins to follow me out. "Go on ahead. I'll be right there. I just need to change out of these stinky clothes," I say with a smile.

"Okay," Aggie says with a shrug, but she seems reluctant.

"I'll be fine. I've been here over two weeks now. I'm sure I won't get lost." I gently stroke her flowing brown hair, identical to my own.

I've still been keeping mine in the city's mandatory braid, but Aggie always lets hers flow freely and I find a part of me green with envy. No matter how jealous, I still can't break the habit. Aggie's stomach answers for her with an impatient grumble. She wraps her small arms around me. I'm still taken off guard by her open displays of affection, and I catch myself looking around for spying eyes before I return the hug. She smiles brightly at me. "I'll save you a seat!" she yells while she scampers off down the hall.

I chuckle at her energetic optimism before heading to my room. Most of the rooms and hallways are abandoned with everyone in the mess hall for lunch, but I hear some voices coming from a room up ahead. I am about to tiptoe by when I hear Anton's voice and decide to eavesdrop. There is more going on than he is telling me and I need to get to the bottom of it.

"How are the plans progressing within the city?" Anton asks.

"Things are about the same." The voice is female and familiar, but I can't place it. "If not perhaps, reverting slightly without her deviations, no matter how small. Also, that friend of hers is no longer intermixing, and he is the only one she has had a significant effect on so far."

There is a moment of silence, but I can hear the soft ruffle of paper before Anton speaks again. "Hmm, we need to reinsert her as soon as possible, but there is still the issue of that boy. Is there any way we can work him to our advantage?"

"His ties run too deep and we can't trust his motives. I'm not too worried about it though. I've taken care of the situation," the female says with a sick delight in her voice.

She better not be talking about Cameron. I hope he is all right. What did she mean she has taken care of the situation? I quietly run down the hall and around the corner when I hear their footfalls approaching the door. After leaving the room, they head in the direction of the mess hall, so I continue in the opposite direction to my room with dark thoughts spinning through my head, making me dizzy. That's it, I need to leave. No more playing around here. It's been long enough for the People to forget what I did. How did I let myself become so attached here? I don't belong here, I belong with Cameron.

I pack a small bag with some extra clothes and fruit. I don't have any places to hide the pack from

Aggie within my room, so I take the pack down the hall and hide it in one of the storage closets. While I walk back to the mess hall, I contemplate taking Aggie with me. Before I reach the table where Aggie and her friends are sitting I decide against taking her. I know she needs me, but with her emotions unchecked and her loose tongue, she won't last a day surrounded by People. I'll need to find some paper to write her a note before I go. Maybe she will forgive me if I explain why I can't take her with me.

The rest of the day flies by without incident and I now lie in bed, wide awake, listening to the rhythmic breathing of Aggie. She'd just fallen into the breathing pattern of someone in deep sleep a few minutes ago. I quietly get out of bed and slip my shoes over my shoulder, where they hang by the laces I tied together. I told Aggie I was too tired to change into pajamas so I am still fully dressed in my creamy scrubs. She accepted my statement because it wasn't the first time I've done it. I leave my goodbye note on my bed for her to easily find tomorrow before sneaking out into the hallway.

My plan is not a very good or thought-out plan, but I need to try. I head to the locked entrance doors. I remember a smaller door off to the side of the large doors. Perhaps I can pick the lock and slip out. I have familiarized myself with the rounds of the night guards. The trek to the exit is stop and go to avoid those guards. I reach the door and my heart starts to live again with the prospect of being with Cameron. I throw caution to the wind momentarily and that is my downfall. I run straight into a guard who has his wits about him more than I do. He is a Boston-type Clone and he's wearing black clothes, like my training clothes, and he's got armor on too. Before I can react, the guard's fist connects with my face and sends my head back into the wall behind me.

"I've got a curfew breaker in sector one," I hear him say with Boston's voice into a radio on his shoulder.

I get my bearings and go on the offensive. The first punch I throw is hesitant because I feel like I'm about to hit Boston. It barely catches the attention of the guard, and I think it makes him angrier. He pulls out his baton and activates the electroshock feature. I've never seen one used before, but my gut tells me whatever the tip touches will receive enough electricity to take down a bull. I am able to dodge the first two jabs attempted, so the Clone uses the baton as a club. I block a swing with my forearm and curse from the pain, but the guard left himself open, so I take the opportunity to present him with a left hook. I don't hold back this time and he stumbles back a step before regaining his balance. He charges full throttle, but keeps himself protected better. I don't have to work as hard to deflect his advances as I do when battling Rhino, but I can feel my fatigue wearing on me. Suddenly, it feels like something else has taken control of my body, and intense pain flows through my every nerve ending. I fall to the ground in uncontrollable spasms. Anton now stands above me with a disappointed look on his face and an active baton in his hand. The bastard snuck up on me.

"We had high hopes for you, Alabaster. Looks like you need a lesson in loyalty and respect." Anton's look of disappointment fades into one of unholy bloodlust. "Ten lashings and two weeks' solitary confinement," he says to someone. I still can't get control of my body, which continues to twitch intermittently, to see who he is ordering around, but I soon find out when massive arms lift me off of the cold concrete.

I cry out in pain. Every movement sends intense waves of agony through my body. Rhino carries me to another part of the compound unfamiliar to me. I'm in too much discomfort to note the route we have taken, but we wind up in a cavernous arena with rows of seats surrounding a dirt rink with two posts in the middle. Rhino sets me down and others begin to tether my arms to the two posts. I scream again when

I am lifted off the ground to a standing position by my arms. All my body wants to do right now is curl up into a little ball, but I am being forced to stand on the tips of my toes with my arms stretched high. Everyone leaves the room with the exception of a single guard at the entrance.

It seems like an eternity, but my body finally stops twitching and most of the pain subsides, but I still feel achy and stiff. My arms have stopped tingling from blood loss from being suspended above my head and have now gone numb. I am barely conscious enough to notice a flood of rebels filling the auditorium-style seats. One of my eyes is swollen shut from the fight with the Boston Clone.

Rhino approaches me and acts like he is securing me, but he slips a tough piece of leather into my mouth. "Bite down. It'll help," he whispers before leaving me at the center of attention.

Anton then enters the chamber and the audience goes silent. "This woman is charged with breaking curfew and assaulting one of our guardsmen." Woman, not Clone. How rebellious of him. "She is new here, and as such, she will be serving a harsh punishment to deter her or anyone else from following in her footsteps. You are all here to witness what happens if you disobey the rules set in place to keep you safe. This woman"--Anton points at me and spits--"this woman will receive ten lashes and two weeks in solitary." Gasps fill the auditorium. "Yes, I know it seems harsh, but this is a harsh world we live in. Let her punishment take place." Anton walks over to a front-row seat and Rhino walks behind where I stand. I hear the whip crack in a practice stroke, and then another followed by more pain than I have ever experienced. I know Anton wants to hear me scream and cry for help or mercy, so I bite down on the leather to stifle my anguish. At the next stroke, I bear down harder, but I can't stop the tears from coming forth to spill my agony for all to see. Anton leans forward with a wicked smile, and I stare right back without blinking. The next stroke falls within the gouge of its predecessor and I can almost feel my teeth connecting through the leather. Rhino is not taking it easy on me for sure. Blood begins to trickle down my back and sides. Only seven more to go. I hear Aggie cry out, which almost breaks my resolve. When I reach the eighth lashing without crying out, the look on Anton's face is enough to keep me strong enough to bear the last two. His jaws are clenched, his face is red, and he leans back with his arms crossed in fury. Anton wants to hear me scream and beg for mercy. The ninth and tenth strokes come quicker than the rest, as if Rhino is just as ready to be done with it as I am. A sigh echoes through the crowd as everyone releases their tension simultaneously. The leather is in three different pieces, and I spit them all out into the dirt without breaking eye contact with Anton.

"Take her away!" Anton yells.

I fall hard to the ground when my tethers are cut. I wasn't expecting the sudden movement and pain, so a small gasp of misery escapes. I open my eyes to see Aggie running toward me, but she is swatted down by an armed guard. I make to get up and go to her, but my shredded back makes my movements sluggish and painful. I mouth the words "Go, it's okay" to Aggie, and she nods and retreats. The butt of a gun comes down on my face, knocking me back to the dirt, but I am still conscious when I hear Rhino's sledgehammer fist connect with bone and flesh then a body hit the floor. Now I have one swollen eye and another that is giving my world a red tint. Even though he is taking great care to handle me gently, I hiss from the torment of Rhino lifting me off the floor. Anton is nowhere to be seen, and I am thankful, because I look around to see a full auditorium of rebels standing with eyes on me and their fists on their heart. I nod with respect and allow a single tear to fall. I am soon whisked out of the chamber by Rhino, and I quickly lose consciousness from the pain.

Chapter 24

I awaken in a dark, cold, drab room. The only light comes from a small crack at the bottom of what must be the door. I have no idea how long I have been unconscious, but I don't have a chance to figure it out before another bout of blackness takes over.

I wake up again, and the room is darker than before. The light that was under the door is now vanquished. I can't make anything out within my solitary cell. It smells of urine and feces and I pray I am not the culprit, but I know I am the only suspect. Time passes, and I am unaware of if I am asleep or awake in the dark silence. It makes no difference if my eyes are open or closed, the room is too dark to distinguish, and the rare moments of dim light under the door are like a taunt, cruel and unfulfilled. I wake up with my back against the cold concrete which is at first a relief, but when I try to move, I realize my wounded back has stuck to the surface, and I scream in agony as I pry myself off. I feel the warm trickle of fresh blood down my back.

I know I have slipped into insanity when I see Cameron lying next to me on the soft satin sheets of his bed. I let the hallucination take me away. He runs his hand through my hair and his lips brush mine. His endless pool of blue eyes send me plummeting to depths I never imagined. Cameron's hands trail down my side and up again, teasing me.

I almost scream when bright light fills my room. After my eyes adjust, I realize it is not a bright light, but a small candle. However, with my light-deprived eyes it seems blinding. Aggie is holding the candle and Rhino is standing guard at the door looking out into the hallway for any threats.

I am briefly puzzled when I hear Rhino say, "Hurry, treat her, then get out."

I realize what he is talking about when I feel Aggie's small hands rubbing a slave on my back. At first I scream from the pain, but I reel it in when the cold cream soothes my back and Rhino shushes me from the door. Aggie places a kiss on my forehead and whispers, "One more week, Alabaster, only one more." Then she and the light are gone and the door seals me back into my dark misery.

I can't believe what she said. I have only been in here for a week. One week, just one. It feels like a year. How will I possibly survive another? That question is easily answered the next night when Aggie and Rhino return and Aggie treats my back again. I now feel like I am able to move without extreme pain, but I am still cautious. I am also not experiencing the hallucinations any more. I am uncertain if I am pleased or disappointed by that. It was wonderful to see Cameron and to feel like he was here with me.

When the door opens again, I am disappointed to find Anton with Rhino instead of Aggie.

"Are you ready to play by my rules now, Alabaster?" Anton asks with unwarranted victory in his voice.

"Never," I barely form the words, and I don't recognize my own dry, raspy voice.

"What was that?" Anton asks, but this time, his voice is void of the victory and rather acidic instead.

"Never," I say louder and with more conviction. "I will never play your game."

The lighting still isn't that good, but I can tell Anton's face is red with fury. "Fine then, you can stay here for another week, and we will see how you feel then."

The door slams shut with an echoing noise so loud, my sensory-deprived head screams with the agony of being overwhelmed with sound. I curl up in the fetal position and cry until my eyes burn and my throat is hoarse. Aggie and Rhino continue to come in over the next week and I use their visits to count down the extra week of solitary.

Chapter 25

Two months have gone by since I last saw Cameron. My heart aches with the absence of his presence. I was only with him for a few days, but it felt like years. When I was with him it felt like I had found a missing part of myself. When I am finally released from my solitary confinement, I can barely walk, so two of Anton's rebel lackeys drag me to my former room. The pain caused by the overly bright lighting makes me vomit. I find it funny that I used to think the lighting was dim, because right now it feels like the lights burn with the force of a thousand suns. I am unceremoniously dropped on my hard cement bed. Panic and sorrow wash over me when I realize Aggie's bedding is missing. The door slams closed behind my escort and I hear the lock engage. Great, I'm out of solitary, but this isn't much better. I wonder how long I'll be locked up this time.

Why is this all happening to me? Why are these people rebelling? I don't understand why there needs to be a rebellion anyway. The city functions smoothly.

There is little to no violence amongst the People. Everyone is clothed, fed, given a roof over our head, we are given a family, and most importantly, we are given a purpose in life. Sure, the Clones are often taken advantage of, but that is what we were created for. It is our purpose, our function. Without us, the city would cease to exist.

Apart from the few demented People, Clones are treated humanely by the People. It's all I have ever known, and I cannot fathom the city operating so smoothly without the separation between People and Clones. Even though this is the belief I have been raised with, a small voice in the back of my head keeps trying to tell me I am lying to myself. I have always been lying to myself. The life of a Clone is no life at all. The voice whispers to me to look at all of the non-essential, non-functional grandeur, petty possessions, and the over use of resources that I have witnessed the People waste in my lifetime. People like Cameron. I tell the voice in my head to shut up. It's the way it is meant to be, the way it must be, the way it was created. I force myself to stop thinking about all of this rebel propaganda. I miss Cameron. I yearn for him. I want nothing more than his arms wrapped around me and his lips to be on my skin once more. How can the People be wrong? If the People are wrong, that makes Cameron wrong, and there is nothing wrong about Cameron. I have been treated far worse by these rebels who claim to be fighting for freedom than I have by any one of the People. Why did I let myself be fooled by the rebels? I feel betrayed.

Cameron is the only reason I exist anymore. A hollow feeling swells in my chest, yearning to be filled with Cameron's love. I am too overcome with grief to do more than let my anguish flow out in a steady stream of tears. I shudder when the crying causes the torn skin on my back to pull. It is healing, thanks to Aggie, but there are still scabs. I gingerly walk over to the sink and wash myself. I am covered in filth. Someone was considerate enough to leave a crisp new set of cream-colored scrubs for me, so I change out of my filthy pants and shredded shirt.

I barely react to the sound of a thousand bees resounding for half a second through my chamber. It's an alarm signaling the unlocking of my cell door. When the door opens, I use my peripheral vision to see a tall slender man with brown hair and untrustworthy brown eyes standing in the opening. I know it is Anton due to the regal manner in which he holds himself, like a man with power who only thirsts for more.

"Have you calmed down yet? You are welcome to stay with us and be safe. However, we cannot have you running off, potentially risking everything we have worked for, everything we have built. After all, you are a significant cog in our plan. Our cause is what you were created for, your Essential Function you might say. Without you, it still may work, but its completion will be far more difficult and less plausible. I implore you to see reason, Alabaster."

I still have not acknowledged Anton's presence. I have regained control of my tears, so I can remain void of emotion. I do not trust this snake with anything I consider to be weakness.

"Well, if you won't listen to me, I hope you will listen to someone else. You have a guest, my dear."

Anton bows back slightly, letting a feminine figure enter into my cell. I look up with interest at the newcomer. Just as fast as I closed off my emotions, I turn them back on. I spring off of the concrete bench and into the arms of my mother. Anton has disappeared and left the door open. I don't attempt to make a break for it. I am too happy to be held by my mother. I also remember how deep inside the facility this cell lies. There would be no way I could make it to freedom without being noticed. I share the longest hug with my mother that I have ever had with her. I don't even care about the scream of protest my back emits. When we break apart, my mother cups my face in her hands to check me over. When she is satisfied with my wellbeing, she kisses my forehead. She gives me another swift hug then turns and stands beside me. My mother drapes one arm over my shoulders, above any tender areas, and leads us out of the cell.

We walk down the hall looking more like sisters than mother and daughter. We are the same build and perfectly proportional, so my mother's arm fits seamlessly around my shoulders. We walk in silence for a few minutes until I stop abruptly and look at my mother with concrete seriousness.

"Cameron, did you find Cameron and tell him what happened? Is he okay? I need to go to him, Mother. Please, help me. I need to talk to him."

I can't believe I forgot about the message I asked my mother to deliver to Cameron. I become a little hysterical as the connection with Cameron pulls on every fiber of my being. My mother again cups my face in her hands and looks me in the eyes. It is as if looking into a mirror. I slightly clam down, but not measurably. It never occurred to me how, even though we look exactly alike, my mother's hands feel so different upon my skin than my own. Or how different my mother's steely gray eyes are. They are the same color, yes, but they have seen different things than my own. They open into a completely different soul than my own.

"Cameron? Who is Cameron?" my mother asks with a puzzled look furrowing her brow. "Oh, do you mean Dr. Staunton?" Her face brightens as she recalls our last conversation.

"Yes, that is what I meant. Dr. Staunton, did you deliver my message?"

"I did as you asked and I found him for you. I only told him as much as he needed to know without betraying our mission here. He is under the impression that another Person has claimed you. He seems to understand. You do not need to worry about him any longer. He definitely is not worrying about you. You can now devote yourself to the cause."

I feel as if my heart has been ripped from my chest. I crumple to the cold floor crying, but there are no tears left to give. How could he let go so easily? I feel betrayed, used, and worthless.

"You see, darling, this is why we were created. We are nothing more than a manufactured roll of toilet paper. They use one square to wipe their shit, and then throw it out because there is another one ready and waiting patiently for the same fate. They don't even care about us. They cannot love us. That boy never cared about you, let alone loved you. Don't waste your potential on him. Join me in the rebellion, and together we can make them all pay."

I feel so weak. I struggle not to believe what my mother says, but find no reason to doubt it. She has no reason to lie to me, and Clones were designed to be truthful. There is a voice in my head that is laughing at me right now. It is the same voice that told me from the start that the implausible fairytale happy ending I had imagined with Cameron was doomed from the start. Boston had been right all along. Boston, he is still trapped in the city. My focus instantly changes from pitying myself to freeing my devoted best friend. A new energy fills my body, the energy of a rebel reborn from the ashes of slavery. I rise off of the ground and stand tall. An energy fueled by hatred, vengeance, and scorn pulses through me with every beat of my frozen heart. I am physically as tall as my mother, we are identical after all, but my new perspective on reality makes me seem taller. I look my mother in the eye with a fiery passion.

"I will help you with your cause on one condition."

"And what is that?" My mother is momentarily taken aback at the rage she sees in me. The power laced into my every syllable fills my mother with both fear and awe. But she also seems excited because I have finally agreed to help.

"We liberate a particular Clone from his confinement. If you do this, I will do whatever you say."

My mother nods with a malicious smile.

"I will see what I can do, but I do not anticipate any issues. It may take a few days planning, but…"

"No, not a few days, tonight. And I am going with you."

My mother's smile hardens as she nods submissively in concession. It's as if she believes she is no longer the one in charge of the situation, which she is not. Some Clone traits are harder to overcome than others, submission is one of those traits.

"Tonight it is then. Plans will need to be made. You need to eat something. They said you have not eaten a full meal in weeks. You head to the cafeteria, and I will meet up with you short--"

I again cut my mother off. "No, I do not wish to eat. I will be going with you to make arrangements."

I have no need for food at the moment. I am sure my stomach would love it if I indulged in some food, but I currently have stronger demands for my consideration than a stomach grumbling for attention like a spoiled toddler.

My mother shrinks in size, she nods once and turns to lead the way with me at her heels. We no longer look identical, as I walk with determination and power in every stride and my mother like a beaten dog with its tail tucked safely between its legs.

After winding down several familiar passages, we stop outside of a large rusty door. A loud squeal escapes from the hinges when my mother opens the ironclad gateway. My mother submissively bows her head as she lets me enter the room first. There are six people standing around an oval table with a large map of the city in the middle. I pay no attention to the map. I have more important issues at stake. I do see little colored figurines at different points all over the city out of my peripherals. There are five people who stand around the table, pointing and loudly discussing plans and ideas, each attempting to speak over the other. I recognize Anton, Octavius, and Steven. Rhino is standing silently in a corner behind Anton. When Rhino sees me, a flash of regret flickers across his face before being wiped clear of emotion. The other five people look at me, and I make sure my gaze burns into each one's eyes. Octavius gives me an appreciative smile of respect, and Steven gives me a spiteful look of indignation. I don't recognize the other two people, but they are not Clones. I don't care who they are,

I give them an equally abrasive glare. I end my eye contact with the leaders of the rebellion when I reach Anton's wicked brown set. His face morphs from stressed into an eager, thirsty gaze when he sees me standing here.

"I am glad to see you have decided to join our cause, Alabaster. Or would you prefer I still call you Clone A14B45T3R?"

"You may call me whatever you'd like. And I have not yet joined your cause."

I am still full of anger. Fiery rage flickers on my every word as I spit them out. Anton looks to my mother, eyes full of inquiry. She was apparently meant to convince me to agree to his terms, not invent my own. But he still seems pleased that I am considering the notion when I had straight out refused only a week ago.

"She has some conditions, Anton."

My mother produces the words softly. She is beginning to regain some of her previous confidence, but not all. Anton does not seem to notice, or maybe he doesn't care, but I take brief note of the unnoticed look my mother gives Anton. She gives him a look of longing and possibly desire. Does my mother love him? Right now I don't really care either. She can have him. I want to get Boston so that I can get the hell out of here.

"Oh does she? Well then, let's hear what they are." Anton fails at suppressing the condescending tone in his voice, and everyone around the table laughs.

He sounds like a man attempting to humor a child's insignificant ideas. He is gravely mistaken. There was once a time I would feel small and belittled, but that seems like a time long ago. My mother moves away from me, putting some distance between us. She obviously feels the heat that radiates from my body as my anger boils over. Anton's look of mockery falters as he realizes the seriousness of my demeanor.

"Eliana, what are the terms?" Anton directs the question to my mother. Apparently, he is also hesitant to make eye contact with me. Once a Clone, always a Clone.

"She wishes us to rescue a Clone friend of hers. She says he has been claimed by one of the People."

"We will look into it. There are more important matters at stake than liberating one Clo--"

"No, you will do it and you will do it tonight." I don't let Anton finish his sentence.

I feel like my eyes will pop out of my head from my rising anger. I'm the one Anton wants, I'm the one with the control, and I will not be dismissed. Anton is the only one attempting eye contact with me, but with great effort. Even the People in the room are skirting around me with their eyes not nearing my own.

"You say I am an important piece of your plan and, without me, success is likely unattainable. If you want my help, you will do this for me immediately. You will do it without question and without delay, or I will leave to do it myself. You can lock me up forever. You will be forced to. You can lash me a thousand times. For every second you do not do as I say, I will constantly be a thorn in your side. I will escape and I will tell the People of your whereabouts. If you do not act immediately, you had better kill me right here, right now, or you will live to regret ever choosing me to be a part of your plan."

My chest rises and falls with an ever-increasing rate. Everyone in the room cowers at the power I possess as I speak. Anton holds his composure slightly more than the rest, but he too flinches at the supremacy of my words. There is a dead silence in the room as Anton's generals look back and forth between Anton and me as we face off. My vision rotates between clarity and blurry with a red tint as my heart pulsates with intensity. Anton's jaw is clenched. I can see his mind working through all of the possible outcomes of different scenarios.

"All right. We'll do as you ask."

There is a palpable release of tension as everyone in the room expels their held breath.

"We have some of the best strategists alive here in this room. I am sure we can develop a hasty plan of action. Perhaps not a perfectly plausible plan, but a plan nonetheless."

"Good. I am glad we have come to an agreement." A smile of victory spreads across my face even though all of the intensity also remains there and my whole body still radiates fervent hatred.

"Well then, Miss Alabaster, tell us what you have in mind."

Anton takes a seat at the table and invites me to join. After I step toward a chair, the rest of the group takes their own.

I study the map that lies before me. I find the hospital then search the streets for Cameron's home. While I move a little iron figurine from the side of the map, I begin talking. "There is a Clone who was assigned to the same Essential Function as me. Before I arrived here, he was claimed by one of the People." I set the little figure on Cameron's house. "I have been to this Person's house on a few occasions and I can draw a map of the points of access to the house as well as the location where the Clones dwell within the house."

I went up and down so many hallways and opened so many doors, I have a detailed map of the layout of Cameron's home created in my head. I find it odd how my memorization skills, which were meant to make me more suitable for nursing, are so easily adaptable for malicious activities. I purposefully neglected to tell the room of my past involvement with Cameron. It's none of their business, and I prefer not thinking about him right now.

Someone hands me some paper and a pen and I proceed to draw a detailed schematic of Cameron's home. My map is so detailed, if it were life-sized, it would be the exact measurements within a quarter of an inch. After I finish drawing the house's layout, I walk everyone in the room through the lower level, which is the only level we will be concerned with. Five minutes later, a plan is devised. It takes another forty-five minutes to organize volunteers for the impromptu mission. Everyone begins to hustle and bustle, getting supplies and weapons ready. My nerves are as steel as I ready myself. A small part of my heart still believes this is all a mistake. It whispers deep within, telling me that Cameron still loves me, but the angry fire of what my logical side tells me, burns the tenderness out. Rhino hands me my black training outfit and armor with a determined smile.

A large group of thirty or more people stand at the farthest end of the catacombs. I have never explored the cavernous room, but at the far end, there is a set of stairs leading down. This room is no exception to the lackluster lighting of the rebel compound, so the lighting is dim, but I can see everyone's face clearly enough. I can make out a few former patients and several other faces I've seen in passing, but a majority are unfamiliar. Only half a dozen or so seem to be equipped to go. Anton hollers for everyone's attention from a platform near the stairs. They are all soon quieted as Anton captivates their complete attention.

"All right everyone, the time has come for our victory. The pieces of the plan are finally fitting into place. For a key piece to cooperate," Anton glares at me with a pause, "We must risk our lives and our mission to gain her trust and her help. We had better be going. Darkness is our only ally tonight."

I see Aggie trying to strap a gun over her shoulder. "Hold up there, you aren't coming," I say while removing the weapon from her shoulders.

She gives me a look of rage, but I'm not backing down. I can't let her put herself in harm's way. And with her limp, she won't be able to keep up. I try to give her a hug, but she steps away with tear-filled eyes.

"I only want you safe, Aggie. I couldn't live with myself if something happened to you out there," I say, but she is as stubborn as me. "Hey, what if you get a welcome-back victory party going. I know you are the best decorator in the whole compound. If anyone is capable of throwing together an impromptu party, it is you."

Aggie cheers up slightly. "You are right, I am," she says before eyeballing the catacombs, imagining a glorious party.

Anton finishes up his inspiring pep talk. There are some cheers and people start hugging and patting each other on the back. I rebuke a hug from my mother. "I don't know you, Eliana. Everything about you has been a lie. I never want to see you again."

I turn my back on Eliana and follow behind the seven other people who are going on the mission. I don't look back to see the hurt I left upon Eliana's face, and I honestly don't care.

Chapter 26

Those who have volunteered to assist in the rescue mission head down a hallway leading to the darkened staircase. Everyone is wearing dark clothing, which makes them hard to see in the gloom. The tunnel walls are formed from large rough stone and the stairs are also made with stones that are not standardized or smooth. I follow cautiously behind. I do not want to lose my footing on the steep, uneven stairs. When I finally make it safely to the bottom of the precipitous stairwell, I jog to catch up to the group, who easily scaled the stairs and are now a fair distance away. The strong smell of raw sewage singes my nose hair as we embark deeper down a dimly lit tunnel. The sparse lighting in the sewer casts a sickly green aura on our group. My legs ache from the exertion I force upon them to keep up with the well trained rebel soldiers. I have been caged in that small cell for the past few weeks with little opportunity to stretch my legs and I wouldn't have taken the opportunity anyhow with how painful my back was. The tight fitting body armor chafes my sore back.

Back when I was in the city, I probably walked ten miles a day at the hospital. I was definitely in better shape than I am now. Even after my vigorous training with Rhino, I still have a difficult time keeping up with the group. The last few weeks of solitary confinement have taken their toll on me in more ways than psychological.

When the rough uneven ground turns into smooth concrete, Anton, in the front of the group, moves from a brisk walk to a steady run. I push through the heaviness of my leaden legs and follow behind. Rhino trails to the back of the group and runs with me after giving me one of his many nonsensical grins. After my legs shake off the lethargy and fall into a fluid motion, I am able to keep up. The exertion of energy helps me to release all of the pent up tension that has been building in the last two months of captivity. Running with Rhino makes me more aware of my surroundings, because I feel like he will attack at any second, but it also makes me forget about my aches and pains. It feels good to finally be able to do something useful. My inner voice tells me I was useful to the rebels when I worked in the infirmary, but I tell myself anyone could have done it. My lungs expand to their full capacity as I breathe harder. I feel good, I feel free.

We have run in silence for what I suspect has been a half hour. My body began complaining ten minutes ago by way of a stitch in my left flank. As we reach our destination, Anton slows down and the rest of us follow. I place both arms over my head to relieve the pinch in my side, but the following pinch from my back makes me flinch. The line of rebels consolidate into a small huddle around Anton, who places a finger to his lips in a signal of silence. Anton looks up a ladder extending high above to a round manhole. I clinch my jaws and nod once in understanding, as do several others. Of the eight volunteers, five are Clones and the other three are not. One of the People is a woman with flowing blonde hair and fierce blue eyes. I have seen her wandering around the rebel complex, mostly in the company of Anton. She is usually dressed in something a couple sizes too small with her busty chest exposed for all to see, but right now she is garbed in black clothing that covers her entire body. We are all wearing similar black garb, and no one has more than the skin on their face showing.

I have never seen the other two People in our group of volunteers before tonight. They are both men and they are identical. They are not Clones, but they share the same facial features, body type, strawberry blond hair and the same shade of summer-wheat hazel eyes. I have heard of twins amongst the People before, but I have never witnessed a set prior to these two.

Octavius, her arm fully healed, is another member of our skimpy rescue squad, but Steven is not. I doubt he would ever do anything to aid me, but I am happy he's not here anyhow. I would feel like I needed constant supervision of my back, knowing he would likely strike there. There is also a Clone who is the same base type as me, but she has a nasty scar peeking out of the collar of her shirt and a mischievous smile.

Rhino heads up the ladder first, and easily moves the heavy disk away from the hole as if it were made of foam. He leaves the manhole uncovered and comes back down the ladder. He nods and gives a grunt while he moves aside for Anton to exit first. After exiting the stench of the sewer, Anton disappears momentarily. When he returns, he signals the rest of us to follow. We orderly file out with Rhino at the tail end of the caravan. Rhino helps a few people make it up to the high first rung, me included. I am the last, other than Rhino, to scale the ladder. When I am halfway up the ladder, I look down the way I came and almost fall from slight vertigo at the long drop to the cement at the bottom. I shake the feeling off and tighten my grip on the rung. Before the world twisted, I realized Rhino still had both feet firmly rooted to the floor of the sewer.

"Aren't you coming, Rhino?" I softly call back to him. I hear a gruff grunt from below and look down once more to see Rhino shake his head from side to side once. The view down doesn't affect me this time, but I tighten my grip on the rung regardless. I assume he stays behind due to the fact that his shoulders are too broad to make it through the small hole above. After all, his shoulders were touching the sides when he climbed up the ladder moments ago and the manhole has a smaller circumference. Rhino gives me a nod of his head to remind me of the mission and to get me moving forward again.

I am the last one through the hole. It takes my eyes a few seconds to adjust to the brightness of the streetlights before I see everyone making their way down the street to the dark alley which runs beside Cameron's home. I get a dizzy feeling of déjà vu as I stare at the grand front of Cameron's home with the enormous mahogany double doors. It seems like only yesterday I stood in front of those doors, excited to see Cameron and to know why he called on me. I realize I have taken a few steps closer to the front door rather than following the rest of the group when I hear a whistle. I look over to see my lookalike waving me to follow into the alley. I take one more look at the double doors before I rapidly shrug off the urge to approach the front and I follow the others into the alley. I try to ignore the knots that have formed within my stomach from the mixed feelings I'm experiencing. I take a deep breath of the fresh city air to clear my head, but it's my heart that needs clearing.

When I am finally in the alley, Anton opens the side door which leads into Cameron's kitchen. The People have grown too accustomed to the lack of crime within their city, so Cameron's door is unlocked. Anton checks the kitchen for safety before he motions for me to lead the way. I move past the other rebels. A few of them tremble with excitement, or fear. I know not which, and right now is not the time to ask. I find myself trembling slightly as well and I don't know my own answer to that question.

"In and out, just as we planned. The cameras have likely given us away and I'm sure the police force is already on its way," Anton whispers to me.

I nod in understanding and lead on through the dark and vacant kitchen. We dare not turn the lights on, but the open back door allows some illumination from the street lights outside. I warily walk across the golden hardwood kitchen floor. Every footstep seems so much louder than it really is. I navigate around the kitchen table to the door at the other end. When I reach the door, I open it to reveal the magnificent marble entryway with the large double doors at the other end. The entryway is only slightly brighter than the kitchen because of the glossy finish of the floor-to-ceiling marble and the glistening crystals of the chandelier above. If I thought my footsteps were loud going through the kitchen, I was mistaken. The footsteps of each rebel now measurably echoes through the grand hall, even though we all tread lightly. I soon arrive at the door under the stairs that Cameron told me leads to the basement and where his Clones sleep. I open the door, which releases a soft cry of protest. Everyone freezes with ears perked. Silence ensues and everyone expels a silent sigh of relief when nothing happens. Anton passes me and leads everyone down the stairs.

I have not yet ventured into the basement. Where to go from here is unbeknownst to me. I follow the group down the rickety wooden stairs. I find it odd that such meticulous attention to astounding detail was paid to the home above, but none at all below. The wooden walls and stairs smell of mold and mildew. I can see wisps of cob webs swaying in a phantom breeze from the ceiling. At the bottom, I really start to trail behind as everyone else hurriedly checks door after door. My nerves falter and I feel sick to my stomach. The humid basement air constricts around me. My heartrate elevates and even though I am breathing harder, I can't seem to catch a breath. I purposefully lag behind even more and head back up the stairs when I am confident no one is looking. I hunger for fresh air. My head has become foggy and my entire body trembles. I stumble down the entrance hall and back through the kitchen door. The exit is in sight. I am halfway through the kitchen when a familiar voice stops me dead in my tracks.

"Alabaster?"

I turn around to see Cameron standing in front of the open freezer with a frosted bottle of dark liquid in his hand. He looks horrible. His eyes are swollen and bloodshot. He apparently has not shaved in several weeks because his face is covered by a scruffy beard reminiscent of brown moss on a tree. The light from the open freezer glistens off his bare chest. His plaid pajama bottoms are stained. Cameron drops the bottle and leaves the open freezer. He walks toward me as if I were a hallucination. I do not move toward him, even though my whole body is pulled by an irresistible force. When Cameron reaches me, he places a hand on my cheek as if he still doesn't believe it's me. Tears fill his bloodshot eyes when he accepts my presence as reality. At his touch, my body stops its trembling as does my concept of time, space, reality. I try to resist the magnetic force which draws me closer to him, denying the union nature intended. This isn't reality. He doesn't love me, does he? His soft thumb glides across my check which is wet from the tears spilling from my own eyes. Just before my resolve completely fails me and I throw myself into Cameron's arms, he crumples to the floor like a limp rag doll. Behind him stands Anton with a syringe incriminatingly held in his hand.

"What did you do to him?" I cry hysterically.

"Don't worry, I didn't kill him. It is only a sedative. He is sleeping restfully. By the looks of it, he needs it," Anton states as he prods Cameron's unconscious body with the toe of his boot.

Cameron just slumps back over with dead weight, but I can see his chest subtly rise and fall with steady breathing.

"We have your friend. Let's get out of here before the police arrive," Anton says, addressing me along with the rest of the crew who have just entered the kitchen.

I remain there, holding new tears at bay, gawking at Cameron's limp and unconscious body. Anton grabs my arm tight enough to bruise and pulls me with him. I try to pull my arm away and I feel something in my shoulder give that I know shouldn't. I lash out at Anton and use some of the training I received from Rhino. I only have one good arm because Anton just dislocated the other, but I use it to break Anton's nose. He releases me and I drop to my knees next to Cameron.

"Fine, stay here and face the Police Clones alone. We're leaving," Anton says angrily. He holds his hand to his nose in an attempt to staunch the flow. He looks to the rest of the group and jerks his head toward the door, ordering everyone out.

I stay prostrate on the ground, stroking Cameron's hair. It is much longer than it was last time I saw him. It also has a layer of grease and grime, making his once wheat-colored hair appear more amber brown.

A gentle hand rests upon my shoulder. I try to shake it off, but I am softly lifted to my feet. I turn and bury my face into the familiar embrace of Boston. He leads me out behind the rest of the rebels. I look back toward where Cameron lies and tears stream down my face. My heart, which previously felt as if it had stopped beating, beats again. Every step farther from Cameron, I feel my heart throb in protest. I try to pull away from Boston to return to Cameron when

Dimitri appears from the entry door of the kitchen. He is swiftly kneeling by Cameron's side. Dimitri looks up at me and gives me a reassuring nod of Cameron's wellbeing. I need to leave. Dimitri looks away from me as he starts tending to Cameron. I still desire nothing more than to fall on the floor next to Cameron, but I finally turn away as Boston's persistent pulling wins out.

There is chaos in the street. One of the members of the rescue party lies facedown and motionless in a scarlet puddle. The silver-gray eyes that match my own stare blankly into the dark abyss of space. There is no more mischief found on that face. I want to vomit, but Boston pulls me harder. Three members of our rescue mission are already in the manhole, safely out of sight. Bright flashes of light escape the barrel of Anton's rifle as he discharges cover fire.

"Get over here! Let's go, come on!" Anton calls to Boston and I.

It seems like a mile from where we stand in the alley to the manhole where our only chance of safety rests. I hunker down with Boston, who is using his body to shield me. We make a run for the manhole at Anton's feet. Boston catches me when I stumble over another lifeless body. I think it is one of the twins, but I don't have time to check.

I don't hesitate to jump into the hole as bullets wiz by my head. I know the fall with likely break my ankle or leg, but that will be more acceptable and easier to deal with than a hole in my head. I now realize the real reason Rhino had stayed down below rather than going to the surface. As everyone jumps in with no time to utilize the ladder, Rhino catches them. It still amazes me how quickly such a large person can move. I am securely standing on my feet as Rhino reflexively catches Boston. The other three group members have already turned tail back to the rebel compound as cowards. Anton is the last one to jump down.

"Let's go, that's everyone." Anton shouts as Rhino sets him down

"I only counted six, what about the other two?" Rhino inquires as he looks up the tunnel above.

"They are gone. Hurry or we will be too," Anton orders while setting off down the tunnel.

Anton's pace increases with Rhino in tow. Boston holds my hand and coaxes me onward. The four of us are shortly running full speed down the tunnel. Rhino slows slightly until Boston and I are ahead of him and he brings up the rear. Rhino tosses a canister of tear gas over his shoulder as we run. I am impressed at Rhino's skill as he nimbly sets up a tripwire with incredible speed. He barely skips a beat and is still matching the speed of the rest of us. And while I am short on breath, Rhino seems perfectly at ease, enough to throw a grin and wink at me. We turn down many different tunnels. Occasionally, Rhino takes a different turn only to meet back up with us at another. I'm not positive, but I don't think this is the same way we came. My legs feel heavy, my side is pinched, and my lungs burn. At least all of the new pain has made me forget about my back and my heart, for the moment that is. I feel like I have been running for more than an hour when we finally make it safely back to the rebel compound. With the labyrinthine system of the sewer, the possibility of the People or the Police Clones finding the compound is improbable, especially with Rhino's fine work with the tripwires.

We walk back up the dark stairway into a flurry of applause, hollering, and back pounding, which makes me flinch each time. I am quite out of breath and out of willpower. Somewhere in the chaos of congratulations, I realize Boston's fingers are intertwined with mine. His familiar touch sends comforting waves through my tension. No matter what happens, I know he will always be there for me. Aggie went all out with the decorations, but I can't find her in the cacophony.

Someone hands me a red plastic cup with a dark liquid inside. It smells bitterly sweet. I am parched after the fast-paced long-distance run, so I take a big gulp of the cold liquid hoping it will quench my thirst. After one swallow, I choke and begin coughing. All of the people around me start laughing and clapping me on the back some more. I swear under my breath from the pain. Didn't these people just witness me receive those lashes three weeks ago? The liquid burned my throat making it feel raw and causing my eyes to water. I feel the burn all the way down to my stomach where it hits with a splash of pain. I cough and I hand the cup off to Boston who is smart enough to only sip the caustic fluid. I soon recover, but I stay away from anymore dark liquids.

Boston doesn't release my hand and he has the red cup filled a few more times while we wade through the partiers. He has gotten to the point of swaying and he seemingly is finding it hard to stay on his feet. His hand holding mine has morphed into an arm around me. It wouldn't be much of a problem, but he has placed total reliance on my small body to support his mass. Boston no longer sips the liquid. Instead, he swallows chug after chug of the volatile substance. Where I was always trying to keep the rebels at a distance and not grow attached, Boston has gone the opposite direction and has set his heart on meeting and befriending every last rebel here. Aggie is still nowhere to be seen, but it is well past curfew, so it's for the best. Speaking of curfew, some sensible people start shooing everyone off to bed.

"Come on, Boston. Enough celebrating for you. Let's get you set up for the night." I drag Boston out of the crowd to find an empty room for him to crash in. He will need to sleep this off for a while.

"Thanks for saving me, Alabaster. I love you. Did you know that? I do. I love you more than I love any other person in the entire world. No, the entire universe!" Boston starts off whispering in my ear, but his ability to monitor the volume of his voice proves ineffective, resulting in him yelling into my ear.

I crash hard into a wall when Boston's larger mass overwhelms my balance as he stumbles with every step. It doesn't help that my vision and motor abilities are delayed from my own reaction to the drink I had earlier. My shoulder cries in protest from the collision with the wall. It is the same shoulder Anton pulled earlier. I can actually rotate it now, but at this point I am sure something is torn within the joint. My shirt feels like it is sticking to my back and I keep hoping it's because of sweat and not blood from my wounds reopening.

Boston attempts to give me several kisses, but fails. Due to both the fact that I have successfully dodged each attempt and that he is probably seeing two of me. I know this because many of his attempts have not been anywhere near my face. I finally get him into a vacant room and plop him onto the concrete bed. He lands with a groan and instantly passes out.

"Good night, Boston. Get some sleep. I'll see you in the morning."

I bend over to apply a friendly goodnight kiss on Boston's forehead. He momentarily wakes, grabbing me around the waist and pulling me down on top of him.

"I love you, I do. You love me, too. I know it. You just don't know it yet, but I do. That's why you came to rescue me. You could not be without me any longer. And now, now we will be together forever."

Boston tries kissing me again, but moves too slowly and with inaccuracy in his drunkenness. I easily dodge his advance again. His body must not be responding to his commands, and I effortlessly slip out from under his arm and leave the room. I look back and Boston is already sleeping soundlessly, hanging halfway off the bed. I am too tired to get him back on the bed properly, so I close his door and sluggishly make my way down the hall to my own room.

Chapter 27

I enter my room and breathe a sigh of relief when I see Aggie curled up on her blankets. She is out cold and I am too tired to risk waking her, so I don't kiss her goodnight. I shut the heavy metal door behind me with a squeal from the hinge. Anton had the lock disabled after I promised to help his rebellion. All of the heavy metal doors in the rebel compound require a minimum of one can of oil each because they all seem to squeal. When the door latches, the revelry from the party is muffled out. I can still hear the rhythmic thrum of the bass from the music through the walls. The people trying to enforce curfew must have given up. I try to process what happened tonight, but my brain isn't functioning properly. After quietly pacing the length of my room a few times, I lie in my bed and stare up at the cold cement ceiling. I feel trapped. This morning, I wanted to help the rebellion because I hated Cameron for what my mother told me, but now, after seeing him, seeing his misery, I don't know what is true and what's lies. It was obvious Cameron is in pain, and I feel broken because I am the one who caused it.

I do not bother closing my eyes to find dreams. I know what will come. I would once again be in the warm loving arms of Cameron. Maybe I should have drank more and passed out dreamlessly like Boston. I don't know when exactly, but exhaustion overtakes me, and a dreamless sleep finds me soon after.

Chapter 28

The next day, I wake early. Aggie is still sleeping, so I let her be. The hallways are empty, and the rebels are still fast asleep or worshipping the porcelain goddess. That's what I've heard it called when someone is expelling the toxic liquid from the previous night's celebration into a toilet. I find my way back to the room with the heavy metallic door where the city map lies. I discover Anton there studying the map alone. He is wearing a similar uniform from last night, but this one is clean and devoid of the stench of the sewers and the horrors of bloodshed. He doesn't seem startled by my presence.

"You didn't tell us of your attachment to the enemy." Anton speaks without looking up at me.

I do not flinch at his blunt statement.

"You didn't need to know. All you needed to know was the fact that an innocent Clone needed your help. My past feelings for someone I barely knew were of no concern to you, nor the rescue mission." I lie, he buys.

"Well then, we held up our end of the bargain, now it is your turn."

"Fair enough. What would you have me do?"

Anton's smile grows evil. "Go home."

Fear grips me. "What? If I go home, I'll be removed. I broke the law! Several laws in fact."

"Don't worry about that. We have resources within the Clone tracking systems. You have been absolved of any and all crimes. You are to go home, go to work, and return home again. No detours. Get back into the routine of your Essential Function."

"That's it? That's all you want me to do? How do you expect to change anything if you have me doing exactly what they want?" My fear is replaced by anger and confusion.

"You will change things just by following your routine and being yourself. That is the most important part. Do not let society tell you what to do. Do what you feel drawn to."

"Your logic is flawed. I am drawn to do what I was programed to do, which is also what society tells me to do."

Anton laughs deeply with malevolence that makes my skin crawl.

"You still don't understand, do you? You are different. You are drawn to do what you are programed for, yes, but it is not what society has told you. You were not programmed by the same rules and laws as the rest of the Clones."

Anton pauses for effect before continuing, but some of the conversations I've overheard begin to make sense.

"You were created by the People at the Clone Sequencing Center like the rest of us, but your genetic structure was constructed differently. We had someone who was loyal to our cause infiltrate the CSC. She was instructed to sabotage a handful of embryos by not removing a few mandatory behavioral traits. Traits controlling free will, passion, hatred, curiosity. She was then not to add the mandatory genes influencing submissive drone-like behaviors. Basically, you were to be created as normal as any Person. Of course without the same conception methods used to create a Person, but with the same unaltered genetic makeup. For an added bonus, we gave you some additional genes not found in your Clone type, hence you fight as good as or better than a Police Clone.

"The saboteur was able to watch you and half a dozen other sabotaged embryos grow and mature into babies for nine months inside of your incubators. However, a short time after you were all detached from your incubators, her sabotage was discovered. The People destroyed all of the manipulated infant Clones. Fortunately, you somehow passed inspection and our ally was able to secretly send word to me of your Clone number before they removed her from society. With that information, I was able to hack into the city's mainframe and assure your placement with Eliana and the monochromatic Clone she was paired with.

"Eliana's job was to encourage and help you develop your abnormal tendencies, but to do so subtly. We did not want the People to discover your flaws and have you removed. Eliana may have done too well with the secretive part. I had hoped you would have turned more Clones than just the one boy. Boston, did you call him?"

The story Anton is telling me starts to line up with memories from my past. In so many memories, I have hesitated acting because I wanted to do something opposite of what a Clone should. My heart and my head have always been at war. I remember chasing a green butterfly in a field when I was three. When I was seven, I recall looking up at the clouds in the sky and imagining they were animals while my classmates were studying their feet. I remember my mother encouraging me to do things like stealing a pencil from school or picking a flower to keep as my own and presenting me with gifts like an embroidered butterfly. I was praised by my mother, not punished, when I pushed my brother for no reason. I had stealthily tried to make several friends at my mother's bequest, but no one returned my amity. No one until Boston that is. He was always a model Clone until I started clouding his judgement. In reality, it is my fault he was incarcerated, it is my fault his life is ruined. And then I came here and I discovered my talent to fight. Without any training I was able to spar as an equal with a thoroughly trained Police Clone.

"What do you mean *turned more Clones*?" I ask.

If that is what I did to Boston, I'm not sure I want to do it to anyone else.

"It comes from a theoretical concept called *Mirroring*. Clones have many traits removed, but they also have several traits added into the mix. One of those added traits is critical in getting Clones up and running into their Essential Function as rapidly as possible. It is the *Mirror* gene. We did include it into your genetic makeup because without it, you would have stood out as a slow learner and removal would have been imminent. Clones learn from other Clones what to do, say, and how to behave in any number of situations. The gene gives new Clones the ability to mimic their expected behaviors by how other Clones act and react. That is why the People organize family units rather than having all of the young Clones growing up together and potentially learning bad habits or not learning the proper way to act. There is a lot more one-on-one training in a family unit. Do you see where I am going with all of this?"

Unfortunately I do see. I am meant to lead the Clones in an all-out rebellion. Anton expects me to build a Clone army to take down the People and follow him. I nod in understanding, but I know I cannot do it. I will not do it. I know many of the People are evil, but not all of them. Cameron is not evil. He is so good and full of love. I feel like I have to believe there are more like him. I also don't find the idea of Clones usurping one suppressor for yet another comforting. I can't fathom this man who stands before me ever being as kind and gentle as Cameron. Anton is more like Leroy, power hungry and malevolent. I keep my expression placid as I nod in understanding, but I refuse to let power fall into this man's grasp. Of that I am sure.

"You'd better get going. You've got a long day ahead of you. You will be leaving late tonight. We need to make sure everything is in order before we send you back. We have limited control of the cameras throughout the city. We plan on keeping them off of you as much as possible, leaving you with more freedom to act as you will. But with last night as testament, we can't control them indefinitely. We had hoped for another fifteen minutes of control last night, but we only had about five. We lost two of our best in the retreat because of it, because of you. Just keep that in mind. There are those who would sacrifice their very lives for our cause, our success, and for you. You are their hope. Don't let them down."

I again nod in understanding. What Anton doesn't know is what I understand. By doing what he wants, I would be letting all of the rebels down. I remember them all standing with fists on their hearts in a sign of respect after my lashings. So many grateful rebels I treated within the infirmary. They all deserve better than Anton.

"If you would excuse me then. I shall leave you be," I reply.

"And, Alabaster." I had turned to leave, but I stop when Anton continues talking. "When you go back into the city, I advise you to stay away from that Person from last night. I wouldn't want anything unfortunate to happen to either of you."

I can sense from the tone in Anton's voice and the evil in his eyes that this is meant as a threat, a promise. I nod compliantly again, but I am slowly losing my composure. I again turn to leave, but Anton begins speaking yet again. I don't turn around this time. I don't want him seeing the anger and defiance rising to the surface.

"I will have Rhino escort you through the tunnels when it is time to leave. There is an exit near your Clone dwelling."

I proceed closer to the door.

"Oh, and Eliana will be accompanying you. So I would suggest you take some time to try to patch things up between the two of you. The last thing I want is for you both to be removed due to domestic violence."

My fury rises near its boiling point, but I am able to hold it in with significant effort. It's not what I feel I should do by nature, but it is what my Clone training has taught me, so I embrace that side for the moment. Anton may want me to do what I feel when I am in the city, but I am positive he does not want me to do it here, or with him.

"I will do my best. Thank you for your hospitality and generosity, sir."

I momentarily turn back to Anton to flourish a dramatic bow and as sweet a smile as I can muster. These actions are only possible by me embracing my Clone teaching. I turn back to my escape from this insanity and rush through the open door.

Chapter 29

When I return to my room, I release a furious scream from my frustration and anger. I then remember I left Aggie sleeping in the corner, but when I look over, she is gone. She probably went to breakfast. I hate being a pawn in someone else's game. I hate it more than I hate Leroy. Boston must have heard me scream from his room down the hall because he stampedes bare chested through the door acting like I am on fire and in need of rescue. I feel as if I'm angry enough to be in flames. My blood boils with fury. Boston relaxes when he realizes my life is not in peril, but then he begins laughing at me, which only pours fuel onto my anger.

"What are you laughing at?" I snap.

"You are really cute when you are angry. You get this little crease right here."

Boston touches an indented line above my brow with his thumb. He then moves his hand around to touch my cheek and seriousness encases him.

"I meant what I said last night," he says softly.

"You were drunk last night. You don't know what you said."

Boston pulls me closer to him. His presence calms my indignation as he emits a comforting aura. I still receive a tinge of excitement from the contact with Boston's bare skin, but it's not like the explosion of desire Cameron ignites. Boston leans in for a kiss and I let him. Maybe I can forget this plan of Anton's and the rebel's and the look on Cameron's face last night. Maybe I can stay here and settle down with Boston. Maybe I can erase Cameron from my memory. I know it would take time, but Boston would at least ease the pain, the longing.

Boston's lips quiver slightly as he presses them against mine. His light-brown eyes study mine to check and see if he is crossing any forbidden boundaries. I can't blame him, because I've rejected him once before. Boston starts to kiss a little harder, with more passion while his hands caress my back, drawing me nearer. I moan slightly from the pain of my back, but Boston takes it as pleasure. He becomes brasher, and I try to return the affection, but I just can't. I pull away. This is not fair to either Boston or Cameron. I could give my body to Boston, but never my heart. It belongs to Cameron. I may be able to erase the memory of Cameron from my head, but my heart will forever remember. It will forever be his. No. No matter how much pleasure I may receive, I cannot give Boston my body either. It just feels wrong. Boston needs someone who will not only give him their body, but their heart and soul should be his as well. He deserves more than me, he deserves someone better than me. I look solemnly up at Boston with watery eyes.

"I can't, Boston. After everything that's happened, I still love Cameron. My mother, I mean Eliana, said he didn't seem to care when she informed him I could never return to him. Is that true? The way he looked last night has me doubting the truth in her statements."

Boston looks destroyed by his continued rejection from me. I hate seeing him like this. It breaks my heart. Even though I don't love him like I love Cameron, I still love him. It still pains me to see him in pain. He flops down on my concrete bed, deflated of life. I sit down next to him and lean against him.

"I wish I could tell you Eliana was truthful. I wish I could tell you Cameron had many women over that very evening, but that would be a lie as well. Cameron came home immediately after Eliana broke the news. He locked himself in his bedroom with a bottle of whiskey. He only came out when his bottle was empty. Cameron would get a new bottle and go back to his cave of sorrow and solitude. Dimitri hardly left his side. I helped clean vomit from the floors and whatever else it landed upon. Cameron has destroyed every piece of décor in his room. Furniture is toppled and sheets are torn to shreds. I have never seen more sorrow, more pain, more suffering from one individual. I was wrong about him, Alabaster. Cameron is a broken man without you. He really does love you."

Tears burn as they well up in my eyes while I listen intently to Boston. I wrap my arms around him in a friendly embrace. He returns the friendliness of the hug without pursuing more.

"I need to be with him. Please, help me, Boston. You are the only one I can trust here. You are and will always be my best friend." I look up into Boston's softened eyes.

"I will do whatever you need, Alabaster. I will forever be there for you, you know that."

Chapter 30

We stay in the comfort of each other's embrace for a long time before Aggie comes running in to the room. I'm sure it's already lunch time. She sees Boston and me, and backs away with embarrassment plastered to her face.

"Hey, Aggie, wait. There is someone I want you to meet." Aggie stops her retreat and smiles shyly. "This is my best friend, Boston."

"Hello, Aggie, it is nice to meet you. Alabaster has told me so much about you." I haven't told him anything about her, but he has always been amazing with kids. I never knew why he didn't get assigned to be a pediatric nurse.

Aggie giggles shyly, but says nothing. I can't remember a single time Aggie has been so quiet when awake. I mean, that girl even talks in her sleep.

"It's lunch time so I came to find you," she says in a whisper.

"We had better be off then," I say before standing up. The three of us walk toward the cafeteria with arms around each other in friendship. We make a brief pit stop by the supply room to get Boston a clean outfit. He picks out a multi-pocketed pair of black cargo pants and a fitted black cotton T-shirt.

It's been a long time since I was in the cafeteria, and the chatty girls I usually sit with scoot over to make room for both Boston and I, as Aggie's place is already set. Now, as I sit next to Boston, I feel lighthearted and merry. For the first time, I join in with the chattering of the girls. We are all laughing and lively. Boston keeps looking around the cafeteria wide-eyed. The effect of so many People and Clones sitting with one another as equals is just as stunning to him as it was to me the first time I took it in.

I take a long look at the people I currently share a home with. Seeing I did not want to form any attachments, I usually kept my head down. I am slightly taken aback at the citizenship of the rebels. There is such a diverse crowd combined in this one room. I have a momentary lapse of judgement. Maybe the rebels are on the right path. Maybe this is how the city should be. I quickly revert to my previous stand on the rebellion issue as the image of the deceitful, power hungry, malicious Anton comes barreling back to me. There is no possibility of the city winding up like this small cafeteria with a man like that at the forefront.

I pull myself back to the here and now. Anton says I'm leaving tonight, so I'd better enjoy this time. I get a little lost in the multiple conversations of the girls when my mind starts wandering off on another tangent. How do the rebels get food, electricity, running water? Within the city everything is connected and delivered. But all the way out here, how do they have any resources? I decide I will investigate, but after I fill my stomach, which is growing louder with growls by the second.

I finish my meal, but Aggie has struck up a conversation with Boston, and I feel it would be rude to interrupt, so I look around the emptying cafeteria again. Over at the next table sit a few People and some Clones. The table bustles with conversation as everyone talks freely. I smile at the ease of it all, but my smile falters as I realize one of the people I thought was a Person at the table, is in fact, a Clone. I made the faulty designation because the Clone is like none I have seen before, but at the same time, she is like one I have always seen. The Clone is my type, but at least eighty years older, with hair a shimmering river of silver, the same shade of her eyes. Her joints are swollen and knotty. The Clone's face has beautiful folds and curves as a testament of the years the woman has lived. Boston casually elbows me to stop me from staring at the woman who kindly smiles back at me. I have never seen a Clone over forty-five, as their physical attributes begin to individualize them and their bodies begin to deteriorate from the years of continuous hard labor.

"So where does all of this food come from?" Boston's question brings me back to my table's conversation. Why hadn't I thought to ask Aggie that? I know Boston has been asking many questions throughout lunch, some of which answer a lot of my own. I never knew Boston was so inquisitive. That is very unlike a Clone. I wonder to myself if he learned that trait from me? I knew Aggie was a well of information, but I never thought to tap into it.

Apparently, the rebels get their water and electricity because they hacked into the city's lines. The city's food conveyor belt has always come this far, but it was long ago disabled. The rebels get their food because they simply reactivated the food transit system. Rebels on the inside make sure food is sent to the compound. The People don't realize they are feeding and taking care of the dishes of the rebel forces.

Boston and I finish with our meal and clear our dishes as we are accustomed. Everyone else also takes care of their own dishes, People included.

Aggie had to go finish the chores that she always puts off until the end of the day, so Boston and I leave the cafeteria alone and walk aimlessly around the rebel compound. We make it to the double doors of the exit, and the smell of fresh air and flowers calls to me. Boston and I take a step in the direction of the doors, but the guards step into our path.

I am about to turn away when I hear Anton say, "Let them pass." The guards step out of the way. "One of you follow them, but they can have can thirty minutes." Anton faces me. "Thirty minutes, no more."

I nod in gratitude, but I have no desire to escape right now. There is no point. I will be back in the city by tomorrow. And after Anton's threat, I don't know if I even want to go back to the city at all. I have little doubt that Anton will harm Cameron if I don't follow his orders. I don't know if I can be so close to Cameron and keep myself away from him.

Outside, there are so many beautifully flowering trees surrounding the dilapidated building of the rebel compound. The pure beauty of nature strongly contrasts with the cruel, cold, structure of the manmade building. Boston and I hold hands as we silently saunter through the glade as the sun peeks through the pink and green canopy above. The slight breeze sends pink blossoms floating gracefully through the air along with the sweet smell of spring.

Boston and I do not talk. We hold hands while walk in the silence of lifelong friends who already know everything about each other. We each know what the other is thinking as clearly as we know our own thoughts. I wonder to myself for a moment if I could live like this. Could I be content abandoning my true love, Cameron, to stay here at the rebel compound and live with Boston, my lifelong best friend? The thought is swiftly abolished again by my deep yearning for Cameron. The sun's rays stretch across the sky as its head sinks lower beyond the horizon line as if it does not yet want to leave this day in the delicate hands of the moon's beams. Boston and I reluctantly head back to the compound when the sun finally gives up the fight and disappears. It hasn't been quite a half hour, but Boston and I are done out here.

The guards shut the compound doors behind Boston and me. Octavius is there, ready to lock the doors for the night.

She smiles at me. "Good luck out there, Alabaster."

I return the smile. "Thanks" is all I can think of to say.

Boston and I begin to walk toward the rendezvous point, which is the catacombs. I contemplate finding

Aggie to tell her goodbye, but I don't want to hurt her feelings again, because I won't be able to take her with me and she will want to come.

Boston and I continue to hold hands and walk in silence. We have communicated in silence for so long, we no longer need words. We can read each other's subtle expressions, as well as understand how the other feels. When we reach our destination, I see Rhino, Eliana, and Anton waiting at the top of the stairs that lead down into the intricate sewer system below. I don't look forward to the stench that awaits me in the dark depths beneath the city. I am comforted when Boston gives my hand a reassuring squeeze. I feel better that he is going with me. That is, until I see Anton approaching us, shaking his head.

"He can't go with you. Too many People witnessed his violent behavior. There is too much risk that he will be recognized. Plus, the scar above his eyebrow is as noticeable as an elephant in a tutu. He will be removed the second the People set eyes on him."

I stubbornly shake my head back at Anton. "No, he goes or I don't."

Boston turns me to face him. "No, Alabaster, you need to go. Anton is right, I am a risk. You need to do this. I will be fine. The last thing I want is to endanger you. I will find a way to help you from here. Last night

Anton gave me an invitation to join the city's camera hackers. I will not let you down. I promise. I will be your watchful guardian angel."

Boston smiles down on me with the protective love of an older brother. I reluctantly give Boston one last hug, and rise to the tips of my toes to present a kiss upon his soft cocoa cheek.

"Take care of Aggie for me, please," I implore.

Boston nods solemnly with a dutiful smile. "I would do anything for you."

After one last glance back at Boston, I follow Rhino and Eliana into the dark.

Chapter 31

The morning is still young when Eliana and I arrive above ground a few yards from the house we have shared my entire life. Rhino stays below and will be headed back to the compound as soon as Eliana gives him the all clear. The sun has barely peeked its golden head over the horizon. No one is out on the street. Eliana gives a whippoorwill whistle, signaling Rhino we are safe, then she and I walk in silence down the street. We reach the door of our dwelling and quietly slip in. There is not yet any food in the delivery chute, and the house is still.

I head directly to the shower to clean off. I have not had a shower since the one I shared with Cameron. At the rebel compound, I mostly used the small sink in my cell and a small bar of soap to take care of my hygiene. The cold water of the shower is refreshing and rejuvenating, even if it's not as luxurious as Cameron's hot water. After my cold shower, I wrap myself in a thin white towel. I fall back into my routine and scan my barcode at the hallway laundry chute and wait patiently for the chute's door to lift, revealing the usual light-blue scrubs of my required uniform. My heart is racing, but no alarms sound and no Police Clones are pounding on the door. Perhaps Anton did wipe my slate clean.

For some unexplainable reason, I am excited about wearing my scrubs again. It will be nice to have something on that makes me feel normal, well, almost normal. I take my clothing bundle to my bedroom to dress with a slight hop in my step. I know part of me is excited by the prospect of seeing Cameron again.

When I am done dressing, I head back down the hallway and to the kitchen. I receive the food dishes and set them on the table. I fill a mug with coffee that Eliana started brewing when we first arrived home. I sit down in my usual place at the table and begin eating my farina before going to work on the accompanying banana. I am going to miss the bacon from the rebel cafeteria. The coffee fills me with happiness as it warms my body and eases the slight headache I acquired in the rancid sewer tunnel and from a lack of a good night's sleep.

My brother emerges from the bedrooms first. He is already dressed in his navy-blue work uniform.

"Good morning to you, brother. I hope sleep found you well last night."

He raises an eyebrow at me. We have never really attempted small talk with one another before. Or any talk for that matter. He doesn't seem startled by my presence either. It's not uncommon for Clones to go missing for any length of time.

"Yes, it did, thank you," he replies politely.

I figure now is as good a time as any, so as my brother sits at the table, I proceed with my mission. "You look like a Thomas. I think I am going to call you Thomas from now on."

Thomas's hand grabs his blue textbook and pulls it tightly to his chest with a look of someone who will soon have his whole reality stolen away from him. A look of panicked fear is plastered to his face as the color drains out.

"Wh--why would you do that to me?" Thomas inquires with a slight stutter as tears begin to well in his eyes.

"You are my brother. I love you and want to call you something special. I won't tell anyone, don't worry."

I smile at him with a wink. Thomas opens his mouth to continue on, but bites his tongue as our father enters. He is wearing the same overly starched charcoal-gray suit and tie he is required to don. I know better than to start a revolution with my father. It would be over before it had a chance to begin.

Anton may be keeping the cameras off of me, but, from this distance, Anton would prove useless at keeping my father off me. My father would likely explode and kill me on the spot if I gave him direct eye contact. I don't want to imagine what he would do if I gave him a name. He would likely kill Thomas as well for the simple reason that he had witnessed a crime of such severity. After all, the number-one rule is: No Clone shall be named. There are Clones who are allowed to have a name, but the name is given to them by the People, like Dimitri. And, those who are named are typically claimed Clones who are kept separate from the general Clone population.

My father and I dutifully finish our breakfast in silence. I keep giving Thomas a reassuring smile as he sits as pale as a ghost. He has barely touched his farina. He is still stunned, and doesn't seem to know what to do with himself. He has set his book back on the table, but the hand that rests upon it has white knuckles due to the tight grip he holds it with. The three of us are already clearing our dishes when Eliana enters. I still cannot bear looking at her, so I hurriedly toss my dishes in the chute and head for the door without any goodbyes. That is not abnormal anyway, no one in my family ever says hello or goodbye.

When the fresh morning air hits my face, I feel rejuvenated. How can all of those people at the rebel compound stand not being in the fresh air and not having the warmth of the sun lick their face? I take a deep breath and a spark of excitement ignites in my chest as I head to the bus stop and on to the hospital. It almost feels like my first day all over again. Boston mentioned that Cameron had not left the house the entire time I had been absent, which means he also didn't go to work. However, I still hope for his presence at the ER today, even with Anton's warning. There is no one who is still within the city that I trust enough to send word to Cameron. No one who would understand why I needed to contact him. I would trust Boston, but he won't do me much good from the rebel compound. It's harder knowing I am so close to Cameron and have nothing but Anton's threat stopping me from going to him, than it was to be so far away and impossible to be with him.

I board the bus and head to the back, where I stand. The trip is swift, and I arrive, without incident at the hospital. I had been a little worried when the bus stopped at the Owl, where Leroy seems to consistently spend the night, but he didn't board.

Entering the ER is surreal after my experience over the past month. No one seems to notice me, nor my absenteeism. Falling back into my routine is the easy part. The hard part is going to be influencing the Clones to defy their ordained programming. I decide to start slowly by giving direct eye contact to People while other Clones bear witness. I then escalate to a few comments to this Clone or that.

"You look nice today," I whisper to a colleague. "May I sit with you at lunch today?" to another. "I like how you braided your hair today, would you be able to do mine like that?" I remark to a Clone who is my look alike.

The Clone self-consciously feels her hair with a natural paranoia of someone who thinks their hair may be on fire. I continue smiling sweetly and the Clone soon smiles back, sensing the safety in me. With the exception of my father, I know none of the Clones will turn me in, because Clones are designed to avoid conflict. Turning me in would necessitate a great deal of time spent in interrogation and questioning. That is not a pleasurable experience for a Clone. No one wants a spotlight placed on them.

After a few weeks have passed, I become frustrated by the lack of *Mirroring*. Anton made it seem as if my fellow Clones would begin to replicate my abnormal tendencies, but as of yet, I have noticed nothing. However, the Clones are changing. The signs are subtle, but I slowly start to notice. Many Clones are slightly curling their lips upward in noticeable smiles. I overhear two Clones making plans to sit at the same table for lunch. I have greater reassurance when a redheaded Clone tells me the light-blue color of my uniform brings out the gray of my eyes and makes them sparkle. I smile brightly as I give the Clone a hug. As of yet, I have not made physical contact with any of the Clones at the hospital. At first, the Clone tenses up in fear and uncertainty, but relaxes after a moment and returns the hug. This action is the spark which ignites the revolution.

The Clones all begin showing signs of affection such as hugs and hand holding. The effect has rippled outside of the hospital now as well. A Clone on the bus gives me a friendly handshake as he asks where I work. He tells me he works as a janitor in an office building. The man looks like Anton and my father, but he has the same kind look behind his eyes as Dimitri. He wears a dark-green jumpsuit. We continue on with a pleasant conversation until People begin giving us menacing looks. Most of the Clones are careful to only break the law away from the eyes of the People. However, a few Clones are either brave or careless, as they hug or present a kiss upon a cheek in plain sight of a Person. The only consequence I have seen thus far are some unhinged jaws of a few witnessing People, but those are easily corrected with some wire.

I decide to take it to another level, and I risk giving a few more Clones a name of their very own. I now have a redheaded friend I call Juniper, Felix is a younger and kinder version of my father, and Scotty, my lookalike, is quickly becoming one of my best friends. It is rather easy, as we share the same genes, and so the same likes and dislikes, the same sense of humor, and the same opinions. It is much like reading each other's mind as our minds work in a similar fashion. Scotty makes me think of Aggie, and I hope she doesn't hate me for leaving her. However, with the dreamy way she looked at Boston, I think she will settle for my replacement.

I met Scotty while we were both in the supply closet collecting necessary items to restock the supply carts in each patient room. I had made a silly comment about going through gauze so fast, I suspect the patients are eating them. When Scotty started cracking up, I added it could be due to the fact that the gauze tastes better than the food the hospital has to offer. Scotty and I laughed so hard I snorted a little. After that, Scotty and I have hung out and talked every day at the hospital. I wonder what my father would do if I invited her over for dinner sometime?

Since the clones have begun *Mirroring*, the hospital cafeteria is much louder with the additional talking added by the Clones. I sit smiling at my creation with Scotty at my side. I have not shared the truth of the rebels and the tampering with my genes nor my mission with anyone, including Scotty. However, I have not shared many pieces of my life with Scotty. Especially pieces about Cameron. I have told her about being in love with someone, but I have never mentioned the person to be one of the People.

Chapter 32

I feel a constant pull to Cameron. I continuously wake up in the middle of the night screaming his name. After waking up in a sweat this morning, I decide to get up and take a shower. I feel sick to my stomach. I attribute the nausea to the lack of sleep. I take my time and let the cold water soothe my nerves as the icy droplets pelt my back, which is completely healed but severely scarred. The towel is abnormally rough on my skin while I dry off. I feel quite lethargic while I dress in my regulated uniform.

After I enter the kitchen, I start a pot of coffee. I imagine I will need two cups to kick start my day today. However, as the rich aroma fills my nostrils, the urge to vomit overwhelms me. I run to the kitchen sink, knowing the toilet is too far. My throat burns as my stomach expels its acidic contents. The shoulder Anton hurt nearly a month ago still aches occasionally, but I ache all over right now. The flu has long ago been eliminated, but my symptoms are flu like. Lethargic, sore muscles, and nausea. The only thing I am missing is a fever.

Breakfast arrives punctually with the usual oatmeal which today is accompanied by an orange. I take a few mouthfuls of hot cereal before giving up on any hope of settling my stomach. I clear my dishes and leave for work earlier than necessary. I plan on going to the health clinic for a checkup prior to going to start my shift. I head down the street and sway unsteadily as I wait for the bus. I slowly climb aboard when the white and green bus squeals to a halt in front of me. I grip the nearest post as if it's the only thing holding me up, which it is. The urge to sit in a seat or curl up on the floor is almost irresistible. I am positive no People will be boarding at the Owl because it's too early for normal life to begin today. This feels like the longest bus ride I have ever endured, but we finally reach the hospital. I enter the hospital's main entrance and head in the opposite direction of the ER, toward the clinic.

At the clinic, I am given an anti-nausea shot by a redheaded Clone and sent on my way without much else. I am a couple of hours early for my shift, but I head to the ER to start anyhow. I have nowhere else to go and nothing else to do. I check in at the front desk where the smiling Clone attendant happily adds me to the current shift list and shows genuine concern at my sickly pallor.

"Are you certain you are able to function? You look terrible, dear," the attendant inquires. She is my Clone type.

I try to assure the nurse of my good health, but the nod I give sends the room spinning.

"I, I am fine," I slur as I lose balance. I feel gravity winning the battle as it pulls my body to the ground. I brace for impact, but the pain does not hurt as severely as I anticipate. In fact, all I feel is the turmoil in my stomach, and the clenching as I vomit again.

The world fades to black and I begin dreaming of Cameron. My dream makes no coherent sense to me as I hear Cameron's voice saying something about a gurney, an IV, and help. My dream feels so real. It almost seems like he is carrying me. I wake up in another dream with Cameron sitting by my side, holding my hand and stroking my untamed hair. He smiles down on me when I look up at him.

"You gave us quite the scare earlier. I told you to be more careful due to your incredible gift to attract misfortune," Cameron says with humor in his voice.

I love dreams. They are so real and vivid sometimes. Were Cameron's eyes really that bright? It takes me a few second to realize Cameron's hands are truly making contact with my skin. This is no dream. As Cameron's face comes into focus, I realize he looks like he is still in pretty bad shape. His face is still covered in facial hair; however, it is now neatly trimmed and his hair is washed, but much longer than I remember it. I can smell the scent of his enticing soap and cologne, and he no longer reeks of liquor and vomit. The dark circles under his eyes are still prominent and his face is gaunt. His eyes have a pink tint rather than the crimson color they held last time I saw him.

"Cameron? Is it really you?"

I weakly raise my hand to his face. Cameron helps my hand find its target and kisses my palm. I feel a slight pain from the pull of an IV needle in my arm. I try to look down at my arm, but the room is still spinning. I close my eyes in an attempt to cease the gyration, but with no success. Seeing the room spins with or without my eyes open, I decide to leave them open so I can see Cameron.

"I was going to ask you the same thing. Where have you been? Your mother told me you were claimed, but my father could find no record. I feared the worst until I saw you that night. I had thought you were nothing more than a hallucination stemming from the amount of liquor in my system. However, last week when I had briefly woken from my binge, Dimitri told me it really was you. Apparently, he has been trying to sober me up since your appearance, with little success until that point. After a few days recovery, I checked the ER time cards, and noticed your name has been regularly appearing for the past four weeks, so I decided to come back to work in hopes of seeing you again first hand."

Cameron smiles caringly at me while he continues to stroke my hair. I smile back at him before rolling over as I'm once again overwhelmed with nausea. The anti-nausea shot should have kicked in by now. Maybe it is food poisoning? These days, food poisoning is even rarer than the flu. And if it were food poisoning, the hospital would be overwhelmed by sick Clones seeing we all eat the same food.

"What's wrong with me, Cameron? I feel horrible."

"I don't know what's wrong. You passed out because your blood pressure is too low. I have some blood tests running, so we'll know soon enough. We will get you better and back home with me in no time. I have missed you."

Cameron softly kisses my forehead. Scotty enters my room with a small plastic cup filled with pretty yellow flowers she probably picked from the planters outside of the hospital's main entrance. It's illegal for

Clones to pick flowers. Scotty seems a little caught off guard by the presence of Cameron, but I give her a reassuring smile.

"It's all right, Scotty. This is Cameron. He's the one I told you about."

Scotty still seems a little uncomfortable as she cautiously sets the flowers on the table next to the bed. Scotty briefly holds my free hand and she also places a friendly kiss on my forehead.

"I hope you are well soon."

Scotty gives a warm squeeze to my cold hand along with an encouraging smile before she departs. Scotty's work shift, and mine, will be starting soon, and we both need to get ready.

"Excuse me, Scotty, would you do me a favor?"

Scotty stops dead in her tracks at the sound of her name coming from Cameron's lips. She turns around on her heels and faces him with a wide-eyed, petrified look.

"Yes, sir, what would you have me do?" There is a slight tremor in her voice.

Scotty has learned from me well. She does not look away from Cameron's eye contact, even though she is visibly uncomfortable. Cameron softens his voice and his expression in an attempt to gain Scotty's trust.

"I sent for some bloodwork for this patient here. If you would be so kind as to retrieve the results for me?"

Cameron speaks to Scotty as an equal and not as a subhuman, as most People do. Scotty still seems uneasy, but she nods obediently before departing.

"Is it just me, or have the Clones started acting strangely since I last left the house?" Cameron inquires after Scotty leaves.

"It's not just you, things are changing. Clones are discovering we aren't as different from the People after all."

A disturbed look settles onto Cameron's face.

"Do you disagree? Do you think Clones––do you think I am less of a human than you?" I slightly regain some of my stamina as I am filled by irritation with Cameron.

Cameron blushes with embarrassment.

"No, it's not that. I think all Clones deserve to be treated better. I always have, and stand by it more so since I met you. It's the rest of the People I worry about. People like Leroy and my father. Sure there are some out there with the same beliefs I maintain, but we are few and far between. I fear violence and bloodshed are eminent if this escalates. I don't want to see anything happen to any Clone, least of all you."

I accept his explanation, and I know he's right. It is only a matter of time until the People start to react to this uprising. Even though there is a current of dread deep within, I begin to feel better. I tentatively sit myself up in the bed. Cameron pulls his stethoscope over his head and listens to my heart and lungs. The close proximity of his hands to my breasts makes my heart rate increase.

"I'm feeling better now. I had better get back to work. Maybe I'll see you at lunch?" I both ask and implore a lunch meeting.

Cameron smiles and gently sets his forehead against mine. Every bit of contact with Cameron's skin sends tingling sensations crawling across my own.

"Lunch? I was planning on changing your assignments so you will be the nurse of all my patients so I can see you all day."

The color returns to my cheeks as I blush with a giggle.

"And then tonight, you will be coming back home with me, and we can start making up for lost time."

Cameron releases the stethoscope and places a hand on the bed beside me. His other hand now rests on my waist as he leans in closer. My heart hammers against my chest with anticipation. Why did I wait so long to see him again? How in the world did I manage to stay away? Cameron hovers close to my lips as our eyes study one another. I finally cave in first and connect my lips to his own. We kiss briefly, because we both know this is not the place for further interaction. Cameron helps me out of the bed, supporting my weight until he is satisfied I am capable of standing on my own. He still has an arm around my waist for support when Scotty runs in, flushed and out of breath. The look of panic in Scotty's eyes instantly worries both Cameron and me. The fear sends a chill down my spine dragging my stomach down with it.

"What's wrong, Scotty? What did the tests show?" My voice waivers with insecurity. The terror radiating from her is almost palpable.

"You need to run, Alabaster. Now. There is no time to explain. Go to the Owl and ask for Astrid. She is my sister and will take care of you. I will come as soon as I can."

Scotty looks over her shoulder as two very large Police Clones and the constable who delivered Boston to Cameron's house enter the ER. The constable heads directly to the center desk where he speaks to the Clone attendant who helped me earlier.

"Go now, hurry. I will slow them down. See you soon."

Scotty gives me a hug as a tear crawls down her cheek to the corner of her trembling lips.

"I love you," Scotty whispers in my ear as she breaks the hug.

Things really are changing. So slowly I have barely noticed the change, but everything has changed. Love is definitely not a normal or natural feeling expressed by Clones.

Luckily, I am feeling much better as Cameron and I take the back exit from the ER. Cameron is still supporting a lot of my weight, even though I don't need it any longer. His worrying doesn't bother me and neither does his closeness. I finally have a feeling of completeness again.

The cool morning air is refreshing, but it fails at washing away the heavy dread filling me. Cameron and I walk down the alley toward the main street up ahead. When we get out to the street, we freeze before immediately turning back down the alley. The entire hospital is surrounded by the Clone Police force and their cruisers. Cameron tightly embraces me like this is the last moment he will ever spend with me. He is caught off guard when I push him away and kneel down on the bumpy cobblestone. I desperately try to lift the circular manhole cover, which I plan to use as our escape.

"What in god's name are you doing?" Cameron asks, bewildered.

"Saving your butt. Why don't you get down here and help!"

Cameron follows my demand, and together we lift the cover. I am again amazed at the raw power Rhino possess, as he was able to easily lift a similar cover with no effort. Together, Cameron and I remove the heavy piece of iron, but it takes a substantial amount of effort from the both of us. I climb down the ladder first and Cameron follows after. He slides the cover back over the manhole. It seems easier than lifting the cover, because Cameron does not have to pull against the greedy needs of gravity. Once at the bottom, I lead on through the sickly green-lit tunnel. I am now familiar with the stench within the tunnel, but it still brings back some of my previous nausea. Cameron can't stomach the smell at all and vomits. I give him a moment to clear his stomach of its worldly possessions before grabbing his hand and leading him away again. I remember the map of the city from Anton's plan room, which I committed to memory the time I was in the room alone with Anton. I have to apply that map to the incongruous twists and turns of the sewer, but I figure it out, and it only takes twenty minutes to get to an exit near the Owl. It would have taken far less time had Cameron not stopped to vomit another two times. The manhole cover takes both of us pushing before it budges high enough to slide away. I jump when a redheaded Clone grabs my arm, assisting me out of the cistern.

"Hello there, you must be Alabaster. I am Astrid. Scotty has told me so much about you. She sent word to me about your need of sanctuary. Come inside, quickly."

Astrid gives me a warm hug. She looks exactly like every redheaded Clone, but she smells beautiful, and has many jewels hanging on golden chains from her neck and sitting on bands around her fingers and wrists. Her ears have multiple piercings, each with golden hoops ranging in size. Astrid has brightly colored powder on her cheeks and eyes, as well as thin black lines which outline her eyes. Astrid's eye lashes appear inhumanly long and luscious. I'm unsure if I have ever seen anyone as beautiful as this woman, even though there are many other identical Clones. As with the Police Clones being allowed to be scarred, Clones from the Owl are apparently allowed ornamentation such as jewelry and makeup, but only inside the confines of their Essential Function. That's probably why I have never seen a Clone with so many embellishments. Astrid is hardly wearing more than a postage stamp, which her ample bosom and supple butt cheeks attempt to escape. Cameron wriggles his way out of the manhole. He takes in Astrid with less interest than I did. He is preoccupied looking back and forth to either end of the alley. Astrid leads us through a heavy metal backdoor, which in turn leads down a red painted hallway. The lighting is very dim and loud music echoes through my head and body, sending vibrations to my core. We follow Astrid, who leads us into a room, just as vibrant a red in color.

"You may want to change into this. If anyone comes in here, it will be more believable that you are supposed to be here if you are wearing this than if you are in the light-blue scrubs of a nurse," Astrid points out as she hands me a lacy dark-blue and black bundle.

I nod in appreciation before swiftly replacing my wardrobe. Once I have removed my clothing, Astrid takes the light-blue scrubs to dispose of them. She shuts the door behind her when she leaves. Out of respect, Cameron has turned his back while I make the change of clothing. When he turns back around, his breath has gone missing while he looks at me and gawks. The darkness of my brown hair, which is now out of its usual braid and cascading down my scarred back, along with the dark lingerie makes my skin pearly white and my gray eyes stunningly prominent.

"What? Why are you looking at me like that? I feel so naked. Maybe Astrid has something more I could borrow."

Cameron has already walked across the room to me, halting my worry as he holds a finger to my rosy lips, silencing me.

"You look fine, incredible in fact." Cameron comments thirstily.

I open my mouth to say something, but Cameron's soft lips are already pressed firmly against mine. His mustache tickles my nose, but I don't care. I wish I hadn't spent the effort squeezing into this tight baby doll as Cameron's hands caress my barely covered rear end. The ultra-thin material separating our skin has suddenly seemed to become incredibly thick as it separates my body from Cameron's. His kisses move from my lips down my neck and to my collarbone. The firmness with which Cameron caresses my derrière pulls the top of the lingerie lower, causing my breasts to spill over. My hands are eagerly making up for lost time while they run up Cameron's shirt. Any worries I had are pushed aside to consider another time. Cameron pauses his caressing kisses long enough for me to pull the white T-shirt over his head. After the obstruction is removed, I scratch Cameron's back as I desperately pull him closer to me. I don't remember Cameron pulling it down, but my garment now lies uselessly around my ankles. I am suddenly self-conscious about Cameron's hands on my back. He pauses on the scars and he turns me around to examine.

"What happened to you, Alabaster?" His soft fingers trace the rough scars.

I turn back around and take his hands. "Nothing I can't survive. Don't worry about it. It's over now."

"I'm sorry I couldn't find you." His eyes glisten with tears. "I tried for weeks, but there wasn't a trace to be found. Even my father, who is a high-ranking official, had no leads to follow."

"No apology is needed. I love you." I kiss him, but he doesn't kiss back.

I kiss him again with persistence and he reluctantly drops the issue of my scars before we resume where we left off. He backs me toward the bed, which is not as large or extravagant as his own, but it will do. Hell, the floor would do for all I care right now. My arms cling frantically around his neck, holding Cameron's lips against mine, fearful of any further separation. Cameron's hands fumble with the leather belt around his waist. He gets the leather belt off and manages to unfasten his pants as we fall softly on the bed. I giggle while Cameron fights with his unruly shoes, which are stubbornly not releasing his feet and, therefore, his pants. Cameron finally kicks it all off and returns his complete and full attention to me. He still has his boxers on, but I can feel the bulge within. He hovers above me and I place my hands on his chest.

Before kissing me again, Cameron stares deeply into my eyes, with his own eyes sparkling. "I love you too," he whispers breathlessly.

I smile up at him before pulling him back down to me without another word from either of us. Our nearly naked bodies rub together, and every part of me is on fire wanting more. That is, until Scotty and Astrid open the door in a fluster. Cameron swiftly rolls off of me and pulls the blanket up to cover our au-naturel bodies.

"I told them you left the hospital, but the cameras, the cameras must have spotted you from the alley. The building is surrounded and they are coming for you, both of you. Astrid has barricaded the front door of the Owl, but that will not last long. I am sorry, Alabaster." Scotty is in tears.

I jump out of bed and pull the scandalous clothing back on. I wish I had more, but this is all there is available to me at the moment. Cameron also gets dressed swiftly. Scotty gives me a hug.

"You need to leave, Scotty. I don't want you to be caught helping me." I pull away from our hug and look her in my identical eyes.

Scotty nods reluctantly and turns back to Astrid and the door to leave. I can't figure out how I was caught. I have been so careful and subtle with my influence on the Clones' behavior. Even if the People have noticed a change, there is little chance it would lead them back to me. A thought occurs to me, did they discover my abnormal DNA from the blood work Cameron ordered today? Before Scotty leaves the room, I grab her arm to stop her.

"Wait, Scotty." She turns around to face me. "Do you know why they are after me? Did they find something from my tests?"

Scotty can't stop the tears from flooding out as she nods in confirmation. "You are pregnant."

Astrid, standing at the door, takes a sharp intake of breath as she stares at me with hazel eyes bulging. Scotty turns away and drags Astrid, who is still staring at me, mouth gaping, out the door. Scotty slams the door shut behind her before she can see the solemn expression spread over my face and before I can ask anything more. I place a hand on my stomach as it suddenly feels full of lead weights. I want to vomit, scream, cry, and laugh, so I do nothing but slowly sit down on the bed in shock. Clones are not supposed to get pregnant. It is impossible. They all have every reproductive gene removed. They are created sterile, infertile, barren.

"How could this happen? It's impossible. There must be some mistake. Maybe they mixed up the blood sample with one from a Person. Maybe you had a false positive. That happens all the time."

Cameron still stands on the other side of the bed as he thinks to himself out loud, attempting to reason out the impossibility.

"No, I don't think it is a mistake. You once asked me what makes me different than any other Clone you've met. I didn't know then, but I do know now. I was not created like every other Clone. I was tampered with as an embryo by the rebels who stand against the People. Rebels who want to overthrow the current system. I imagine it to be quite possible I ended up fertile."

My voice is void of any emotion.

"Rebels? What rebels?" Cameron inquires.

I haven't looked at Cameron since Scotty left. I haven't stopped staring at the door where Scotty stood when she broke the news, which usually brings unsurpassed joy to a woman, but has only brought me fear and unsurpassed sorrow. I'm sure Cameron doesn't know how to handle such implausible news. It was enough to rock his world with the possibility of a

Clone becoming pregnant, but adding in a group that wants to rebel is probably more than he can handle at the moment. I can feel Cameron's eyes on me, waiting for a response, but I don't know where to begin.

There is a long, drawn-out moment of complete silence in the room. I can't even hear the music from the hallway anymore, but the silence is suddenly cut short by a commotion beyond the door. I am pulled out of my stupor by the pandemonium. The door to our room topples to the ground as two Police Clones use more force than necessary to enter. Cameron reacts fast to the danger and dives over the bed to slam his body into the first of the Clones, but to no avail. The Clone isn't even fazed by the collision. He places Cameron into a headlock and does not release until Cameron stops flailing, unconscious. I have no time to react. Or maybe I do, but my entire concept of time and space has left me. I know I would be able to fight a single Police Clone because I've done it before, but three Police Clones are currently crammed into this room and other wait eagerly outside in the hall. Somehow, I am in restraints. I wouldn't have put up much of a fight anyway. There's no fighting this now. What's done is done, but my shock still remains, suffocating me. There is no point to resist arrest. Rhino's brethren are just as strong and nimble as he is, and there are too many. I give up. I know survival is no longer achievable. It's not even an option. It never was. A hysterical laugh escapes me as I am yanked up from the bed and led through the door.

Even though I did not resist arrest, I decide to continue to stay true to myself as I compliantly walk out with my head held high rather than bowed in submission and shame. I have gained control of myself and no longer laugh, but a defiant smile pulls at my lips. The sound of Cameron's feet dragging somewhere behind me rips through my chest, but I hide any sign of weakness to portray strength. Through the crowded hallway, I am unable to see him. Word of my predicament must have traveled, because the Owl Clones are all trying to get a look at me and whispering amongst one another.

When we exit the red-lit interior of the Owl, I am loaded into the back of a black SUV police cruiser. Cameron is thrown into the backseat with me before the door slams shut. His head lands softly in my lap. I subtly move my fingers to his neck to look for a pulse. I release a minute portion of the tension built up in my chest when I find the soft rhythmic thump of life.

Chapter 33

As the cruiser nears the city hall building, located in the heart of the city, Cameron finally begins to stir. I do not realize it until he places his hand upon my face and smiles up at me.

"You are the best thing that has ever happened to me. I will love you until the day I die and beyond," Cameron whispers so the constable in the front passenger seat can't overhear. I look down on him in my lap and hold back the forming tears.

"Don't talk like that, you will survive this. My fate won't be as fortunate, but you will go on. You were only doing what People do with Clones. You had no idea what I was, other than another source of pleasure and entertainment. This is what you will tell them, because it is what I will tell them. You need to live on. If you really do love me, do me this last and final request, live." I look away from him and out the window toward a solid-looking marble building and my impending doom.

"How can I live without you?" Cameron implores.

"I will always be with you, because I too love you until death and beyond." I smile down at him and force as much encouragement and fearlessness as possible into my words.

The cruiser stops and the doors open, filling the gloomy car with sunshine. Cameron sits up and gives me one final kiss before we are ripped apart. Cameron struggles for release, but I again hold my composure and my head high. There are many Clones gathered outside of the city hall complex. Some are going to and fro, doing their Essential Function, but there are others who seem out of place. It is as if they are there to observe. I see a few of them whispering to one another as they point and stare at me. I wonder if word of the life growing in my womb has spread this far already.

Cameron and I are separately led up a staircase in the front of the looming white marble building. The sun beats harshly against the white marble making it seem like it is glowing. We continue on between two enormous white marble pillars that dwarf even the large Police Clones before we reach the glass front of the building's entrance. If I were astonished by the beauty of Cameron's bathroom, I no longer have words to describe how this building makes me feel. The grandeur of this entrance makes his bathroom seem like a dirty bedpan. The floor is constructed of a dark marble with golden swirls throughout. The towering walls are white marble with complementary golden swirls continuing up to a golden encrusted ceiling. Chandeliers of gold dangle like small earrings, but each one is larger than the Police Clone who currently nudges me forward because I have slowed down in my awe.

The constable leads us on down another two hallways before I lose sight of Cameron who is led into an interrogation room. I give Cameron a stern, imploring look, telling him to do as I asked. With his jaws barred, Cameron gives me a slight, defeated, nod of his consent. More tension is expelled from my aching chest. As long as he is safe, as long as he will live. I don't care about my own fate, only Cameron's. Mine was written by Anton and the rebels years ago.

I am soon led into an interrogation room of my own. I obediently take a seat and wait as the door is shut behind me with a screech. The room is cold. It is not just the temperature that is cold. The atmosphere is designed to exert power and dominance over me. The black walls seem to close in menacingly. The floor is concrete, but it is also midnight black. The ceiling is a soulless depth of darkness, void of any forgiveness. There is a single fluorescent tube light on one wall.

It causes me more depression as the darkness of everything else seemingly attempts to swallow out its existence. I can relate.

The wall I am facing beholds my reflection on a mirror. I don't understand the purpose or function of a mirror in an interrogation room. I decide to utilize it for my own benefit to better monitor my facial expressions. The chair I sit in is metal, cold, and very hard against my back. My mostly bare skin stings from the contact with the icy surface. There is a table in front of me, also metal and bolted to the floor. I notice a camera in the corner of the room. I know the government has me monitored on a screen sourced from this camera, but I imagine Boston is watching as well. I am not certain, but just in case he is, I give the slightest expression of apology. I am confident the expression will be missed by the People, but Boston has known me for so long and knows me so well, I am positive, if he is watching, he understands it.

The only door opens with a loud scream that echoes through the room and causes me to flinch slightly. The constable enters the room and sits in the chair opposite the table from me. I can slightly make out the features of his face, but his figure is slightly silhouetted by the light behind him. He does not look at me for a moment while he flips through some papers in a manila folder sitting in front of him on the table. The sound of the papers shuffling is the only noise in the room, and with each new page turned, I find myself wincing. When he finally looks up at me, the constable is not surprised when I do not look down, breaking eye contact, as a Clone should.

"You have been a busy woman, haven't you?"

I find it curious that he didn't say "Clone;" he rather chose the noun "woman" in reference to me.

"Of course I have been busy. I am a Clone. We have nothing else but to be busy."

"Ah yes, but you have gone above and beyond your call of duty. Have you not?"

The constable raises an eyebrow at me, pausing for a response. When I say nothing, he looks back at his papers and continues on.

"You have corrupted a promising young member of the People. You have led countless Clones astray with your behavior. There is also a written complaint about an instance where you apparently assaulted a Person. The computer's report has gone missing, but the original paper copy has been sitting on my desk for well over a month now. And to top it all off, you have somehow managed to be impregnated. You do understand the consequences for your actions, do you not?"

This time he does not pause for an answer. I wouldn't have given one anyway.

"Unfortunately, your fate is not going to follow the normal removal protocol, due to the severity and extent of your violations. The powers that be want to make an example of you. They hope that, in doing so, we will not need to eliminate a largely corrupted portion of the Clone population."

The constable again looks up at me and folds his hands atop his paper pile. I am not sure if I really did see it, but when the constable first looked at me, I think I caught a glimmer of sorrow in his solemn gray eyes.

"I would have it no other way, sir. It was I and I alone who broke the law. I would pray no one else would be punished for my wrongdoings. And as for the fate of the young man who was arrested with me, he had no part in my actions. He was indeed misled, but innocent. He did not know of my capacity to bear children. If he had, I am certain he would have used protection or not had me at all. All he did was take what he wanted, as any upstanding Person would do." I speak flatly.

"He said much the same and has, in fact, already been released." My shoulders relax slightly at the good news. The constable doesn't notice my reaction and he continues, "You are scheduled to be removed tomorrow afternoon in the main courtyard of city hall. A firing squad has been selected as the method of choice. The entire city will be mandated to attend, Clone and Person alike. An officer will show you to your cell now." Great, another cell.

"Thank you, Constable."

I bow my head slightly and raise it to again meet the constable's eyes.

"Have a nice evening, sir," I wish with a slight smile. My words cause that flicker of sorrow to momentarily flash in the constable's eyes again. I am sure of it this time.

The constable stands and escorts me out of the room to a Police Clone officer who awaits out in the hall to take me from there. The look of regret is still on the constable's face and it seems to intensify slightly with every passing second. It's as if he is sympathetic to my actions and my fate for those actions. Cameron must be right about other People feeling as he does concerning the Clones. I give the constable one last smile before turning away and following the Police Clone officer.

As I am escorted to my cell, I am led through a busy office with twenty Clones, each seated at a desk, with their eyes at a computer screen. Each of the four different Clone types busy working are dressed in identical black slacks, white button-down linen shirts, and red ties. Each desktop is empty other than a computer screen, a keyboard, and a pile of papers. As expected, there are no family pictures or personal memorabilia anywhere in sight. Each Clone has their fingers dancing lightly upon a keyboard. The flurry of clicking and clacking emanating from the typing fingers comes to an abrupt halt as every single Clone stops to look up at me. Most of them stare at my face, but I catch a few staring at my belly. My hands subconsciously move to protect the life growing within from their gazes. Their eyes follow me until I am out of sight. The soft pattering sound commences once again, but fades away as I am led farther down the hallway.

The large Clone officer opens a solid door revealing a small room with a cot in one corner, a meatal toilet in the other, and a sink built into the wall. It is much like the cell I was in at the rebel compound; however, this one is slightly smaller and far more depressing. Probably because I know my fate beyond these four walls. At the rebel compound, I figured I would be released to live again. But with this one, there will be nothing left of me after I depart. There is a small barred window on the far wall, too high for me to see out of, but it is open, allowing for the breeze to pass into the chamber, as well as the harmonic song of the birds. I smile slightly. At least this cell has a window. However, that almost makes it more depressing, because now I will get to see, hear, and smell the wonders of life that I'll be leaving behind.

The Clone officer places his large mitt-like hand on my shoulder, escorting me in. before he releases and closes the door behind me, he gives me an ever-so-slight comforting squeeze on my shoulder. I turn to him while the distance of the opening shrinks and see a single tear well up in each of his large blue eyes as they twitch to prevent the watery escape. The Clone blinks quickly several times and the tear drops disappear. I give him a reassuring smile as the final gap is closed. I am amazed how quickly all of the Clones have changed. It started with a small spark at the hospital and it has spread throughout the city like a wildfire. The Clones were like a water-deprived field of wheat. When one small spark of love and hope occurred, the whole field instantaneously went up in flames. I only hope there will be some who remain after the fire is snuffed out.

Chapter 34

I lie face down on the cot and finally release my anguish. I muffle a cry with my face buried deep into the pillow. I don't cry for myself. I have accepted my fate. I cry for those who I will leave behind, for the unknown fate they shall each face. How will Cameron deal with this world without me in it? He barely kept his sanity when he thought I was claimed by someone else even though he still believed I was alive. How will he handle the sorrow when I am truly gone? Boston with his constant love, who would give up his freedom and his life for me without hesitation. Scotty with her quirky sense of humor and never-wavering loyalty. What will become of her? And Aggie, dear, sweet, innocent Aggie. I didn't even say goodbye to her. I know Anton, Eliana and the rest of the rebels will celebrate my death as a martyr, using it to influence others to follow in their plight. I cry until my tears run dry. When the ache in my chest lessens from a searing pain to a dull throb, I roll over onto my back to stare at the bland concrete ceiling.

I am delivered a small tray with half a grilled cheese sandwich accompanied by a glass of water for lunch. I nibble it, but am unable to finish, as my stomach is uneasy. I resume my reverie, staring at the ceiling, until another tray is delivered some hours later. This time a bowl of stew with another glass of water. My stomach has eased slightly from the tension, and I am able to finish the stew. I even wish there was a bit more when my stomach gives a greedy growl. Someone comes and collects the food tray after each of my meals, but I pay them no mind. I now sit on my bed and study the plain wall. For all of the magnificence of the lobby, this cell lacks any interest. However, as the evening wears on, the oranges, reds, purples and pinks of the sunset paint a beautiful mural upon my otherwise bland cell wall. I would choose the subtle splendor of this wall over the pompous extravagance of the gold-encrusted marble of the lobby any day. I wait, content in watching the warm colors change as they dance upon the cold cement. So free, so full of life.

A soft pattering noise breaks my trance like reverie, pulling my attention to the floor beside my bed. A wadded paper ball still rocks back and forth on the floor from the slowing of momentum. I pick up the wadded ball and open it. Inside are written two words in blue unfamiliar handwriting.

Thank you.

I duck as another ball comes hurtling in. I open that as well. It has the same two words in a different color ink as well as different penmanship. I pull my bed closer to the window with a screech from the metal bed legs rubbing on the concrete floor. I climb up onto the bed and stand on the tips of my toes while pulling on the bars to try to get a glimpse of the world outside of my cage. All I see are People and Clones walking to and fro. No one remains to take claim of the note deliveries. While I am straining to see outside, a Clone passing closely by my window places a fist to his heart before he tosses yet another paper through the bars. The Clone doesn't appear familiar to me. I don't pick up this new delivery because I see yet another Clone shoot a folded paper airplane with surprising accuracy through the bars of my window. As I watch, several other Clones do not throw messages, but they do place a fist to their heart while they give me a slight nod of acknowledgement and respect. After a few minutes of observations and added notes, I sit and collect my deliveries. I read each and every one as more continue to arrive throughout the evening and into the wee hours of the night. Each contains the same two words, each in different handwriting. I find it peculiar that we as Clones do not share the same exact handwriting. Some are elegant cursive, others are a scribble, some are bubbly, and others yet are stiff.

I am uncertain why these Clones would be thanking me. Perhaps they recognize my hand in the subtle rebel efforts? Even after the curfew bells toll, I continue to receive my precious notes. These Clones are risking too much to deliver them to me.

Sleep is no good to me again tonight. It's chased off by nightmares of my loved ones dying tortuous deaths. As each one dies, their final cry is "Thank You." Before I realize it, the morning sunshine is peeking through my barred window. There comes the sound of my cell latch opening as the door swings out on its hinges. A small dark-haired woman delivers a breakfast tray with the usual breakfast items I am familiar with, oatmeal and a fruit selection. Today it is a half grapefruit. There is also a steaming cup of black coffee, which usually has the greatest appeal to me, but the strong smell makes me gag. I nod a thank you to the woman, who does not seem to notice or care. I hurriedly rush to the toilet to expel the turmoil from my stomach. After my stomach has nothing left to offer the metallic bowl, it continues to twist and cramp. I take the coffee and grudgingly pour it down the drain and run the sink water to wash it down.

"What a waste," I say out loud to myself.

I take small nibbles of the oatmeal, but it does not sit well. I know I need something in my stomach to give it some peace, so I try the grapefruit. It not only fills my stomach, but it also relieves the queasiness slightly. Throughout the day more notes appear, but with less regularity than the night prior. I continue to collect each one, reading the same two words over and over again.

Chapter 35

I had accepted my fate yesterday, but after waiting alone for so many long hours, fear has begun to seep into my entire body. I can feel every inch tremble in trepidation. As the hours crawl by, I dread what fate has chosen for me. I don't even look at what's delivered on my lunch tray, but I do consume its entire contents. I sit on my bed, bobbing my legs up and down on my toes while I hold the pillow tightly to my chest and stare blankly off into space. The afternoon wears on, but there is no dinner delivered. Faint pinks begin to illuminate my cell wall again, bringing the procession of the sunset dance. I know it's only a matter of time before they come for me. As if on cue, the door to my cell opens with a screeching cry of protest, as if it too does not want me to fade away from this world.

Great, I think to myself, another thing to let down and disappoint. The constable and another man stand in the doorway. I find it a bit curious that they are without a Police Clone. The constable is wearing the same trench coat he always wears, but the other man is wearing a very finely tailored black suit and tie as if he is prepared for an exclusive formal event. The only thing throwing off his elegance slightly is the black bowler hat atop his head. The light in the hallway is behind him, silhouetting his features. The constable begins speaking to me, drawing my attention away from the other man.

"The time has come, Clone number A14B45T3R. If you would like to change out of your current garments, I have brought you a clean outfit." The constable offers me a small bundle.

I gratefully take it with a polite nod. I had forgotten I still wear the risqué dark blue and black lingerie. The constable closes the door for me to change in privacy. There is a white T-shirt and faded blue jeans as well as white undergarments and tennis shoes. I struggle to remove the tightly fitting bodice. It was a lot easier with Cameron's assistance. The new clothing slips on easily enough. The T-shirt fits perfectly, without any folds or wrinkles. The faded blue jeans must have been custom made for my Clone type, because they also cling to my form smoothly, but not tight. I run my fingers through my long silky brown hair for the last time. I don't have a tie to hold it back in a braid, so I leave it free and flowing. Aggie would have liked it that way. Every female Clone has their hair pulled back when in public, because it's the law, so I find it curious I'm not supplied a tie of some form. I choose not to worry about it. This will be my last act of free will and rebellion. I leave the stack of notes in a neat pile upon my pillow. My stomach has given only slight morning sickness today and most of that was when breakfast arrived. I'm pleased that it is not overwhelmingly aggressive at this point. I want to walk with honor and I would be unable to do so if I were vomiting and fainting the whole time.

The door opens once again, and I walk through the opening of my own volition. The constable directs me to follow him. I now get a better look at the man accompanying the constable, and pause to do a double take. The man, who is a member of the elite People, strongly resembles Cameron. He is in his late forties and his wheat-like golden hair is clean cut and covered by the bowler hat. The man has had his eyes hidden under the shadowed rim of the hat, but as I stare open mouthed at him, he lifts his eyes to me. My heart plummets into my stomach as I realize his eyes share the same deep blue-green depths as Cameron's. He is approximately the same height as Cameron, but his muscles are leaner and not as pronounced. The man has a slightly different nose, but other than that, their bone structures are the same. This man is Cameron's father, of that I am certain. At the look of recognition on my face, the man gives me a very familiar half-smile that sends an unpleasant chill up my spine. However, where Cameron's smile is full of love, this smile is full of malice. Suddenly, I want to vomit again.

The constable gives me a nudge to reclaim my focus to the task at hand. He leads me down the hall I walked yesterday. Cameron's father trails closely behind, humming a melancholy tune. There is no one present in the room which had the twenty Clones working the day prior. The building is empty of both People and Clones. We don't continue upon the route I took through the imposing lobby yesterday. Instead, we veer down a hallway to the left, and exit the building through a glass front lobby leading to a large courtyard. The courtyard is full of both People and Clones, but they are segregated. The People are around the back and the Clones are closer to the far end of the courtyard where there is a clearing. That must be where I am headed. The powers that be want the Clones to witness firsthand what happens to those who break the law. As I walk through the People, I am welcomed with jeering, snide comments, and spitting. I continue to walk with my head held high in dignity.

I will never again bow to anyone. I am comforted by the scattered People who give a solemn nod of respect and regret, but they are few and far between. When I reach the section where the Clones stand, I hold myself stronger. Every Clone has me as their one and only focus. They do not shout, they do not cry, they do not spit. They are Clones, they are not meant to have emotions, so they conceal them. However, I know what each is feeling because they all have their brow furrowed in concern and their eyes forsake their placid exterior. Some place a fist to their chest when my eyes pass over them. I smile the brightest smile I can muster, encouraging the Clones and assuring them that I am not sorry for what I have done, and I am not afraid of what's to come.

I walk to the far side of the courtyard to the place void of people I saw earlier. I calmly take my place against a white brick wall. Before I turn back to face the spectators, I take in the beauty of the last sunset I will see. The courtyard is still bright enough to distinguish facial features, but shadows cast a strong contrast of colors. In the front row of my audience stands the constable and Cameron's father along with a line of twenty Police Clones armed with semi-automatic rifles. Each one is basically identical, but simultaneously different. Each has had differing experiences leading up to this point in their lives. Each Police Clone has small and large scars worn on their bodies to remind them of their past mistakes and failures. I realize that every Clone bares scars. The Police Clones are the only ones permitted to bare them on the outside, but all Clones have them somewhere on the inside. They are emotional scars. Scars of abuse, hate, neglect.

"READY!"

The constable begins the count. At this moment, I discover the one thing that sets one Clone apart from another. The People can try all they want to dehumanize the Clones, but they will never succeed. The soul finds a way to shine through, to make itself known.

"AIM!"

The Police Clones raise their rifles, every barrel points to my heart. I silently pray each bullet stays true, to relieve the aching throb I have held captive within. I remain standing tall and proud. I do permit one lone tear to escape, to solemnly roll down my cheek. My eyes remain wide open and fearless. I want to take in every last sight, every last sound, this life has to offer.

"FIRE!"

I flinch ever so slightly, but feel no pain. The accuracy of the Police Clones is impressive. I am dead before I even hear the guns fire. Before I feel a single bullet pierce my skin, I am no more.

However, I soon realize I can still feel the gentle breeze, hear the birds singing the song of spring, and smell the bloom of flowers from somewhere within the courtyard. I open my eyes, which I didn't realize I'd closed. I'm still standing, facing the line of Clone officers. However, their weapons are lowered and the crowd of both Clones and People stand silently behind them. The Police Clones each give me a respectful nod with a fist over their heart before they drop their weapons and disperse into the crowd of Clones. They couldn't do it. They could not kill me. I let out a small gasp of laughter that echoes through the silent courtyard.

"Get back here! You have a job to complete," Cameron's now-red-faced father orders the Police Clones to no avail. They aren't going to return. He looks imploringly to the constable, who shrugs helplessly as he attempts to conceal a laugh.

Cameron's father calls to the back of the courtyard where the People stand uncomfortably.

"Are there any willing volunteers to finish this? Come forward and claim a weapon."

Fifteen men come sauntering up and pick up the rifles. Cameron's father smiles and shakes the hand of a few of the volunteers. I am not surprised to see the face of Leroy among the volunteers. He actually looks sober for once. His shirt is neatly tucked in and there are no stains on the storm-gray polo. He looks up at me and smirks, so I raise a finger and tap my nose with a smile. Leroy's nose has become crooked since I last saw him. I assume it is because of the kick I delivered. Leroy's smirk quickly disappears, I assumed right. Many of the men don't seem to have any knowledge of how to hold their weapon, let alone how to fire it. None seem to understand the power over life and death they control with the inanimate object. After a stern look from Cameron's father, the constable spends a few minutes instructing the volunteers how to use their weapon. I flinch as the constable fires a demonstration shot, which echoes through the courtyard. The bullet hits the white brick façade that stands behind me, only a few feet away from my head.

After the constable is satisfied in the competence of the volunteers, he lines them up before me. Cameron's father eagerly gives the commands to the firing squad this time.

"READY!"

I take a deep breath.

"AIM!"

I close my eyes.

"FI––for god's sake, get out of the way boy!"

I open my eyes to reveal the hypnotic eyes of Cameron right in front of me. Tears pour out of my eyes and I shake my head from side to side.

"No, no, no, no, no. What are you doing here? I told you to live, live for me. I can't do this knowing you will be dead too. Why, Cameron, why?"

Cameron takes me into his arms.

"Because I can't live knowing you are dead. Better we both die together."

Cameron bends down and kisses my rosy lips while wrapping his arms securely around my small frame.

"Cameron, son, get out of the way. Come stand with the People, where you belong," Cameron's father yells across the expanse with annoyance in his voice.

Cameron does not turn around to his father as he replies, "I am exactly where I belong, Dad."

"Suit yourself. If you do not come away now, you die too," Cameron's father callously calls to Cameron.

I look over Cameron's shoulder to see three of the People drop their weapons, Leroy included. But there are still twelve standing at the ready. In reality, it only takes one. Cameron's father begins the count again.

"READY!"

I don't care who is holding weapons any longer as Cameron again kisses me and his kisses become more intense. We both have tears streaking down our faces and seeping into our kiss.

"AIM!"

Cameron moves, turning his body so it is directly in front of my small figure, futilely attempting to block the coming onslaught.

"Oh come on, seriously? You all need to get out of the way. We have laws, and those laws have been broken, and in accordance with those laws, this girl, this Clone must die in atonement for her crimes. If you do not move, you will all suffer the same fate."

Cameron and I break apart to find ourselves surrounded by a large mass consisting of mostly Clones, but also People. I see a few familiar faces from the hospital. Scotty and Astrid are here, Thomas, my brother, the bus driver who I started calling Skipper just two days ago. I also see the familiar faces of some rebels. Eliana stands next to Rhino and Anton. I quickly scan the faces in search of Boston, but I do not see him. Hopefully he stayed with Aggie at the compound. I feel a slight relief. I don't want anyone to die for me, especially someone I love, and there are already plenty of those here. Cameron holds my hand tightly in his own, reminding me of what I could lose.

"Then change the laws," calls the voice of Anton.

"We can't just change the laws. They were put in place to create a utopia. There is no more violence or murder in our society. No one steals as we are all given everything we want. It is perfect." I can hear Cameron's father's voice, but I can no longer see him. Some People can be heard voicing their agreement.

"Look around you. This is violence and murder if you proceed. Did you know this Clone is pregnant? You will not only be murdering her, but her unborn child as well." I don't know how Anton found out about that, I just found out yesterday.

At this new information, the people in the crowd gasp and a low murmur builds in volume. I see a few more of the People with the rifles gasp as they gawk at me before laying their rifles down. There are still eight People armed. A couple of them seem to have forgotten they are holding a weapon, and one man holds it tighter as if he is concerned about the current predicament. I don't blame him, I am too.

"Don't listen to him. Clones cannot become pregnant, it is impossible." Cameron's father announces to the crowd with a false smile.

"You lie. I have the test results confirming it right here." Anton calmly extends his arm with a folded sheet of paper tucked between his fingers.

"Where did you get that? You will pay for stealing, Clone." Cameron's father snarls.

Anton pays him no mind and proceeds to address the Clone masses again.

"And the lack of violence and murder only applies to the People. What about the Clones? We are killed daily for amusement, for pleasure. We Clones don't get whatever we want. We are given only what we need to survive, and that is not living. It is serving. It is slavery. We deserve to have what we want. We deserve to love and be loved."

Anton wraps his arm around Eliana, who seems surprised but pleased. If she only knew he is incapable of loving anyone but himself. I momentarily feel sorry for her. The feeling passes quickly.

"We deserve to choose who to live with, where to work, what to do in our free time. We deserve to have free time. Clones, look around you. We outnumber the People five to one. Let us unite, let us take down the People and make them cower under our rule as we have theirs for far too long. Join me."

Anton raises a fist into the air as he finishes. I cannot take it anymore. The fierce look of a rabid dog I find in Anton's eye makes me sick to my stomach, more so than any morning sickness.

Before the cheering commences too far, I interject.

"No. Stop. Do not listen to this snake of a man. He wants to cause havoc. He only wants you to take down the People so he can rule over you as they have. He doesn't want you to be his equals, but his slaves. There is a better option. We join the People and unite as one humanity. I have seen it firsthand. It can be done. People, you will need to treat us better, like equals. You will need to join us in doing the hard labor we are designed for. Share the workload. I implore you to stop mistreating us. Stop using us, killing us, and treating us like animals. We are all human, we all have a soul. We can join together, we can love one another."

I don't notice Anton's enraged look as he lifts an abandoned rifle and points it at me with deadly accuracy. I finally see Boston and I smile up at him as he runs at me with full speed. I hear a loud bang from the bullet escaping from the nozzle of Anton's riffle as Boston's body instantaneously slams into me, knocking me to the ground. My ears are ringing but I still hear the screams and the commotion of people running in chaos through the courtyard.

Cameron kneels down and gently rolls Boston off of me. I sit up to see Anton pinned to the ground by Rhino, who is pummeling his face, and Eliana stands screaming next to him. I then look down at Boston. There is a scarlet pool increasing in size under his body. Cameron rolls him back over onto his side revealing the source of the blood. There, in the middle of Boston's back near his shoulder blade is a large, expanding crimson blotch. Boston's face is twisted in agonizing pain. Cameron tears Boston's shirt open to find a large wound between his shoulder blades near his spine. Blood spills out at an alarming rate. There is no exit wound. Boston coughs and blood splatters out, speckling my white T-shirt. A small trickle of blood spills out of the corner of his mouth. Cameron looks up at me and shakes his head gently with remorse. I already knew there was little hope, but Cameron's confirmation causes my heart to slam at my chest. I start to cry as I pull Boston back into my lap. I can feel his blood soak into my clothing, but I don't care.

"Why did you do that, Boston? You are so stupid," I sputter between sobs.

"You know why I did it. I love you, just as much as he does. I told you I would die for you." Boston coughs more blood and struggles to get his words out. "The world would lose too much if it lost you. You are one in a million, I am one of a million." More blood oozes out both his back and his mouth. "Live and love on, Alabaster."

Boston reaches up and touches my face one last time before his hand falls heavily to the ground. I grab Boston's lifeless hand and hold it back to my cheek.

"No. Boston, don't leave me! Boston, stay here, don't go, Boston." I sob into Boston's stagnant chest.

Cameron wraps his arms around me tightly. I begin shaking from hysterical sobs. Tears are streaming from my eyes, blurring the mayhem happening around me. Someone comes and tries to lift Boston's body, but I will not release him. Cameron pulls me off of Boston's lifeless body and cuddles me close. I bury my head in Cameron's chest and continue crying. I hit Cameron's chest a few times, not because I blame him, but in an attempt to transfer my pain somewhere else. Cameron understands and does not flinch away. He just rocks me back and forth while stroking my hair.

Anarchy ensues. The entire courtyard is filled with People and Clones fighting to the death. It has reached a point where no one knows who they are inflicting their brutality upon. Clones are beating People as well as other Clones. Many People are fighting Clones and other People. Rhino has moved on to another faceless victim, who is no longer recognizable as Clone or Person, because Rhino has reduced the facial traits to a mound of ground beef.

The rifles have been lifted and the echoes of gunfire resound from the shadows.

"We need to go. Now." There is a sense of urgency in Cameron's voice.

I shake my head *no* into his chest. Someone lights a cloth which is peeking out of an emerald-green glass bottle with liquid soaking into the fabric. The bottle is lobbed into the brawling masses. Heat encompasses my body, drawing me back into reality as the shattering bottle causes a fiery explosion. I find it hard to breathe while I witness human figures writhing in agony as they are swallowed by the hungry flames. Cameron lifts me to my feet, and I follow willingly this time. He keeps me pinned against the wall as we edge toward an arched exit nearby. Cameron's body shields me, both from experiencing and witnessing the violence commencing.

Chapter 36

I feel Cameron jolt and shudder as if in pain more than a few times before we escape through the arch. The cool evening air hits us and we drink it in. It is as if we went through a portal into another dimension when we passed through the arch. A world untouched by violence. The sound of agonizing cries can be heard, but the wall makes them muffled and surreal. I want to crumble to the ground again, but Cameron pulls me farther away from the cacophony. I don't know where he is leading and I don't care. All I can feel right now is sorrow. If I had only kept my head down and mouth shut when I first met Cameron. If I only let Leroy do whatever he was going to do. If I had only accepted the punishment for fighting back. If I had only lived by the rules set forth for me and every other Clone, Boston would still be alive. So many lives are being extinguished and I feel it is all my fault. Despair and guilt make my body feel like a ton of bricks are tied to me and I have been thrown into the ocean. I gasp for air as I struggle to breathe. I feel like my lungs are filling with water rather than oxygen. I fall to the ground while Cameron pulls me along.

I didn't realize how quickly we were moving. I skid several feet along the rough cobblestones, collecting gravel in my skin with the force of impact. Cameron barely skips a beat as he scoops me up into his strong arms. I hate myself even more when I realize Cameron is limping while he speeds down the street baring all my extra weight. We reach Cameron's black Mercedes, where Dimitri stands attentively. The battle has now spilled out of the courtyard in the form of a mob. Only the sound of the madness and mayhem has reached Cameron and me, but the danger is fast approaching. Dimitri opens the door and runs to the driver's door without waiting for Cameron and me to load in.

The car's engine rumbles to life as Cameron slides me onto the fine black leather seat. Cameron reaches out to close the door and is forcefully ripped out of the car. An angry Clone with the face of Anton has Cameron by the collar of his shirt and they begin to grapple.

"Run, get out of here!" the Clone is yelling at me.

At the same time, Cameron calls to Dimitri. "Dimitri, drive! Get Alabaster out of here!"

Before Dimitri has the car in gear, a glimmer of light catches my attention. A large, silver blade materializes in the Clone's hand. Before I realize what I am doing, I am out of the car and my body crosses the path of the blade, averting its intended destination within Cameron's chest. All of my guilt and sorrow flood to the searing pain in my abdomen as they flow out of my body in a crimson tide. The Clone is stunned by his mistake long enough for Cameron to gain the upper hand. Cameron throws a punch packed with vehemence, sending the Clone spiraling to the ground, where he remains motionless.

Cameron has not yet realized the damage done by the Clone's blade. He turns around and sees my hand at my stomach, inadequately concealing the injury. I can feel the color draining from my face as Cameron's also falls pale. My face pales from blood loss, Cameron's from the severity of the situation. I smile weakly at Cameron before my strength fails me and gravity takes over. Gravity is a bastard. Cameron is sluggish from shock, the fight, and his own wounds, resulting in his inability to reach me in time. My body is already in such agony that the solid cobblestones don't feel harder than Cameron's cloudlike bed. I am still conscious when my body is lifted into the back seat by Cameron and Dimitri together. I'm pretty sure I have hit my head, because I can feel a warm sensation spreading.

I begin to feel like I am dreaming. The world around me fades away while I slip into unconsciousness. When my vision returns, I have a new vantage point above the car, where I'm floating. I look down through the car's roof, which has become invisible, at my still body. While I watch from above, Cameron rips the lower portion of my shirt apart, revealing a bubbling crimson geyser three inches above my naval. Dimitri goes to the trunk and retrieves a black bag. After entering the back door across from Cameron, Dimitri gives the bag to him. I can tell the two are talking because I can see their lips move, but all I hear is silence. Utter complete silence. It's eerie. I don't even hear the blood that usually pulsates through my head. Dimitri digs through the bag full of medical supplies. He hands Cameron different items as Cameron's skilled hands work feverishly with the gaping wound. I lazily wonder to myself if Dimitri has medical training. My thoughts become more and more sluggish and less coherent.

At this point I know I am not breathing. I watch the men working as a team to save me. In fact, I don't believe anyone in the car is breathing. The difference being, the men are holding their breath, and I have none. Cameron cleans and proceeds to sew the wound shut. The scarlet river stops flowing as Cameron finishes the last knot. My body's skin is translucent from blood loss. Cameron's shaking red fingertips reach for my body's neck, where they press firmly against my carotid artery in search of a pulse. I can't stand to watch Cameron's pain. There is no pulse to be found. I wish I could touch him one last time. Let him know everything is going to be all right. But that time has come and gone.

I slowly let my spirit drift away as Cameron becomes hysterical. He leans over my body and begins compressing my chest with his palms. The crack of cartilage snapping does not hinder his resolve as he presses deeply. I try to depart, but I'm suddenly tethered to my body. Cameron continues to push my chest in after every release. His lips seal around mine and he forces air into my deflated lungs. Each breath draws me closer, urging my soul to once again be one with my body. My soul aches to once again be intertwined with his. Cameron continues to compress my body's chest fervently, even when Dimitri tries to make him desist, he continues. Cameron's vision must be blurred from the tears visibly flowing from his eyes. He throws Dimitri's comforting hands off and proceeds to lock his lips to my body's now-blue-tinted lips with one more breath. I am so close now, I can almost feel Cameron's touch once more. Cameron rests his tear-saturated cheek against mine as he breathes hard.

His lips are near my ear when he whispers. "Come on, Alabaster. I know you have more fight in you. Don't leave me now, not like this." His thumb brushes a lock of hair from my face.

Cameron applies one last kiss to my body's cold mouth, but this one is filled less with air and more with love. That is what I needed to draw my soul back into my body. I gasp as my lungs fill with the stuffy air of the car's sleek interior. My eyes open wide and sound crashes around me. Cameron smiles with a laugh and he wraps his body around mine. His entire body trembles with laughter and the exhaustion of emotional turmoil. I give an involuntary whimper as the distant memory of pain becomes a reality once more. Cameron releases me with a worried look. I smile up at him with a love-filled expression.

"I'm fine. I'm here. Don't worry, I won't leave you again." I use all of my remaining strength to raise one hand and place it upon the back of Cameron's head, where my fingers twist gently in his soft hair.

"I didn't think you left me before." Cameron's brief smile doesn't reach his eyes before it fades back into a frown of concern. The chaos of the revolution is now only yards away. The Clone who stabbed me begins to stir on the sidewalk.

"Dimitri, we need to get her home immediately."

Chapter 37

Dimitri was already in the driver's seat with the car in gear before Cameron even spoke. Dimitri's foot pushes the pedal to the floor, where it remains. I lie across the back seat propped up in Cameron's lap. I begin to feel better as my heart pumps more blood out into my deprived body. Cameron holds me close and keeps asking me if I'm well. I smile up at him reassuringly, but I don't think I've got him convinced. With Cameron's help, I sit up to look out the window. I don't know how long I was unconscious, but the sun has fully set and the moon begins to peek its head over the buildings.

To get home, we must drive through the mob which has overflowed from the courtyard. People and Clones alike are breaking into homes, pilfering everything not nailed down. Cars have been overturned with tires in the air like a dog expecting a belly rub. Amidst the havoc, a little girl stands holding a small ragged teddy bear. She's no older than three. The girl has long lovely golden hair. Her dirty face is streaked with the reminder of tears which have since stopped flowing. She reminds me of a younger Aggie, but she's not a Clone. I have regained more of my strength, but I am mostly fueled by adrenaline as I open the car door and proceed to exit the moving vehicle. Dimitri slams on the breaks as soon as he realizes my intentions. I think long enough to wait until I can safely exit the car, but I still stumble slightly. I quickly approach the child. Cameron follows me out, but Dimitri remains in the idling car. I kneel down to the girl's eye level.

"Where is you mommy and daddy?" I inquire of the little girl while holding the girl's fragile hand in my own.

The girl's other small hand extends a finger to a nearby car. I release a slight gasp of horror, because the car has been devoured by flames, and now rests black and smoking. The little girl's chin quivers, so I pull her close. Cameron gently pulls on my elbow, urging me back to safety.

"We need to get out of here. It's not safe."

I wince from pain as I lift the little girl. "She is coming with us."

Cameron reluctantly nods and takes the small figure out of my arms. The three of us are in the car, and Dimitri already has the car moving before the door is shut. An angry mob of Clones flood the streets. They throw bricks, bottles, and rocks at the black Mercedes while it passes. A few unfortunately brave souls decide to stand in front of the moving vehicle in hopes of halting its momentum. Dimitri is merciless as he presses harder on the already-floored gas pedal. The little girl shrieks while the bodies thud loudly against the hood of the car and bounce over the roof.

As we approach Cameron's home, the mobs lessens and the streets seem normal, other than the ghostly absence of people. The light of distant fires flicker eerily on the buildings. Dimitri pulls up onto the curb with just enough space to open the car door and enter the house. He and Cameron rush inside. I sit holding the young girl in my lap, rocking her slightly while stroking her honey-toned hair. The girl is silent with a glazed look in her sapphire blue eyes.

"What is your name, sweetheart?" I inquire of the little one.

"Olive," she whispers in response.

"Don't worry, Olive, we're going to be safe." I say it more to assure myself than to comfort the child.

Burning fear courses through my veins when I look out the back window to see the blood-crazed mob working its way down the street in our direction.

"Cameron, Cameron!"

I yell into the house with panic laced into every syllable. I grip my stomach as the force of yelling sends shooting pain from my gut. Cameron and Dimitri appear and both toss large duffel bags into the backseat with Olive and me. Dimitri wields an old-fashioned shotgun, and Cameron has a pistol tucked into his pants. Dimitri climbs over the top of the car and heads straight toward the mob.

"Dimitri, what do you think you're doing? Get in the car, let's go!" Cameron pleads from within the open double doors of his house.

"It has been a pleasure working for you all these years, sir."

Dimitri briefly turns back to Cameron before going head-on toward the mob. Cameron looks at me and Olive with indecision written on his face. Cameron's jaw sets firmly. He slams the car door and climbs over the roof in pursuit of Dimitri. Before Cameron's feet hit the ground on the other side, Dimitri opens fire into the mob, a loud crack echoing through the street. He already has the shotgun cocked and ready as three Clones fall to the ground and others are wounded. Cameron lands his feet on the ground and starts toward Dimitri, who fires into the hoard again with similar results. I open the car door on the street side to follow after Cameron. I close the door after I exit to keep Olive safely away from the gunfire. I catch up to Cameron, who is still a few yards behind Dimitri, who prepares yet another round. The mob has realized the aggressor's presence and the few who have guns of their own begin to loose bullets in Dimitri's direction. I take Cameron's hand and pull him back to the limited safety of the car. He doesn't budge, too focused on Dimitri. There are only a handful of Police Clones, not nearly as many as I would have imagined, but none of them are carrying the guns. The result is poor aim, as the guns are fired without accuracy. A bullet grazes Cameron's shoulder, but he barely notices.

"Dimitri! Come on, we need to get out of here!" He calls one more time for Dimitri to come back.

"I am buying you time, sir. Get Alabaster, your baby, and the child to safety. This is what I must do." Dimitri doesn't even look back at us while he fires into the crowd again.

Dimitri takes down a few more of the mob's number, but there are so many, it is like trying to stop a flooding river with only one sand bag. Cameron reluctantly allows me to pull him back to the car. His bicep is bleeding slightly, but it doesn't seem to bother him, as he keeps looking back to his loyal butler

Dimitri. I feel like Cameron has finally realized the close bond he has with Dimitri. More like the bond of father and son rather than Person and Clone. From what I saw tonight, Dimitri definitely loves Cameron more than his own father, who was willing to have him killed. The mob is dangerously close to Dimitri now, and those without guns begin hurtling objects at him. He is not daunted as he's struck with rocks, bottles, and a sterling-silver candlestick. He continues to reload, fire, and repeat.

Cameron is still hesitant, and keeps looking back to Dimitri, who is now dangerously close to the mob. On the outskirts of the mob, I spot a Clone, a Boston lookalike, holding a dirty brown bottle with a white cloth extending out of the opening. Dimitri does not see the Clone, but the Clone doesn't seem interested in Dimitri. The horror of the night turns into slow motion when I realize the Clone's intentions. As the Clone makes a break toward the Mercedes, he lights the cloth and whirls the bottle at the idling car. The bottle shatters with a blast strong enough to push Cameron and I back a step. The blast encompasses the entire car in a single fiery burst. I can't breathe. I am filled with frozen terror rather than the heat from the nearby blazing inferno. Little hands pound upon the glass of the car with no hope. Even though my ears are ringing from the force of the explosion, I can hear an ear-piercing scream cut through the night, but the following silence cuts deeper.

The mob pauses for a brief second, but soon resumes its assault. I involuntarily shake from pure terror, overwhelming sorrow from what I just witnessed, and from the tremendous pain of the knife wound in my abdomen. Cameron takes my hand and leads me down the street, away from the horror. I follow like a blindfolded horse being led from a burning barn, trusting Cameron to lead me to safety. We make it a few blocks down the street and dive into an alleyway. The loud blasts of the shotgun cease as the pounding of many feet hitting the pavement takes over. Dimitri has fallen. Cameron pauses briefly, looking back over his shoulder. I can tell by the look in his eyes that he is going through an internal conflict of flight or fight. I gently squeeze his hand to remind him of the danger we are now facing. He looks down on me and clenches his jaw with resolve. I know as well as he does that Dimitri is gone, and if we go back we will be too. Even with my training, I wouldn't survive a fight against so many. And there is more than just me to think about now.

Cameron and I continue down this alley at a sprint until we are abruptly stopped when it dead ends at a red brick wall. Cameron jumps at a fire escape ladder, but he can't reach it. He then digs through boxes of trash and rubbish to find something to utilize as a weapon. I stand there in a daze. How can all of this be happening? How can people act this way? How can Clones act this way? I finally come to my senses when my eyes focus in on the round covered manhole of a sewer entrance. I grab Cameron's arm and pull his attention to our only hope of escape.

Chapter 38

Cameron and I silently work as a fluid machine, lifting the lid, and slipping into darkness. My stitches pull with the effort, but I barely notice. I've grown numb from the trauma of this night. Cameron slides the cover back into place before meeting me at the base. We are both running on adrenaline, and I don't feel any pain as we take off. We swiftly create distance between us and the bloodthirsty hoard. The mental picture I have of the sewer map is still as fresh in my mind as the stench I wish was not currently singeing my nose hair once again. We run with no direction for a few minutes before I take over and start leading Cameron. Since we lost the duffle bags in the explosion, which I wish I could erase from my memory, I determine we need supplies first. I head to the only place I know of that has not only clothing and food, but medical supplies. The hospital. It's risky, but I don't know any alternatives. I navigate the dark labyrinth with Cameron trailing behind. Neither one of us can run full speed due to our injuries, and without the motivation of an angry mob right at our heels. Our adrenaline is running thin. We hobble as fast as we can, but both of us pause and hold ourselves up with the slimy sewer wall every hundred feet or so. My stitches pull and pinch with every motion.

"Where are we going, Alabaster?" Cameron asks between breaths.

"The hospital, so we can get you patched up and grab any supplies we can find. I don't know how long this will be going on."

Cameron nods with a smile. "Good thinking."

Cameron is at least able to hold his stomach contents down this time in the sewer. We are soon under an upward-leading tunnel I am confident leads to the street at the hospital's front entrance. Cameron climbs the ladder first and pushes up on the heavy circle with enough force to barely crack it. He peeks out to see if our route is clear and safe.

"Shit."

"What is it? Are we not at the right one?"

"No, it's the right one, but the fights have already reached the hospital. It doesn't look like many people are going in and out of the hospital though. Maybe it will be empty inside. Do you know of any sewer exits in the alley?"

I close my eyes to better visualize our options.

"I think there is one near the delivery entrance."

Cameron gently lowers the cover and scales down the ladder. I lead on again down a few more tunnels. Cameron climbs up the new ladder. He peeks out before climbing back down to me.

"It seems like the coast is clear. Do you need help going up the ladder?" Cameron rubs his injured shoulder. I can see the blood soaking through.

"I should be all right. I will take it slow. I probably need help getting to the first rung though."

"Okay, make sure you don't pull those stitches."

Cameron leans down and kisses my forehead. Vibrant tingling spreads from the point of contact. When he stands up, he gives me one of his half-smiles, which lifts my spirits slightly. The smile still doesn't make it to his eyes, which are overflowing with concern and grief. Cameron hurries up the ladder ahead of me to open the manhole then he scurries back down to help me climb. I peek my head out and double check the safety of our route. Cameron helps me out first, but he exits right at my heels. Cameron slowly lifts me to my feet and we stay in the shadows as we head toward the service door a hundred feet away. I jump several times because of the loud commotions that keep coming from the front of the hospital building. We safely reach the door.

Cameron opens the door and peeks his head in. "Stay out here for a second. I want to make sure the coast is clear and I'll be right back for you."

I don't release his hand. "No, don't leave me alone. We will be better off together."

I start hyperventilating with the prospect of being separated from Cameron. All of my fears suddenly vanish when Cameron's lips are suddenly on mine. The world fades away and my distress vanishes.

I didn't realize my eyes were closed, but they lazily open when I hear Cameron's voice say, "I'll be fine. Stay here." He runs his thumb across my cheek bone and I press my face against it. Before I know it, his hand is gone and the door clicks shut.

Only a few seconds have gone by and I am distraught. I would have rather stayed with Cameron. He is gone for what I think is much too long, but is probably only a few minutes. I grow impatient and become jittery from worry. The noise from the main street grows steadily, so I decide to follow after him. I open the heavy service door to a hallway, which is only illuminated by the flickering emergency lights.

"Cameron? Cameron, where are you?" I call out his name no louder than a whisper.

Cameron does not respond, so I make my way down the dark and eerie hallway. My nerves are fried and I jump at every sound, no matter how soft. Terror courses through my veins as I hear more than one set of footsteps echoing down the hallway around the corner. I jiggle the locked knobs of several doors in search of a hideaway. I dash back down the hallway from which I came, assuring my feet fall silently upon the tiled floors. The rubber of these tennis shoes muffles my footfalls, but they do squeak on the linoleum. The footsteps down the intersecting hall are nearing the hallway I am in. I'm still too far from the service-door exit to make it before the owner of the footsteps is upon me. My heart is beating so fast, I feel it may explode. Before the footsteps have completely rounded the corner, a hand appears out of nowhere and covers my mouth, silencing the scream I try to produce. The hand pulls me through a nearby doorway which closes softly behind me, and I begin to cry. The hand holds me while the footsteps pass by the door without hesitation. When the hand releases its hold over my mouth, I whip around to face my captor. With a sigh of relief, I find Cameron in front of me. His hands are now on my hips, and he pulls me close into an embrace. I release a few more gentle sobs as I snuggle my face into Cameron's chest. He smells of smoke and blood, but I can still smell traces of his fading cologne. It reminds me of better times. I look up at Cameron, and he kisses my forehead. He holds a backpack that is so full, it is bursting at the seams. Cameron releases me and peeks out of the door before turning back to me.

"Come with me. We need to go up to the third floor," Cameron says with some urgency.

"Okay, but we've got supplies. Shouldn't we find safety? What's on the third floor that's so important?"

"You'll see." Cameron's half-smile reappears, and just a spark of it reaches his eyes before the concern once again overwhelms it.

"I think the elevators are inoperative. Can you make it up the stairs?" Cameron inquires with concern.

"I'll be fine." I stand taller in defiance, and wince slightly from the pinch in my stomach.

Cameron takes a concerned step closer. "I can carry you."

I hold one hand up to stop his approach and the other is on my wound. "I will be fine, Cameron, let's go. We need to be getting out of here."

I stubbornly push past him and head toward the stairs. Cameron trails behind, but quickly catches up. He places his arm around my waist protectively. I make it up the first flight of stairs with little strain or effort. Midway up the second, I slow down as my stitches indignantly pinch at my stomach. By the time I reach the landing of the second floor, I am running short of breath. Cameron sweeps me off my feet and carries me up the last flight. I notice he still has a limp in his step. Cameron sets me down at the third floor landing next to the heavy fire door. He gently pushes the door open a crack and checks for any signs of life.

Cameron takes my hand while we cautiously enter the maternity floor together. We walk by the nursery, which normally has the People's newborn babies. The nursery for People is much smaller than the one for the newly delivered Clones. People still have babies naturally, but not nearly in the massive numbers Clones are produced. The nursery is currently as deserted as the rest of the hospital. I release a lungful of tension. I couldn't stand the prospect of seeing any more lifeless bodies, especially not those of innocent infants. Cameron guides me into a small room with a bed in the center, accompanied by a machine with a computer screen. He gently removes the remnants of my red-stained, once-white T-shirt and brushes his fingers down my bare shoulder. Cameron places a soft kiss on my shoulder as he lowers me down onto the bed.

"Now really is not the time for this, Cameron."

"I don't know what you are talking about." Cameron smiles with mock innocence before he continues on. "I just wanted to make sure I closed everything properly so you do not have any internal bleeding."

There is a slight pause before Cameron softly adds. "Besides that, I want to check on the baby."

I had almost forgotten the fact that I am pregnant. I place my hand protectively on my stomach.

"Do you think it will survive?"

I feel sick to my stomach. The knife went into my abdomen dangerously close to where my uterus is. It doesn't take much to lose a baby with a trauma like this.

Cameron's smile fades into a very illusive expression. His doctor training kicks in because he doesn't want to let on what his education tells him is most probable.

"I won't know until I look. At this point, I am more concerned about your welfare."

I sense the distress Cameron is attempting to conceal as he turns away from me to turn on the machine. The machine luckily has backup power and whirs to life.

"And the baby's welfare? Tell me the truth, Cameron." My question comes out sharper than I had meant, and Cameron flinches slightly.

"The odds are not in our favor, but I have seen many unlikely things happen."

My heart sinks as I take in the sadness in Cameron's eyes. I relax on my back as much as possible with the tension and pain coursing through me. I stare up at the bland ceiling while the equipment hums softly. I flinch when Cameron removes the taped gauze of my bandage from my stomach. My porcelain-white skin is covered with sticky blood, so Cameron takes a wet rag and cleans me, taking extra caution around the stitches. He checks the stitches and gently cleans the area. He then squeezes a clear, pasty liquid on my stomach, which sends a cold chill up my spine. Both Cameron and I take a deep breath in as Cameron places the head of the ultrasound sensor near my belly button and spreads the gel around. He checks the knife wound first. There are a few moments of silence as he navigates the sensor around my stomach to take in different angles.

"There is no internal bleeding." Cameron states and his shoulders relax slightly.

"Okay. And?"

Cameron is still silently holding his breath, as am I. He appears to be worried, which causes me to panic slightly. My heartbeat flutters with anticipation and my body tenses. Cameron releases a large gasp of breath and starts weeping as he squats down to the ground with his head between his legs.

"Cameron, what is it? Is it okay? Is everything all right? Cameron, talk to me!" I say with panic.

Cameron composes himself before he stands back up and places the sensor back where he pulled it off. He turns the screen so I can see it. There, on the screen, is a small alien like creature with barely formed arms and legs. I see one little tiny leg kick, causing me to join in Cameron's tears of joy and relief. Cameron pushes a few buttons on the keyboard, and a soft rhythmic thrum fills the room. We both smile with a laugh as the anxiety is released. The uterus seems to be completely intact. Cameron presses a few more buttons, and another small machine prints out a black and white image. Cameron hands me our baby's first picture before he helps me up to a sitting position. While I study the photo and trace the little person's image, Cameron wipes the goop off of my stomach with a towel. He gently applies a new bandage over my stitches. Cameron pulls a light-blue set of scrubs out of his new backpack. It's my usual work uniform. I slip the keepsake gently into a front pocket of the backpack. Cameron assists me in pulling the new top over my head. I wince when I raise my arms to slip them into their intended holes of the shirt. I put the scrub bottoms back in the bag, because these jeans are comfortable and not too defiled yet. After I am properly clothed, I draw Cameron closer to my body. He is so warm against my coldness. I hug him until some of his warmth thaws my inner chill. I run my hands down his back to his rear. Cameron cringes when my hand hits a moist spot on the fabric of his pants. I hop off the table and turn him around to examine the spot. There is a hole in his jeans surrounded by a crimson halo.

"What is this?" I inquire.

"It is nothing. Don't worry about it. I am more worried about you and the baby. We need to get going. We can take care of me later. I'll be fine."

"Nonsense. Drop your pants and let me be the judge of that."

"It is not really a good time for that, Alabaster," Cameron replies with a cocky smile and a mocking tone.

I give him a stern look of annoyance. Cameron reluctantly drops his drawers as he rolls his eyes. He turns around and bends over the hospital bed that I was lying on a moment before. I discover a small hole in his lower right cheek. It is small enough that blood has ceased to flow from the opening. I suspect it to be a bullet wound, and my lifetime of medical training tells me the bullet is still lodged within the fatty tissue. I believe it to be from a ricochet because a full speed bullet would have caused more damage. I riffle through a drawer and find a silver set of forceps.

"This is going to hurt."

I don't give much warning before I insert the tips of the forceps into the hole. I dig around as Cameron muffles a few pained groans into the backpack. The metal forceps hit upon an equally hard object within the tissue. I pinch the foreign object within the mouth of the forceps and pull it out. I then give Cameron a playful slap on his bare rear before pouring some alcohol over the now-bleeding puncture, causing Cameron to jump from the sting. I place a bandage over the wound. I also examine the graze on Cameron's bicep. It is only a shallow scratch, so I utilize the alcohol once again. The wound does not need stitches. I place another piece of gauze secured by a hot-pink strip of CoBand encircling his bicep.

"There, now you will survive," I diagnose with a smile.

Cameron turns around and gingerly pulls his pants back up. He moves to hold me close. We are once again reminded of the ever-present danger we are still in when a loud crash comes from out in the hallway. We freeze and silently stare at the door. Cameron slowly moves my body behind his own. I still peek out around Cameron's arm. Muffled voices work their way through the thin hospital walls. Cameron and I hold our breath, but we can't control our loudly pounding hearts. The voices slowly fade away without entering any rooms. Cameron and I both release our captive breath, and Cameron turns around to face me. He presses his forehead against mine and we look into each other's eyes. We are both exhausted, and the prospect of moving again is daunting. My body feels stiff and heavy.

"We had better get going. It's not safe her," Cameron whispers to me.

"It is not safe anywhere," I reply.

"Then let's just keep moving."

"Can't we just leave the city and run away? There must be something more beyond the fields. We could find a new city somewhere else."

Cameron looks back at me with panic evident in his eyes. "We can't leave the city. There is nothing beyond the fields. They really didn't teach you anything, did they?"

"We were only taught what we needed to learn for our Essential Function. Any sort of curiosity or diverging thought was either frowned upon or removed."

"Well, we will just leave it at *there is no hope for us beyond the fields*. I will tell you more when we aren't fleeing for our lives"

Cameron kisses my forehead and takes my hand to lead us out of the room. His kisses always seem to make me momentarily forget what I am thinking. He barely cracks the door open to scout out the hallway's safety. When he is comfortable with the absence of danger, Cameron leads me out of the room and directly toward the staircase. He does the same safety check at the next door. The stairwell appears empty, but I know that could change at any second. There are indeed people in the hospital, and those people will want to go to different floors. Seeing the main power grid is out and the hospital is running on generators, the only way to reach another floor is by stair.

Cameron and I quietly, but quickly, go down the stairs. When we reach the landing of the second floor, we hear the resounding echo caused by a door slamming far above us. We briefly stop and listen for a moment. The soft sounds of a scuffle are audible from several floors above to my pricked ears. Cameron and I quicken our steps and, in doing so, we aren't as silent. We halt again as the scuffle intensifies into a loud brawl between two people. Cameron and I look up for any signs of the altercation in time to see the dark shape of someone being pushed over the railing and plummeting to the ground floor with a short scream that is cut off by a stomach-churning crack. My gaze follows the body's unfortunate descent to destruction.

I look back up to see a red-haired Clone looking down on us with hateful eyes ablaze. I don't recognize the Clone and doubt the Clone knows me either. The look of purely evil hatred the Clone woman bares burns through my soul, sending chills down my spine. The Clone heads down the stairs with the speed and heat of the desert winds. Her thunderous footfalls echo loudly through the stairwell. Cameron and I both take two or three stairs at a time toward the exit below, adrenaline taking over once again. I move so swiftly, it's as if I am gliding with barely more than a foot skimming the surface of each stair. Cameron and I make it to the base level without falling. However the psychotic Clone has somehow cut the distance between us in half, and she is now only a flight above. There is not enough time to make it out of the stairwell door, the hospital service door, and on to the manhole in the alley without being caught by this madwoman. She will probably be on us before we even exit the hospital. I stop when we pass the corpse lying on the floor. I have a flashback of Boston's dead body lying before me when

I see the blank eyes of the Clone staring up at me. I want to throw up again. My head is spinning from my exertion, and my incision throbs.

Cameron must be thinking what I was thinking about the manhole escape route, because he guides me toward the ER as soon as we leave the stairwell. I know it's risky to venture deeper into the hospital, but I trust him to have a plan. We are lucky enough not to run into anyone else. The bloodthirsty Clone doesn't seem to know her way around as well as Cameron and I do, helping us to regain some distance.

Once in the ER, Cameron ducks behind a privacy curtain with me by his side. He turns on the defibrillator and cranks the dial as high as it will go. Cameron then takes the paddles and rubs them together. The silhouette of the Clone appears on the white curtain. Cameron takes two long strides toward the shadow. At the same time, I pull the curtain aside. The Clone woman is caught off guard long enough for Cameron to press the electrified paddles to her chest. The Clone's hazel eyes roll back into her head as she twitches a few times before crumbling to the ground with a loud thump.

The noise we have made in our standoff sparks the interest of others. I can hear more footsteps approaching. I take Cameron by the hand and pull him out of a dazed shock. Cameron has been trained as a doctor, and he has taken an oath to save lives, and instead, he just took one.

I hustle out of the ER, dragging Cameron behind me. I head toward the cafeteria with an idea. It's crazy, but it is all I have. The cafeteria is empty, but has obviously been raided. I have already worked out the plan in my head. I navigate around upturned tables, fallen chairs, and other obstacles, and I lead Cameron to the dish chute. It will be a tight fit, but I'm certain we'll fit. Cameron seems to realize my escape plan, and he wordlessly helps me up into the square opening. My small frame easily fits with room to spare as I crawl in. Cameron is not as lucky with his broad shoulders. He is able to lie on his stomach and army crawl using his elbows with both shoulders pressed against either side of the tunnel. I hope the tunnel does not taper off at all, otherwise Cameron will be stuck.

Progress is slow, because we are both exhausted and the fit is tight for Cameron. We are also moving slowly to make as little noise possible. The chute is pitch black, and I have a difficult time making anything out, even after my eyes have adjusted. Due to the darkness of the tunnel, I don't see the swiftly sloping floor. I squeal because I am unable to slow my accelerating decent. Cameron grabs for my ankles, but he's unable to find them in the darkness. My fall is cushioned by a mountainous heap of uneaten food scraps. I move out of the way in time for Cameron's body to come crashing out of the chute above. We're both now covered in a mixture of foods ranging from clam chowder to oatmeal to mashed potatoes. I pause to look around, and Cameron slides off the heap.

The emergency lights are all that illuminates the large warehouse. There are no People or Clones here. The pile of food doesn't appear to be very old, because it shows no signs of decay or mold. The rest of the warehouse is pristine with the metal conveyor belt glistening in the dim light. I notice a yellow banana, which is unblemished, in the pile of food. My stomach gives an untamed growl. My last meal was at lunch. I peel the fruit and devour the pale flesh. I see a red sparkle of a half-eaten apple which I have no qualms finishing. Cameron follows suit and eats a few undefiled edibles. He then picks out a few more whole apples and struggles to find space in his already overflowing backpack for the fruit. I look at Cameron and laugh. He is covered in mashed potatoes and spaghetti sauce as well as many other menu items. I slide off the mountain and approach him

"Come here, Cameron. You have got something in your hair."

I begin to pick out grains of rice mixed into his hair.

"I am not the only one." Cameron smiles at me with a chuckle as he removes a long spaghetti noodle from my hair. "Were you saving this for later?" he asks as he holds it up in front of me.

We spend a few minutes picking out copious amounts of food from each other's hair, but once the larger chunks of food are removed, Cameron and I decide it's time to leave. We spot an exit sign and proceed to depart.

The double doors lead to a poorly lit hallway with flickering lights. We cautiously move down the hallway, and soon come to a locker room. We enter in hopes of finding clean clothes. It's a typical Clone locker room without lockers, as Clones have no belongings to lock. Just like Clones, this locker room is identical to the one at the hospital, with the exception of a large shelf full of brown clothing. There is no attendant desk for a Clone to sit and monitor supplies. I grab a bundle and unfold it. The chocolate-brown shirt and top look exactly like my nurse's uniform, other than the color. I head straight to the showers and turn one on. This is the type of shower I am accustomed to, not Cameron. The water comes out with low water pressure and no heat. I smile and disrobe as I prepare to shower. After I hop into the water, letting it wash away the grime, food, and blood, Cameron comes to join me. When the icy water first hits his warm skin, Cameron jumps with a yelp.

"What the hell, Alabaster? You are out of your mind! That water is freezing! How can you stand it?"

I smile at him and shake my head while shrugging my shoulders.

"This is the typical temperature I shower at. We Clones are not important enough to waste precious water-heating energy resources on."

Realization runs across Cameron's face, followed by remorse

"I can see why the Clones would rebel. There are so many things in life that I have taken for granted, when you have had nothing."

"I have always had everything I need. And none of that matters now, as long as I have you."

I playfully splash the frigid water at him. Cameron jumps as it hits him, but then he dives into the water, grabbing me. I squirm away, because he is still covered in filth and I had finally scrubbed the last morsels off. Cameron finally releases me and hastily scrubs off in the icy stream. I am forced to re-rinse the residue Cameron was kind enough to share.

Cameron shuts the freezing water off as soon as he has the majority, not all, of the grime removed from his skin.

There are no towels, so we use the extra sets of brown uniforms to dry off with. The uniforms are perfectly tailored for Clones, so I fit nicely in my set. It may be slightly tight in the stomach region, but that could also be my imagination. Cameron, on the other hand, is not as lucky. He is taller than Boston's Clone type and too broad shouldered for the Clone type like Dimitri and my father. Cameron resolves the issue by wearing a Boston type shirt with broader shoulders, which is slightly too short and shows a little bit of his belly button, and the longer pants designed for my father's type, which I really enjoy as they run tightly over the planes and contours of Cameron's groin and rear. As I pull my shirt down a little farther, I notice the bandage Cameron had applied to my wound earlier is now scarlet in color. I gently remove the tape to reveal a few of the stitches have opened, allowing a crimson river to trickle out. I quickly try to conceal the damage, but Cameron notices the vividly contrasting red that flows across my porcelain skin. Cameron tenses and hurries over to me.

"It is nothing, really. I am fine." I try to pull away from his probing eyes.

Cameron gently grabs me and keeps me where he can see me. Cameron kneels down to examine the extent of the damage. His fingers are still icy from the cold shower, sending chills through my body.

"I think the bleeding is coming to an end. We'll put on a clean gauze pad though," Cameron resolves before turning to retrieve a new gauze and tape from his bag.

To properly cover my wound, Cameron pulls the waist of my pants below my hips. Cameron's close contact to my private areas negated the previous icy chill in my body with a flood of heat. I shudder slightly and place my hand on Cameron's wrist. He smiles knowingly as he is still fully aware of the effect he has upon me. Cameron gently tapes the gauze to my soft skin and kisses my flesh next to the gauze. As he caresses my belly with his thumb, Cameron looks up adoringly into my eyes, revealing a well of tears in his own.

Cameron stands up and cups my face in his hands to place a kiss on my rosy lips. The kiss progressively warms me from the inside out. However, reality works its way back into my mind, and I turn my head, breaking the union of lips.

"We need to go."

Cameron does not take it personally, and he kisses my forehead. He then turns away from me momentarily to grab his backpack.

"All right then. Let's be off," Cameron says with a smile while he takes my hand and we head for the door.

The building appears to be empty still, but we continue on cautiously anyway. I hope Cameron knows the city better than I do. I have never traversed more than three places until recently. Even though I had memorized the city's map at the rebel compound, I only memorized the streets with a bird's eye view. That does little to no good when you are on the street. I still have no knowledge of where the buildings are in relation to others. Anton's map did not have the building names or street names. Before I began my Essential Function, I had only been to my home, school, and the hospital. After I started my Essential Function, I added Cameron's home to that short list. In measures of distance within the city, it's not very far from the hospital, so my map wasn't large. I went to city hall yesterday, but I wasn't paying much attention because I was more concerned with Cameron. I have traveled the city's underground more than I have above. But my knowledge of the tunnels does me absolutely no good when I have no idea where we are starting off. It would be imprudent and dangerous to wander around in the sewer aimlessly.

Several hallways and a few wrong turns later, Cameron and I enter an unimpressive lobby. There is an unmanned front desk and a single faded sofa with two lumpy mismatched cushions. A large wall of windows face the street front, which appears just as vacant as the building. The few streetlights that are operational flicker on and off. It's still the middle of the night. During the hours of curfew, the Clone sector has a majority of its streetlights turned off. Curfew doesn't end until the dawn approaches, and the lights will turn on an hour before the sun kisses the horizon, and then they are off until the onset of dusk. I deduce we must be in the Clone sector, because the streets are not as brightly lit, nor are they as well tended as the streets frequented by the People. While we traverse the sticky linoleum floor of the lobby, Cameron and I try to hide within the shadows. Who knows if there's someone outside looking in.

"We need to find somewhere to stay for the rest of the night. We can't just keep moving forever. Eventually we will be too exhausted to keep on. Any ideas?" Cameron whispers to me.

I contemplate our options for a moment.

"We could try the Owl. Astrid seems pretty non-rebellious, and the Clones designed for the Owl don't seem to be held to the same strict laws as the rest of us. Maybe they won't care about the revolution?"

Cameron pauses as he thinks about the option. "It is a possibility, but the way things escalated, I don't think it will be safe. I don't want to risk it. If I were to lose you again, I, I, I don't know what I'd do."

I reassuringly squeeze his hand. "I am not going anywhere without you."

I stand up on the tips of my toes to place a kiss on Cameron's lips. He wraps his arm around me and smiles down at me with his charming half-smile, which makes my stomach flutter.

"Any other ideas," he asks once more.

I deliberate for a few minutes, which takes all my concentration, because I am always flustered when Cameron is touching me. Being that I am exhausted, it takes an extra amount of effort before I come to my senses enough to think clearly again.

I light up with an idea. "We can go to my house!"

"You want to take me, a Person, through the heart of the Clone sector, and then proceed to take me, a Person, into a Clone home?" Cameron gives me a puzzled glare.

"Yes. I doubt any Clones will actually be in the Clone part of the city, because they will be destroying your portion. We'll likely not see a single soul."

Cameron contemplates this idea, but the look on his face tells me he doesn't find any major flaws in the plan. "All right, you are making sense. Which way do we go then?"

"That is the problem, I don't know where we are."

"I should have figured as much."

"What is that supposed to mean? I don't see you leading the way either." I push Cameron away from me.

Cameron grabs for my hand, realizing he offended me. "I didn't mean anything by it. I just meant you were really not taught the little things. You are one of the smartest, most caring people I know. You are lacking in common knowledge though and it's not your fault. It's due to the fact that you were never taught. Where do we need to get you so that you will know where to go?"

I accept Cameron's explanation and allow him to pull me back into his strong arms.

"Well, I would need to be anywhere on my bus route from my home to the hospital or to the Clone school."

"Hmm, that doesn't give me much to go off. I recall hearing that the food disposal warehouse is in the southern section of the Clone district. So, if that

is true, we need to head northwest. The Owl should
be in that direction, and I know that was on your
bus route, because that was where I first saw you."
Cameron pulls me closer and touches my scarred chin
with his thumb as he finishes talking.

I blush slightly as Cameron stares down at me.

"We had better be off then. It will likely be getting
light soon," I say as I turn away to conceal my flushed
cheeks. "And with the sun, there will be fewer places
to hide."

Cameron gently replaces his hand on my chin.
He turns my face back to him and connects his lips
to mine. The kiss is brief, but fantastic. It leaves me
wanting more, but I know we can't have more. We
must be going. The sooner we get to my dwelling, the
sooner we can rest. Oh, the thought of rest is enticing.

Cameron and I leave the building and cautiously
cross the street and head left. We take a right at the
first street we come to. After jogging down this street
for a few blocks, we take another left. We still have not
passed a single sign of life, which gives me hope that
my plan will work. Otherwise, I am guiding Cameron
to his death. After jogging down our current street
a few more blocks, we veer right. At the end of this
street, the red lights of the Owl are vividly visible,
as well as some large bonfires. My heart sinks. If the

fires have come this far, it means the riots have come this far as well. We slow down and cautiously make our way toward the building. We attempt to skirt the illumination of the sparse streetlights. I try to place any building or feature on the street as we pass, but nothing clicks. We still have not seen anyone, but I know that doesn't mean we won't.

I stop suddenly. Our path is blocked by a large mass. Cameron and I carefully observe the mound to discover what threat it may pose. Cameron whips me behind him. The obstruction is the body of a Police Clone. Cameron slowly circles the Clone, keeping me safely behind him. He finally relaxes when he realizes the Clone is dead, but he does nudge the body with his toe before he is convinced. I turn the Clone over, worried it may be Rhino, but I am relieved to discover it's not him. Before turning to continue on our way, something catches my eye. I kneel down next to the Police Clone's trunk of an arm to examine it closer. There is a web of ivy green lines climbing across the skin of the Clone's arm and torso. The discoloration originates from the same area I removed that cylinder from Rhino's shoulder area. The gangrene color is darkest at that point, and, the farther it goes, the lighter in color it gets, until it is a seafoam green at his fingertips. Just to know, I pull his shirt up slightly.

I can see the lines running all over his chest. I don't know what to make of it, but it causes a deep-seated tension in my gut. I know those wicked lines are what caused this Clone's demise. And to think, if I hadn't removed the object from Rhino, he would be gone too. I hope he is okay.

Cameron takes my hand and gently tugs on it to remind me that we need to keep moving. When at last we are only a block from the Owl, I finally get my bearings and I now know where to go from here. At the same moment, a head peeks out of a window high up in the Owl, spotting Cameron and me, as we unfortunately stand under one of the only working streetlights on this road. The head disappears, but a commotion can be heard from within the building. I pull Cameron down a side street and we begin running furiously. I feel my stitches pulling sharply on my stomach, but I don't have time to worry about them. Cameron is limping, but he is still able to keep up. There is still at least a ten-minute run before we reach the anticipated safety of my dwelling.

If that weren't challenging enough, I fall to the ground and begin to writhe in pain. I'm certain that I have twisted my ankle on the uneven cobblestone sidewalk. Cameron swiftly lifts me up and carries me down the road. He sets me down in an indented building entrance which would be hard to see from down the street where we came. He checks my ankle and I can't help but to cringe as he moves it.

"It's twisted. You shouldn't place any weight on it."

I nod. He is not telling me anything I don't already know. I can't walk on it, let alone run. Cameron leaves me sitting in the corner and he peeks out down the street we left. No one appears to be following us. Cameron sits down next to me, and we relax for a moment to catch our breath.

"You can't walk on that ankle, Alabaster. How far do we have? I don't know if I can carry you much farther."

I bury my head in my hands, crying softly. We still have at least two miles to go, maybe more. My ankle screams in protest, even without any weight on it. The pain from my incision contends with my ankle's fuss. It apparently doesn't want to be ignored, and my lungs are making an effort to win my attention with their agonizing pleas for respite. We can't stay here any longer, so I compose myself and stand. I begin to walk and wince with every ounce placed upon my twisted ankle. Cameron tries to pick me up, but I push him off.

"I will be fine. We need to keep going. We are sitting ducks out here."

"Fine, but let me at least try to help."

Cameron places my arm around his shoulder
to take some of the weight off of my foot. Our
progress is slow as we hobble along. No one seems
to be following us, but that doesn't stop me from
continuously looking back over my shoulder. The
sky begins to lighten as the sun approaches the
distant horizon. We are walking through the ghost
town streets of the Clone sector where the Clone
dwellings are located. I both appreciate and despise
the brightening sky. I appreciate it because none of
the working streetlamps cast enough light to see by,
making it easier for someone to sneak up on us. I
despise it because we will be unable to sneak around
unseen soon. Luckily, we make it to my house without
any more issues. The door is unlocked, as it usually
remains. Clones don't have any possessions someone
would envy. I take my arm off of Cameron's shoulder
to welcome him into my house. The entryway is
far less grand than Cameron's. In fact it is far less
existent than Cameron's. We dodge the table and I
lead Cameron down the narrow hallway. The two
of us collapse onto my small unyielding bed. I am
unconscious before I have time to realize how small
and hard my bed truly is. Cameron and I both lie
on our sides. My body is trapped against the wall by
Cameron's, which is hanging over the edge. I face the

wall with Cameron's arm securely wrapped around me. I feel safer than I have in months. My last thought is that this truly is home. Not the dwelling or this bed, but this man with his arm around me.

Chapter 39

I don't know what time it is when I finally wake up. The power is out, so my alarm clock is as well. Fear and panic fill my mind as I recall everything that happened last night. When I realize Cameron is not in the room with me, I begin hyperventilating. Seconds later, I begin screaming. Cameron runs into the room with a panic-stricken composure. He is at my side, wrapping his arms reassuringly around my trembling shoulders.

"Where did you go? Why did you leave me?" I manage to formulate the questions through strained breaths.

Everything hurts.

"I didn't go anywhere. I was just looking around your house. Seeing if there is anything useful. You were sleeping so peacefully, I thought I would let you get as much as possible. I don't know when we will get much more. I'm sorry."

I acquire control of myself as Cameron holds me close and kisses the top of my head. When I begin breathing normally again, I gently push him away to wipe the last tear from my cheek.

"So did you find anything useful?" I inquire.

Cameron shrugs.

"Nothing useful. You really don't have anything. I had always thought Clones had something. A couch, a dresser, a table lamp, carpet. I don't know what I had in mind, but not absolutely nothing."

"We have a coffee pot. That is something. And an alarm clock."

I tap the blank, powerless clock on the small table next to my bed, and Cameron smiles at me.

"I did find this. I don't think they will be helpful, but they are interesting."

Cameron reveals a familiar blue-bound textbook. I open the hard cover, which reveals dark smudges on the inside. As I look closer, the smudges form to create distinguishable forms of people, faces, animals, and landscapes like none other I have seen. I can see great detail, undistorted by the text which lies behind each piece of artwork. Each page has text topped by a different exquisite piece of artwork.

"This is my brother's book. Where did you find it? He never puts it down."

"In one of the other bedrooms. Under the mattress."

My brother has been drawing. I think back on my memories of my brother. In every memory for the past few years, that book has been in my brother's hand or by his side. I thought nothing of it, other than he was committed to learning about his Essential Function. I never would have imagined him breaking the law by having a creative passion, nor could I imagine him stealing a pencil or pen to accomplish the task. With the time spent on the intricate detail of these, he obviously didn't do it while sitting in class with his classmates and teacher there to witness. I could imagine Eliana committing this act of rebellion, but not my brother. My brother, who cried when I named him Thomas. My brother, who seemed intent on following in my father's strictly law-abiding lifestyle. Deep down, I had always believed I was not the only one who had illegal feelings, thoughts, and desires. Secrets that, if discovered, would be a death sentence. At least I had my mother who knew I was different––even though I didn't––and was there to guide me. Poor Thomas had no one. I can't imagine the stress and loneliness he must have felt by not being able to share his gift and, worse, having to vigilantly keep it secret. I should have been there for him. I am so selfish.

The Clones just needed someone to be the catalyst. Someone to show them it's okay to have passions, it's okay to have ideas, it's okay to have feelings, and it's okay to be an individual. Anton was right about the Clones needing me, but for the wrong reason. He thought I would show them, train them how to be. The reality is, they already had it all within themselves. They only needed someone to show them how to share it, release it, and let it blossom. Someone to give them courage to be themselves. I wonder to myself if it really needed to be me, a Clone, to instigate the change. What if a Person had shown a Clone compassion or treated a Clone as if they were an individual, with respect and equality? Dimitri certainly was different. I could see the deep love and commitment of a father he had for Cameron. But it didn't seem like Dimitri ever told Cameron; it was just my observation. Would this revolution be far less bloody if the People had treated the Clones as fellow humans rather than mindless subjugates?

I realize I have been ignoring Cameron in my moment of revelation when he softly kisses my neck and slides his hand up my outer thigh toward my rear. His other hand closes the textbook with an attention-grabbing clap before he takes it out of my hands. Cameron has my full attention now that his hand has found bare skin on my lower back. I become self-conscious about my scarred back, but Cameron's touch relaxes my worries. My scars no longer hurt, but the healing skin is still more sensitive than the rest, so when his fingers gently crawl up and down my back, they send tingling goosebumps over my entire body. My breathing intensifies as both of Cameron's hands are now caressing my back. His hands momentarily cease their contact with my skin while they work together as a team to unfasten my bra. His lips trace my collar bone. Cameron alternates between soft kisses and gentle nibbles while he moves up my neck. My fingers twist in his soft hair. Cameron's hands cause my shirt to climb slowly up my back as he strokes my spine. We momentarily break apart so I can pull my brown shirt over my head. Cameron takes the opportunity to swiftly remove his own matching shirt. By the time my head peeks out from under my shirt, Cameron is already back at my lips. Cameron lays me down on my stomach and begins to trace each scar with his lips. I feel like he is begging forgiveness for not being there to protect me. I don't blame him, and there was no way he could have prevented it, but he blames himself. After he has covered my back with kisses, he rolls me back over and positions himself, hovering inches above me. I fall into the depths of his eyes and I know there is no coming back. I'm drowning in love with him.

He is being careful not to hurt my stomach, but I pull him closer. My body craves contact with every part of him, no matter the pain. Cameron's hand violates the protective elastic waistband of my pants as it ventures below. I arch my back in pleasure as well as to decrease the distance between our bodies.

I am so focused on Cameron's bare skin against mine that neither of us hear the footsteps coming from the hallway. The bedroom door bursts open with a startling crash. Cameron reacts swiftly and he is off of me with his bare-chested body shielding me from the intruders. I immediately pull my shirt back over my head and fasten my brassiere. I peek over Cameron's bare shoulder to face the invaders. They wear black ski masks, concealing their identities, but I know they are Clones by the shape of their bodies in combination with the shade of their eyes. I also know they are thirsty for blood by the burning hate in those same eyes. After a momentary standstill, the masked assailants approach. Cameron leaps forward at them with the rage of a wild beast backed into a corner. Only two of the masked assailants are able to grapple with Cameron because the room is too small for the other three to maneuver. There are no Police

Clones included in this entourage to knock Cameron unconscious with one blow. He is able to fight well enough to stand his ground. Cameron throws a heavy fist and hits one Clone hard enough to send him spiraling backward. The masked Clone's head hits the floor with unrestricted force. He involuntarily twitches once, but moves no more while a red halo slowly forms around his head.

Cameron is greatly outnumbered and the intruders soon overcome his efforts. I have trouble seeing through my tear-filled eyes and my throat has become raw from my screams. One assailant holds Cameron's arms behind his back whilst another tenderizes Cameron's face. I jump at the closest assailant and begin throwing punches. This minimally trained Clone is no match for me and the genes I share with the Police Clones. He is soon backing out of the room to safety, but he is soon replaced. I deal some damage to this one, but the room is so small, it's difficult to maneuver. Cameron is on the floor being kicked in the gut. When Cameron releases a pained cry, I become distracted enough for the Clone I am fighting to gain the upper hand. He grabs my arm and easily flips me over his back. I am winded when I land on the ground with a hard thud and that's where I remain, sprawled out on my back in front of the merciless Clone. The masked Clone takes the hard toe of his foot and forcefully kicks me in the side. When he kicks again, I grab his foot and twist his ankle and he loses balance and then falls after tripping over the dead body of the first Clone Cameron attacked. Another Clone helps the attacker I brought down back up, and the two of them begin to kick me ruthlessly. Cameron tries to crawl to me, but the relentless assault impedes his advance. I curl into the fetal position, attempting to protect my already-wounded stomach. I receive another three hard kicks before a woman's commanding voice causes everyone in the room freeze.

"What the hell is going on in here?"

The masked Clone assailants turn to look at the woman, and Cameron takes the opportunity to pull my shaking body into his protecting arms. Together we cower in a small corner of the room staring up at the masked assailants. I am unable to see who the woman standing on the other side of our attackers is. I can tell the woman has no mask to hide her identity, but the other figures in the room impede my view. From what I can make out, she is dressed in the same black garb, and has long, flowing brown hair.

Cameron no longer cares about the other people in the room when he sees me holding my stomach where my stitches are. I don't want to move my hands away, so he firmly but gently pulls them out of his way. My body is trembling from the pain. Cameron gently raises my shirt and removes the red-soaked bandage. A few of the stitches have been torn and a constant trickle of blood slowly seeps out. Through teary eyes I can tell Cameron's face is swollen, gashed, and bloody. He rips a corner of the bed sheet off and presses it firmly against my stomach. The wound is open enough to require my stitches to be redone soon. My ribs feel tender. With each breath, pain courses through every fiber of my body.

I jump when I feel a second set of hands upon my stomach. The cold hands are pulling the sheet off of my wound to inspect my injuries. When I open my cringed eyes, I see the woman who seized control command of the masked assailants crouched before me. The woman is talking with Cameron, but the pain muddies my hearing. Through my watery eyes I am able to make out a face as familiar as my own. The woman is a Clone. I am unable to determine if I know the woman or not due to the pain, which is causing the room spin. I roll over to hurl any remnants from my previous meal. The force of my stomach contracting causes the pain in my abdomen to become well known. I can feel more stitches pulling at my skin as they tear open. After I have nothing left to offer, I pass out.

Chapter 40

I come to in a familiar gray cement cell of the rebel compound. From what little I can make out, as my head is spinning, it is my bedroom cell. Aggie's blankets are tidily made in the corner, but she's not here. I look toward the door and see figures walking by the open frame. Another look around the room tells me I am all alone. My ribs are wrapped tightly, and a clean bandage covers newly threaded stitches. I gingerly stand with aching bones and tense muscles. I still feel sick to my stomach, and the room whirls as I approach the door. The world around me closes in as darkness swallows everything I see once again. I cry out for Cameron before the darkness overcomes me completely. I give gravity full control of my body, allowing it to take me captive.

When I again wake up, I am lying upon a white-sheeted hospital bed, looking up at white recessed lights. This room is familiar too. I'm in the infirmary. I have a cold compress against my forehead, reducing, but by no means eliminating, the skull-splitting thrum. I gingerly touch my forehead with gentle fingertips to discover a neat line of stitches along my hairline. As I take inventory of my body and each ache I feel, I discover an IV line protruding from my arm. I feel weak and my consciousness slowly slips away. I futilely try to hold on, but it's as difficult as holding water in a holey bucket. I see Aggie's sweet face, and her mouth is moving, but I can't hear her. My eyes close and refuse to reopen. I am soon oblivious to the world once more.

Chapter 41

When my eyes finally respond and open sometime later, I look up into a light as bright as a thousand suns above me. I am no longer connected to an IV, but I am still lying on a firm hospital mattress. A crisp white blanket lightly covers my body up to my shoulders. I groan as I prop myself up onto my elbows to look around. I am still in the infirmary with callous gray concrete walls. I see Aggie sleeping upright in a metal chair with a blanket. This only means one thing: I am back at the rebel compound; I wasn't dreaming. How did I get back here and, more importantly, where is Cameron?

I can hear voices coming from out in the hallway. The door is slightly cracked. I sluggishly pull my stiff body up and over the edge of the bed. My legs, sore from running, do not catch me as quietly as I had hoped. I freeze in a crouched position, listening for any sign of someone hearing me. Aggie speaks, but she has been known to talk in her sleep. I monitor her for a second, but she doesn't so much as bat an eye.

After a few seconds of silence, I release the breath I took captive and slowly stumble toward the cracked door where the voices come from.

"They want blood. There is no way they will let him live." A man's familiarly smooth voice states.

"If he does not live, she will not be compliant," replies the melodic but commanding voice of a woman.

I can't tell who is speaking to whom. Both voices seem familiar, but I cannot place either. My head is still spinning slightly, which makes it difficult to focus properly.

"Do we even need her anymore? The government is gone. The People are subdued. She no longer serves a function."

"Of course we still need her. Many of the Clones and rebels alike worship her. The Clones think of her as their savor. If she does not go along with our plans, it is likely no one else will either. If she plays along with us, everyone will follow in step."

"We could kill her too. Tell the Clones and the rebels that the People did it. Make her a martyr. That will make them follow us and reduce the headache of trying to control her."

"Haven't enough people already died? Besides, if anyone discovered the deception, we would surely be ruined. The boy has been trained in the medical field as a doctor. Perhaps that will be enough to at least merit his continued existence. So many doctors were killed. We will need him."

"They claim he is a murderer. You saw the damage he caused when your people incarcerated him. He killed that Clone. He needs to pay."

"It was self-defense,"

"Bullshit." The male voice cuts the woman off.

I have heard enough. It is now apparent they, whoever they are, want to kill Cameron and possibly me as well. I need to find Cameron and escape. But how? And where will we go? At this point I don't care. I desire nothing more than to be with him. There is another door across the room, and I head for it with determination. My feet are less secure than normal, causing me to sway as if on a ship battling stormy seas, and I've also got double vision. I pause to vomit as the room spins, but determinedly push on through the pain, vertigo, and nausea. Surprisingly, Aggie is still sleeping like a rock. Sweet thing.

I reach the metallic door and crack it open slightly to see if anyone occupies the hallway. The coast is clear, so I stealthily slip out of the door and head down the vacant hallway. The cold cement floor send icicles coursing through my veins while my bare feet pitter-patter along. Each step sends a chill and pain throughout my body. The hour must be early because the rebel compound is deserted. It's been a month since I was here, but I still know my way around. That's just the way my photographic mind works. I hastily navigate the passages and head toward the prison cell block where I assume they are keeping Cameron.

When I reach the prison cells, I peek into several rooms. Many of the rooms are occupied by People, who are each in extremely poor condition. They are beaten, clothes are torn, and one poor individual does not seem to be breathing. I discover the constable locked in one of the cells. He is not as bad off as some of the other captive People. I finally find Cameron in the last cell at the end of the hall. He is lying on the hard cement bench, staring up at the ceiling. My back aches with the memory of the discomfort experienced on a stone bed. I attempt to open the heavy iron door, but it's locked. I am unsure where to find the keys, which makes me feel helpless. I kneel down and open a small slot in the door. I am once again so close, but so far from Cameron.

"Cameron," I whisper through the slot.

Cameron instantly perks up and looks in my direction. He smiles as he rolls off of the concrete bed and crawls toward the slot that only reveals my eyes.

My heart breaks to see Cameron's face. It is swollen to the point of forcing one eye shut. He also has a few deep cuts that require antiseptic and stitches. Both are things he is not likely to receive any time soon. I remember him looking pretty beaten and bruised when we were caught, but he looks much worse now. It seems to me that someone continued the beating while I was unconscious. We touch fingertips, because that is all the small slot will allow. I cry quietly. I feel so helpless. I have always had my life controlled by the People, but I have always felt in control of what I am meant to do. There have been so many things out of my control lately. Being so close to Cameron, yet unable to be held in his arms is the worst deprivation of control I have experienced yet.

"Cameron, I need to find the keys to get you out of here. I overheard a conversation, and they plan to execute you. They also discussed killing me if I don't do as they say. I will be right back. I will find the keys, and then we can escape." I begin to stand up to leave, but Cameron's voice stops me in my tracks.

"No." Cameron's voice is firm to the point it causes me to flinch.

"What do you mean *no*? I need to get you out of here. Did you not hear me? They plan on removing you, executing you!"

I have stopped crying; however, I am now yelling at Cameron in an escalating whisper. Hopefully no one has heard me.

"You once asked me to lie to save my own life so you could bare the punishment alone. I did that for you, and I am now asking the same of you. Tell them you do not care if I live or die. Tell them I was taking advantage of you due to my privileged status. I want our baby to live, Alabaster, but more than anything, I want you to live. Boston had it right, the world would be a dark place without you."

"I want you to live. I want us to live on together. Besides, you didn't do what I asked. You were going to die with me in that courtyard. I will find the keys, then we will escape this place together."

"And where will we go, Alabaster? There is no place where they will not find us in the city."

"Then we can leave the city. There has to be something more beyond the fields."

Cameron interrupts me, saying, "Alabaster, there is nothing beyond the fields." Cameron's voice has become cold. "Nothing."

"What do you mean nothing? There has to be something."

"No, there is nothing. You never learned about our history, our history as the human race. There was once something more. Something great, something beyond your wildest dreams. But man's hatred, greed, and thirst for power destroyed it all. I assure you that there is nothing now. We are only alive because we are trapped within an enormous protective dome. If you were to step outside, you would be dead within minutes. The air contains no oxygen, but it is full of poison. The temperature is so hot, your skin would melt off of your bones within seconds. There is nothing but death."

I am silent as I process this new nightmare.

"I am still going to get you out." I stubbornly clench my jaws in defiance. "We will just keep moving. Maybe if we get enough supplies we can stay out in the fields or trees or maybe even the sewer, we will just keep moving. We can do it, as long as we are together we can."

"We can't do it, Alabaster, we can't. We will need more supplies. We will need a lot of medical supplies to deliver the baby and take care of you postpartum. It is simply impossible. I would rather sacrifice myself to save you, both of you. I implore you, I beg you, to do me this final request and deny any attachment to me. Take care of yourself and our baby and know I will always love you both."

Tears fill Cameron's eyes, but he does not allow them their freedom just as he does not allow me to free him. I finally nod in concession, but continue to conceptualize escape plans. I cry as Cameron moves back to the cold stone bed after kissing my fingertips.

"Cameron," I whisper through the slot. No reply, no response, he doesn't even move. I close the slot without another word and leave.

I run down the corridors, which are now slowly filling with half-awake bodies. There are more than a few angry shouts as I run into the zombielike bystanders. I run to ease my pain, to numb my hurt. I need air. I need the sun. I need freedom from this constrictive feeling encompassing my soul. Most of my pain dims while I move.

I finally find my way to the crisp air outside. There are no guards at the door today. The sun warms my skin, but does not penetrate deep enough to thaw the icy frost within my heart. The once beautifully blossoming trees are bare, and they look like they are mourning the beauty they once held. I feel the same. I had a beautiful love and now it's gone and I feel bare inside. I keep running at full speed in a direction away from the city, away from the rebel compound, away from Cameron, and away from my heart. I do not believe, cannot believe, what Cameron revealed to me. Sharp rocks and sticks tear at my bare feet, but I don't care. I yearn for more pain to be physically inflicted upon me in an attempt to dull the unbearable pain searing me from the inside out. Pain originating from my knife injury begins to contend for attention as it sends sharp waves of pain up and down my body. I don't care. I don't slow. I welcome the pain and keep pushing.

I run through an evergreen forest until it gradually changes into a barren field. The force of the sun's brutal rays beating down on me does not slow me down as I continue my feverish pace. My lungs ache, yet not enough to drown my sorrow. I wonder how this world could be so cruel. When I was a young girl, I contemplated a greater being who created everyone and everything. I imagined the benevolent being as a kind and gentle fellow who would one day come and whisk me away from my life of servitude. I now wish he were a real being standing in front of me so I could beat, torture, and pummel him into oblivion. What sort of evil, sick, twisted creature would create something and allow it to suffer so much pain? Why would he allow his other creations to treat one another so poorly? I abandon the childish idea of something greater as I release a feral scream at the top of my lungs.

As the scenery changes from barren field to scorched earth, I slow my maddening speed to a halt. I still stand upon the brown dirt spotted with gray stones, but ahead of me there is only blackness. Rolling fields of black. Far off in the distance, I spot the skeletal system of a lost city. I cautiously walk toward the ash-covered ground ahead, but I am soon stopped by an invisible force. I raise my hand up and push my palm out toward the invisible wall. A warmth fills my hand, but it doesn't pass through the iridescent wall. When I pull my hand back, a shimmer runs skyward before disappearing into the clouds. I pound on the invisible dome, screaming and crying with tears streaking my dirty cheeks. An echoing thunder runs up the barrier with a warbling ripple, but the wall remains solid. I feel so hopeless, so lost. Cameron wasn't lying. We are trapped.

However, while I stare out into the distant field of despair, I freeze when I see movement on the forbidden side of the force field. In the death-like abyss, a beautiful emerald-green butterfly with black wingtips flutters gently in the breeze. I smile as I am filled to overflowing with joy and hope. If a butterfly can survive out there, then why can't a human? I smile as I watch the butterfly for a few seconds before it lands upon a jet-black mound of ash. The minute weight of the butterfly combined with the gentle wind current created by its delicate wings disturb the heavy ashes, revealing a beautiful blue iris. The blossom is very small, but very alive.

Author Bio

M. C. Wilkinson grew up in Colorado with a view of the majestic Rocky Mountains from her bedroom window. She moved to Idaho her last year of high school. During an adventurous Fourth of July trip, she met the love of her life on the highway playing leapfrog, and it's been a joyride ever since. Two children and many dreams later, she woke up and started writing *When the Bough Breaks* on her phone.